GRACE AND ALLY

AMY FILLION

For anyone who has ever felt lost. And for those that have lifted them.

ALSO BY AMY FILLION

Adult Novels

Secrets of Spaulding Lane: Nancy

Secrets of Spaulding Lane: Marni

Secrets of Spaulding Lane: Rose

Little Things

Broken and Breaking Free

Children's Books

Fairville: Room of Reveries Book 1

FenneGig: Room of Reveries Book 2

Esmerelda and the Courageous Knight: Room of Reveries Book 3

Wonderwell: Room of Reveries Book 4

SkyTopia: Room of Reveries Book 5

The Ancient Curse: Room of Reveries Book 6

A Magical Farewell: Room of Reveries Book 7

CHAPTER 1

*W*hen her husband left, he took everything with him.

Clothes, shoes, kitchenware, furniture.

Her heart.

He refused to part with the materialistic items, no matter how small or big, that they had built their lives around.

It was amazing what a couple could amass in twelve years' time.

He was older than Grace by eight years. They had met at a Christmas party hosted by a mutual acquaintance when Grace was in her senior year at a small local college on the outskirts of Boston. She was twenty-one at the time, shy, reserved, sometimes mute when her anxiety slithered its way like a slippery snake into her thoughts and took hold, compressing tightly, fully.

Grace didn't have many friends, but not for lack of trying. Her inhibited nature prevented her from approaching a stranger, from approaching even a classmate that she'd happen to see in the dining hall or walking along one of the many winding campus pathways, boots crunching on snow and gravel, breath billowing in front of their faces, hair snug beneath thick woven hats. She recognized familiar faces immediately and possessed the talent of remembering names as well. She'd walk behind them, even beside them sometimes, speaking to them in her mind. *"Hi, Annabelle,"* she'd say. *"My name is Grace. We're in the same abnormal psychology class. Remember?"* And in her head, they'd look her directly in the eye, and their lips would slowly, hesitantly begin to lift until it dawned on them that yes, they did recognize this thin young woman with the long, stringy brunette hair plastered to her cheeks, almost touching the creases of her eyes under her favorite woolen hat, the burnt-orange one that her nana had knitted her before she'd passed just a few years ago.

Her nana.

The ache was still raw, but the hat was a reminder. Of better days. Of better times. When she'd felt comfortable, welcomed, warm in the presence of another.

Loved.

"Oh, yes. Grace," Annabelle would say. *"I remember you. Yes. Abnormal psychology. How do you like Mrs. Greeley?"*

"Oh, I love her," Grace would reply. *"Just love her. The way she smiles all the time, and the way she gesticulates, all arms and hands. She really has a passion for what she does, doesn't she? Her enthusiasm shows. Right?"*

"For sure," Annabelle would agree, a large, genuine smile on her face. *"Where are you headed to?"*

"I was just going to grab something to eat," Grace would say.

She wouldn't have to explain to Annabelle that she still lived on campus, even as a senior. She wouldn't have to explain that her father didn't have the financial means to rent her an apartment, and even if he did, he wasn't paying Grace's way through school anyway. She was doing that herself with a job at the campus library as well as a hefty academic scholarship and several student loans.

And she wouldn't have to explain that she, Grace, didn't possess the social qualities of one that would seek out a roommate or two to share an apartment with. No. Not to Annabelle. Not in this fabricated conversation. There was no need to explain that she lived in a dormitory, had a small room all to herself, and spent the majority of her time in that clean and tidy enclosure with the door closed unless she was in class. Or at the library.

The library she could do. Even if there were crowds of students studying or surveying the various books in the stacks, in the library, she felt at ease. She felt at peace. People didn't go to the library with the intention of engaging in social conversation with friends. At the library, she could almost feel comfortable in her own skin. She was with like-minded individuals, others that shared a passion for the written word. Or so she thought. She hoped.

"*Oh, I'm headed to meet a few friends for lunch, too. Want to join us?*" Annabelle would ask.

"*I'd love that. Thanks.*" And Grace would step in time with Annabelle, the two girls making their way to the mess hall. It was as simplistic as that: say hello to Annabelle, strike up a conversation, eat lunch with her, then meet her friends. Quite easy.

And in her mind, she'd embrace all of this. She'd effortlessly make friends with three or four other women that afternoon. She'd be invited to attend a party that night just off campus, where she'd strike up further conversations with complete strangers, and she'd have no inhibitions in doing so, no anxiety toying with her mind, telling her that

3

these strangers, these fellow students, were looking at her closely, were scrutinizing her. They wouldn't see what was inside. They couldn't. They weren't privy to the words that echoed in her mind, words from her childhood.

Your hair makes you look like a mouse, Grace. Do something about it, wontcha?

Now why would you go and do something like that?

Got any brains in that head of yours?

No wonder you don't have any friends. All the better for me. Don't want them in my house anyway.

No. In these contrived dreams, Grace was a social butterfly. She was an extroverted individual, appreciated by those that crossed her path.

But it was only in her mind; that she knew all too well.

Dana was her name, this acquaintance that hosted the Christmas party at which she'd met her husband. She hadn't initially been inclined to go. She could see it now; no matter how often she'd float away in her thoughts, devising an alternative existence, she could see it. She knew how that party would progress. She'd hold a glass of wine in her hand or maybe a beer. She didn't know if she liked the taste of beer, but to conform to the crowd, she'd partake. What did people serve at Christmas parties, anyway? She hadn't ever really been to one. Not as an adult.

Glass in hand, she'd survey the room from her huddled position in a corner as masses of people congregated around her. She supposed they'd probably all know one other or at least a few other people at the party. It would be easy for them to be merry, to excitedly converse with one another. To genuinely enjoy their time in Dana's apartment.

But not Grace. Grace would feel exposed, naked. She would avert her eyes, train them on the floor. And though she'd like nothing more than for someone to tap her on the shoulder, to introduce themself and inquire after her name, make polite conversation, Grace would come across as surly, bottled, and unwelcoming. She always did. She knew this. Even when her intention was quite the opposite.

Yes, she knew how the evening would progress. She was convinced this was so. And yet Dana's grandmother and Grace's nana had been very close, the best of friends. Grace had encountered Dana several times when her nana was still living. Grace knew her nana had so desperately wanted Grace to befriend someone, anyone. She wanted for Grace what she had with Dana's grandmother: a best friend, a woman in whom she could confide absolutely everything. A woman who would love her no matter her faults. A woman who could crack the facade that she presented to the outer world.

Oh, how Grace would love this for herself.

She dreamed of it often.

But it was hard to have any close friend at all, let alone a best friend, when she shut herself off, when she shut down. When she wouldn't let anyone in, no matter how desperately she wanted to.

It was because of the memory of her nana, though, that Grace accepted Dana's invitation to attend her Christmas party. For two full weeks, she didn't back down. She didn't pick up the receiver of her landline—no cell phone in college for Grace; why would she have needed a cell phone when there was nobody to call?—to ring up Dana and cancel. She held firm even through the nausea induced by her imaginative thoughts about the evening. She had trouble concentrating through class the day prior and through her school work. And she loved her classes, her learning. She was a determined student. And it was easy to complete academic tasks when her social life was next to nonexistent. No. She didn't cancel even then. She owed her nana that much.

After all, she had promised, hadn't she? She had promised her nana that she would try, that she would extend herself.

That she would make more of an effort.

What would her nana have thought if she knew that all of Grace's overtures these past three years had been conjured in her mind?

Yes, she owed it to her nana.

But she also owed it to herself.

The party was on a Saturday evening. Grace had woken that morning to her stomach roiling, emitting sounds that trumpeted its protestation. Her anxiety would do this—wreak havoc with her gastrointestinal system. She was often left feeling utterly appreciative and relieved that her room was just a few doors down from the women's bathroom.

After a morning shower, Grace had holed up in her room for a couple of hours—she was never one to sleep in on the weekends—and attempted to clear her mind so that she might study for an upcoming exam. The attempt had proven futile, and so she closed and locked her door, walked down the first-floor hallway of the dormitory, exited through a side entrance, and made her way through the thick, cold winter air and to the mess hall to grab some breakfast.

She sat down at an unoccupied table in the spacious room. Most of her classmates hadn't changed out of their pajamas; thick flannel and bright cotton prints abounded. Grace was one of only a handful of people that were dressed for the day ahead. She poked at her oatmeal and blueberries. She had thought this to be a good choice: filling, offering sustenance to her otherwise empty stomach. But as she brought the spoon to her lips, her insides protested. Her mouth salivated, and she was afraid she was going to be sick.

Perhaps she should head back to her room and make a call to Dana. Maybe this wasn't such a good idea after all.

But then an image of her smiling nana entered her mind—her nana with her abundant wrinkles, her blue eyes crinkling at the corners with delight—and Grace knew that she had to persevere. It was just a party, right? It really wasn't a big deal at all, not in the grand scheme of things.

She *could* do this!

What she couldn't do was eat. Grace stood from the table and brought her bowl of oatmeal and blueberries to the conveyor belt that was slowly moving dirty dishes along and into the back of the kitchen, where they'd be washed. She felt terrible that she was wasting food—growing up without a lot of money had made her appreciate good food from an early age—but she didn't see a way around it. If she forced the oatmeal down, she was sure to end up in the bathroom.

Grace trained her gaze on the hard white floor and watched as her feet in their winter boots made their way to the front door and out into the cold December morning. She tugged her orange hat farther down over her ears, her hair tickling her cheeks and exposed neck and resting against her jacket.

When Grace entered her room, she kicked her boots off in the corner and sat down on her bed. She sighed. What now? Perhaps she should attempt to study again? The test was on Monday, and it was a big one, worth almost fifty percent of this semester's grade. She wanted to be a teacher and to work with children. Elementary children, that was.

Once they graduated to middle grades and especially high school, they intimidated her. But younger children didn't make her nervous. She loved children. They comforted her. She was good with them. If she wanted to be a teacher, her studies couldn't falter now, not when she was almost through with her undergraduate education.

Grace opened her laptop, a used one that she had acquired at a reasonable price using the money she had earned working at the library, sorting and stacking books. She loved this laptop. It meant she no longer had to trek across campus to the nearest computer lab and type away alongside other financially unfortunate students. And gone were the days when she was one of the only students in a classroom forced to resort to using pen and paper to jot down notes, a bit of an embarrassment that couldn't be helped.

She looked at the screen and surveyed the words she had typed, black against a white backdrop. She tried to concentrate. Instead, she found an image of herself at the forefront of her thoughts, wine glass in hand, bloodred liquid sloshing out the top as an elbow shoved into her arm. Apologies, a concerned expression. Red spreading to stain her dress.

Grace clenched her eyes shut and rubbed her temples with the tips of her fingers. She was being ridiculous. She knew this.

She closed her laptop. There would be no studying today. At least she had all day tomorrow to get her work done, and she knew all the material anyway. She always made sure of that.

Perhaps if she opened her most recent book, she'd be able to lose herself in its pages. Grace lay on top of her comforter and reached over to her nightstand. She lifted her novel and opened to the bookmarked page. When she reread the first paragraph four times over, she knew there would be no concentrating, and she gave in, setting her book back down.

Television then. She'd watch television. If she found her mind wandering, it wouldn't make a difference anyway. It was just the TV. Grace lifted the remote and pushed the on button. Sound filled the empty space, and it pleased her. She needed the distraction.

Grace attempted to watch the TV as her eyes floated to the dress she had hung on her doorknob, the dress she had picked out last night to ensure she was ready for Dana's party. The only nice dress she owned. She wasn't much into dresses these days, preferring jeans and sweaters. She stood from her bed and walked over to the closet door. She lifted the soft material in her hands, perhaps a bit too light for a winter party, but it was what she had, so she'd make do. The dress was black, a universal color and one she was content to wear. Black should help her blend in. She ran her fingers along the body of the dress, looking for any imperfections she could care for. She certainly had the time. But there were none. She had made sure of that last night.

Grace lay back on her bed and began to watch the television again. At this point, it was only noise to her ears, but she stared at the screen nonetheless. It was a welcome distraction from her thoughts.

And thus, the morning passed. Grace headed to the mess hall around noon. Her stomach was rumbling with hunger. Or was that her anxiety manifesting itself again? Either way, she really should get some food into her body. She didn't want to feel weak. The last thing she needed tonight was to faint in front of all the partygoers. That would surely solidify her fate and prove that the nightmares coursing within her head about having a terrible time, about people staring at her, would, indeed, come to fruition. Of course they'd be staring at her if she fainted. Grace wrapped her arms around her thick jacket and pushed her elbows into her stomach as she walked. It would be her, too, wouldn't it? If anybody was going to faint, it would be Grace. It just figured.

The aromas in the mess hall were tantalizing, and Grace found that she truly was hungry and looking forward to eating. The food staff had made their famous mac and cheese, the meal that kids raved about throughout campus, and for good reason. As with many of the other students, Grace loved this mac and cheese—the elbow-shaped pasta was soft, and the cheese clung to the spoon. Delicious!

With her tray of pasta and the addition of an apple, Grace quickly surveyed the room. She found a small empty table in the corner near a set of windows and hurried over before someone else could occupy it. The last thing she wanted to do was ask if she could eat with another person. That would prove awkward.

Grace sat down and picked up her spoon. She brought the cheesy pasta to rest beneath her nose and inhaled its scent. She closed her eyes, and her lips lifted ever so slightly. She spooned a small portion into her mouth and began to chew. It really was a wonderful meal. Grace managed three bites before her stomach flipped, and she rested her palm over it. She dropped her spoon and closed her eyes. She swore she could hear the ticking of the clock behind her, counting down the seconds until it was time for her to leave in her black dress and catch the T to Dana's place. She hated the T. Hated it! So many people crowded into one small space. So many germs. People touching her, leaning up against her. But the T was her only mode of transportation when off campus. She didn't own a car.

Grace attempted another bite of mac and cheese and found she was able to get it down. But that was it. She couldn't force more. She was afraid of the consequences if she did. She wished she could take this meal back to her room, but she had nothing with her, no containers or boxes. She could take the apple, though. That would do. And she had a couple of snacks in her room if she felt the need for nourishment. She wouldn't make it back to the mess hall for dinner; she'd be leaving before then. But she assumed there would be a plentiful array of foods at Dana's. Whether or not Grace would partake was another matter altogether.

Grace deposited her tray onto the conveyor belt and walked out the door and back to her room for the second time that day. She passed giggling girls and wished she were among them. She passed couples hand in hand and dreamed—not for the first time—that she wasn't so shy, so anxiety ridden. She would have liked very much to be in a relationship, something she had never had the pleasure of experiencing before. In the eighth grade, she had been kissed, and she was pretty sure it had been done on a dare, so that didn't count whatsoever. Plus, it had made her queasy. She thought it quite sad indeed that that measly eighth-grade experience had been her first and only kiss.

A tear dribbled down her cold cheek as Grace hastened toward her dormitory. Why did she have to be like this? Why couldn't she be like most of the other students at this school, amiable and playful, making fantastic memories with friends that she'd store away and take along with her on life's journey?

She didn't fully comprehend why she was how she was, but as she opened the door to her room and plonked herself on her bed, she was determined to make the most of tonight. She could do this. She *had* to do this! She'd look people in the eye. She'd make small talk. She would find her voice.

She would!

Grace looked good in her dress. A small mirror hung on the back of her closet door, and she was able to see herself just well enough. Mostly her upper body, but it would do. She was pleased. She didn't wear any makeup. She never had figured that stuff out, and her father's discouraging words from her teenage years echoed constantly in her mind. But she had taken another shower and tucked her dark hair behind her ears, something she rarely did, as she found more comfort when it was hiding her cheeks. Grace didn't own any heels, but she did have a pair of black ballet flats that she slipped on. They'd be comfortable for the evening, even if they proved to be a bit difficult on the wintry sidewalks through Boston.

Boston. It was where Dana lived. Grace knew she'd be able to get herself to Dana's place just fine, as she had been there before, and she was familiar with Dana's particular area well enough since she had grown up just on the outskirts of the city. Her father worked in Boston, not far from Dana's place, and had done so ever since Grace was a small child. It was more the crowds that she was worried about. Crowds of people, swarms of people, she didn't like one bit, and she never felt comfortable late at night, either, so she knew she'd be leaving Dana's on the earlier side to get back to her room.

But she was going. She was off.

And as she stepped foot outside in her flats, dress, and winter jacket, as she stood under the glow of the nearest streetlamp, she was proud of herself.

That first step outside was a big one indeed.

Grace made her way to the closest T station, a walk of about fifteen minutes. She waited for the train to arrive, wringing her hands, the skin of her fingers pressing against the smooth inner surface of her gloves.

Her legs were cold, but there was nothing that could be done about that. She was glad she had her thick jacket to stave off the wintry chill of the December evening, even if only her upper body was kept warm. She was wearing her burnt-orange hat, her favorite. She knew it would mess up her stringy hair, but the hat not only kept her head and ears warm, it also reminded her of her nana, reminded her why she was standing on the platform of the T station at that very moment, waiting for the train to take her into the big city, to take her to Dana's place and a crowd of people she did not know.

The train arrived, and she boarded. Blessedly, Grace spotted several unoccupied seats. She walked toward one and sat down. She wrapped her arms around her chest, pushed her elbows inward, and pressed her knees together. She was shivering.

It took another twenty minutes for the train to arrive at the stop at which Grace would deboard. There was a ding on the intercom, and the announcer declared the name of the station. Grace stood and walked toward the open doors. She followed a small crowd of people onto the platform. A whooshing sound met her ears, and a burst of hot, stale air stroked her cheeks, filled her nostrils. She closed her eyes momentarily as she began to walk toward the exit.

Up the stairs she went and out into the blustery evening.

She wrapped her arms around her chest even tighter and hastened her steps down the rickety sidewalk. A few stray snow flurries touched her nose, her cheeks, then melted on her skin.

Dana's apartment was a ten-minute walk from the T station, and Grace was so cold by then that she was grateful when she arrived at the front door of the brownstone. She knew she was standing in front of the correct door, for this one was a bright red while the others surrounding it were muted browns and tans, and a few were black.

Red. Grace shook her head and grinned slightly. Red to match Dana's exuberant personality.

She could hear the music from her position outside. It seeped out of the cracks in the door, in the windows. She heard laughter and some sort of clang from within. Grace steeled herself, fisted her hand. She lifted it to knock and then dropped it to her side. She sighed. What had she been thinking?

Grace slowly turned to leave, but as her foot hovered over the stair below, the door opened, and a bustle of noise filled her ears, while tantalizing scents pervaded her nostrils.

"Thought I saw you there."

Grace recognized Dana's voice behind her. She inhaled sharply and bit down on her lower lip as she turned around. Dana's smile was wide when Grace looked up at her, her cheeks flushed an attractive pink. Whether from merriment or alcohol Grace wasn't sure, but it didn't matter. She had been spotted, and it was too late to turn back now.

"Come in!" Dana exclaimed. "What are you doing just standing there? Honestly... it's freezing outside." Dana held the door open, and Grace slipped inside.

"So glad you could make it," Dana said, her smile

growing as she closed the door behind Grace. "Not too many people were busy, so we've got a full house tonight, with more to come later. How great is that?"

"Yes." Grace's voice was so soft it wasn't much higher than a whisper.

"Oh, hey there, Grace." A voice with the timbre of a baritone spoke as its owner sidled up next to Dana.

Grace recognized Tommy, Dana's long-standing boyfriend. They had dated in high school then moved into separate college dormitories there in Boston after graduation. When Tommy had acquired his bachelor's degree, he'd found a job in the city while Dana pursued her master's. Dana had completed her studies a couple of years ago and found a job, and she and Tommy had moved into their brownstone just that past spring. Grace was pleased for Dana and her success, both in love and in life.

"Hi, Tommy," Grace replied meekly.

Tommy turned to Dana. "Something I gotta show you," he said, lifting his chin to indicate the direction in which he'd like her to follow.

"Yep. Okay," Dana said before glancing back toward Grace. "Come in. Have fun. Food is over there." She pointed to a table in the corner of the room. "And the drinks are next to it."

"Okay," Grace said as she nodded. "Thank you."

"No problem. Glad you could make it. See you in a bit." Dana turned on a heel and followed Tommy into the crowd.

Grace stood helplessly in front of the closed door for a minute, pressing her arms into the chest of her jacket and stealing glances around the room. Although both Dana and Tommy were only a handful of years older than Grace, many of the people conversing in the room looked to be even further along in age, perhaps in their late twenties. This immediately placed Grace in a heightened state of unease. Would she have much in common with these friends of Dana's and Tommy's if she was confident enough to approach them, to speak with them?

Well, she wasn't going to get far by standing in front of the door, now, was she?

Grace took a deep breath and held it in. She exhaled then walked into the room. Food. Perhaps if she had a plate of food, it would occupy her hands, and she could always turn to it if she found she had gotten cornered. Yes, food would do. She made for the table against the wall, stuffed her gloves in the pocket of her jacket, and picked up a gleaming white plate.

Grace was amazed at the choices on display. Who had made all this? Had Dana done it herself? If she had, then Grace was sure it had taken all day. Before her were mini quiches adorned with melted cheese and red peppers on the top, a quintessential Christmas color. There were stuffed mushroom caps and Brie wrapped in a puff pastry, the cheese oozing out of a triangular slice on the side. Crackers lined the plate. There was bruschetta and an olive and cheese board. There were nuts and various platters of Christmas cookies. Meatballs were submerged in a deep red sauce that was steaming out of a crockpot. There were fruits and veggies, plentiful and bright.

Grace chose some large green grapes and a few slices of cheese. She deposited them on her plate and then scooted farther down the table until she was standing in front of the alcohol. There was so much, most of which Grace had never even heard of before. There was hard liquor and beer, wine and cider.

Grace gently placed her plate on the table and lifted a

sparkling wine glass. She reached for a bottle of red wine, and then instantaneously her mind trickled back to her nightmarish daydream in which someone had pushed into her at this party, and she had spilled a glass of red wine, the liquid dripping down her hand and splashing to stain her dress. Sure, her dress was black. And no, she probably would not be rammed into tonight by a careless attendee, but she would take no chances. She altered her direction and lifted a bottle of white wine instead. She poured a small amount into her glass, knowing that if she only had a splash, it would enable her to more easily make excuses to visit this table again.

With plate and glass in hand, Grace turned around, surveyed the room again, and settled on a vacant corner. She slowly made her way over, careful not to bump into anyone. When she arrived, she settled in nicely. From here, she could see the entire room. Grace looked down and felt quite silly as she realized she had placed herself in an awkward position, for there she was, holding not only a plate of food but a glass of wine as well. How was she to eat the food if her other hand was simultaneously occupied? And then Grace also realized she was still wearing her thick winter jacket and hat.

She looked around, and there just beside her was a small end table, the base for a large lamp. Grace thought it would have just enough space for her to put her plate and glass down. She did so, and then she wriggled out of her coat, stuffed her hat into a sleeve, and looked around again. Where was she going to put it? She noticed several coats hanging by the front door, but that was on the other side of the room, and she didn't really want to dodge the crowd once more. She looked left then right. There was a couch next to the table. She'd just deposit her jacket

17

behind it for now. She was sure Dana wouldn't mind if she did so.

When through, Grace lifted her plate and picked a grape off the vine. She slipped it into her mouth and slowly began to chew. Even though she hadn't eaten more than a few bites of food that day, she wasn't hungry, but she didn't know how else to occupy herself. She finished her grape and then set her plate down, picking up her glass of wine instead. She took a small sip. She stood there in the corner of the room, sipping here and there but mainly pretending to drink often so it would appear to onlookers that she was enjoying herself.

Grace surveyed the room again. Off in the distance, she saw a laughing couple, the woman slipping her arm around her companion's waist, her eyes lifted under long, thick lashes, her lips grinning mischievously. Beside them were two women in animated conversation, one holding a bottle of beer and attempting to gesticulate as she relayed her tale.

Grace looked down, her eyes focusing on the hardwood floor. She sighed before lifting her head. As her eyes scanned the room, they landed on a woman about ten feet away, and Grace realized that the woman was looking directly at her. She wasn't smiling, but nor was there a frown on her face. Her expression was rather blank, in fact, indifferent. Grace didn't know what to make of it. She tried to smile, slipped a hand from her wine glass with the intention of waving, but just as her fingers lifted, the woman turned to the man standing beside her, and the moment was gone.

Grace averted her eyes and looked off into the distance. Her mind began to wander. The music muted in her head, and the gay chatter of partygoers was lost.

"Hey there!"

Grace was startled from her reverie, and she jumped. Dana stood by her side, laughing.

"Sorry about that. Didn't realize how gone you were. Didn't mean to scare you."

"You didn't scare me," Grace replied.

"Could have fooled me," Dana said, but Grace knew she was jesting, so she smiled. "Hey, got someone I want to introduce you to."

"Huh?" Grace's mouth hung open ever so slightly as her brows furrowed.

"A friend," Dana said. "I want to introduce you two."

"Oh." It was the only verbal reply that Grace was able to manage.

Dana smirked. "Gary, Grace. Grace, Gary."

Grace hadn't noticed the tall man standing next to Dana until that very moment, and when she looked over and up at him, she went mute. Her mouth felt dry. Her body tingled. The man was incredibly handsome.

"So good to meet you, Grace," the man said. He stuck out his hand, and Grace looked down at it before slowly slipping hers over to meet his. They shook, and Grace noticed how the man's hand dwarfed her own, how it felt warm and inviting.

"Nice to meet you too," she mumbled.

She wanted desperately to avert her eyes, but she forced herself to look directly into the man's, and when she did, she found she lacked the ability to look away. The man's—Gary's—irises were dark, so very dark, one of the darkest sets of eyes Grace had ever seen. So dark, in fact, that they were mesmerizing. Grace felt as if she could lose herself in their depths.

Gary's palm released Grace's. Grace brought her hand

to rest against her glass, but her eyes remained on Gary's and his on hers.

"Gary is a friend of Tommy's and of mine," Dana explained.

Grace could hear her words, but they sounded far away, distant. "Okay," she managed to reply.

"Tommy and Gary work together," Dana continued. "Not in the same department. Or was it the same one, Gary? I don't remember."

Gary chuckled. "Not the same department," he answered, "but we still work closely together at times, depending on the project."

"Oh, that's right," Dana said. "Now I remember. Don't mind me." She turned to Grace. "So this is Gary. And he's really nice. And I saw you over here and thought I'd introduce the two of you."

"Okay," Grace said again. Could she not manage something else? "*Okay?*" What in the world?

"Dana, Dana!" It was Tommy calling from the other end of the room. "You've got to come see this."

Grace broke her gaze from Gary's and looked toward the shout.

"Wonder what he wants now," Dana said to Gary and Grace, although she was grinning widely. "I suppose I should go on over. Catch up with you two later." And then she was gone, leaving Grace alone with this stranger, this man that both discomfited her and piqued her curiosity simultaneously.

"So, Grace," Gary began. "I don't know anything about you. Dana just grabbed me and dragged me over. How do you know each other?" He took a swig of his beer.

"I... I..." *Come on, Grace,* she thought. *Pull yourself together, for goodness sake!* She took a sip of her wine and then another.

"Good stuff?" Gary teased.

Grace felt her cheeks flush, and she glanced down at her black ballet flats. She inhaled deeply, took another sip of wine, and then looked at Gary. "We grew up together," she said softly.

"Oh? How so?"

"Nana was best friends with Joyce."

"And who was Joyce? I'm assuming this nana you speak of is your grandmother."

Grace nodded. "Was," she said softly.

"Sorry about that. Didn't know she died." Gary took another sip of beer.

Grace shook her head. Of course he wouldn't know. And for that matter, how in the world was he supposed to know who Joyce was? Dana had just told Grace that Gary was one of Tommy's coworkers, so he probably wasn't a person that was privy to intimate details of Dana's life.

"Thanks. And Joyce is Dana's grandmother."

"Ah. It's coming together now." Gary smiled, and Grace found that her lips lifted into a slight grin, much to her extreme pleasure. "So then your grandmother and Dana's grandmother were close."

"Yes," Grace confirmed.

"And you say you grew up together, you and Dana?"

"Um… well… we saw each other sometimes."

"All right."

"I… I…" Grace wasn't sure what to say, how to explain further.

"Looks like you kept in touch, though, yeah? Otherwise, you wouldn't be here."

Grace smiled, relieved that Gary was able to follow her

disjointed statements, and pleased, too, that he hadn't walked away.

"Yes," she said. "We kept in touch. Dana is very nice. She's always been nice. And I don't live far away."

"Is that right? And where is it that you live? What do you do?"

"I'm in school."

"Not high school, I hope," Gary replied.

Grace startled. Did he really think that she was still in high school? But then she saw the sly smirk playing on his lips, and she found herself giggling softly. "No," she said. "Not high school. I'll be graduating college in the spring, this is my last year."

"Ah... good for you." Another sip of beer. "Plans for the future?"

"I can't afford grad school, so..." Grace cut herself off. This stranger didn't need to know her financial situation. She shook her head. "I... um... I wanted to go to grad school, but I can't right now, so I need to find a job. I'm doing well in school, though, so I'm pretty sure I can find one."

"And what is it you'd like to do?"

"I want to be a teacher," Grace said. "Little kids. An elementary school teacher. I like younger children."

"I could never be a teacher, especially with little kids," Gary said with a grimace. "Don't enjoy kids so much. Good for you though."

"Thank you," Grace said. *Ask him something, ask him something,* she silently shouted to herself. "Do you like your job?"

"Yep," Gary confirmed. "I do. This one's my second since graduating. Got my master's... let's see... maybe six years ago now? First job sucked, but this one's good. Good people, too. Hey, Tommy's there, right?"

Grace managed a smile. "Yes," she said. "Tommy has always been nice to me."

"Good to hear it," Gary said. "But not surprised."

"Have you... Dana and Tommy, have they had you over here before?"

"Sure," Gary said. "We get together sometimes, but mostly it's just me and Tommy. After work, we'll get a beer. There's a great place just a few blocks from the office."

"Do you... um... do you live in the city?" She wanted to ask him if he lived alone. Did he have a girlfriend? Wife? She surreptitiously glanced down at his left hand resting against his thigh and didn't notice a ring.

"I do, yeah," Gary said. "Not too far away from here. Got two roommates. Slobs, both of them." Gary grinned. "But I like the company."

"Then it works out," Grace said.

"It does," Gary replied. "Won't be like this forever, but for now, I'm having fun. Love the city. Love my friends. Got a good job that pays well." Gary nodded. "Loving life at the moment."

Grace smiled. "That's very good to hear you say."

"And how about you?" Gary asked. "You happy in school? And where did you say you lived?"

Here it is, Grace thought. *What will he think when he learns that I still live on campus?*

"I like school a lot. I like to learn. I... I live at school."

"On-campus apartment?"

"Um... no," Grace said hesitantly. "I... I live on campus, but in a dorm."

"Oh," Gary said with knitted brows. "I didn't realize seniors did that."

"Um... not many do. I... I'm probably one of the only ones," Grace admitted. "But I like it. I have my own room. And everything I need is there." She looked at the floor. "I don't have a car," she added as if that clarification would excuse her lack of motivation for moving off campus.

"Don't need a car in Boston," Gary said. "I don't have one either."

"The school's not in the city. Just outside," Grace said, hoping this would make her situation more acceptable.

"T is a great tool," Gary said. "Just hop on, and you can get anywhere. Even outside the city limits a bit."

"Yes," Grace said. "I suppose." She lifted her glass to her lips only to find that it was empty.

"What are you drinking?" Gary asked as he reached for her glass. "I'll refill."

"Oh," Grace said, a bit taken aback by the kind offer. "White wine. Any white will do."

"Be right back," Gary said then walked in the direction of the tables.

Grace stood in the corner of the room, clasping her hands and resting them on her stomach. She smiled. Though she wasn't the best conversationalist, and other men and women in the room were certain to provide more stimulation, Grace was proud of herself for having gotten this far. Gary was refilling her wine glass, and he'd be returning to her. They'd have the opportunity to talk some more.

And Grace was determined to make the most of it.

When Gary stood in front of Grace and handed her glass off, Grace thanked him as she looked up and into his deep, hypnotizing eyes. She felt her stomach flutter, but this time, it wasn't entirely the result of her nerves.

They spoke for an hour. The clock continued to tick, the music went on playing. Guests mingled, chatted, drank, and ate. And Grace didn't acknowledge them in the least. Neither did Gary.

Two hours passed, and Grace was thrilled that she had been able to hold up her side of the conversation, shocked, in fact, that she had done quite well, had divulged information about herself to Gary, and had reciprocated in asking questions. It didn't go as well as it would have in her mind, but it went rather smoothly regardless. Smooth for her, anyway. She was proud, happy. Elated, really.

When Grace eventually looked at the clock and realized how late it had become, her eyes widened, and she hastened to deposit her empty wine glass onto the end table and grab her jacket from behind the couch.

"What's wrong?" Gary asked.

"It's getting late. I really need to head home."

"Oh," Gary replied, frowning slightly. "Do you really have to go?"

"Um... I... I really don't like being out too late in the city."

"Oh," Gary said. "Of course. Hadn't thought of that, but of course. You're alone. Why don't you stay a bit longer, and I'll just ride the T over with you, make sure you get back to your room safely."

"Oh," Grace said, taken aback by the offer. And then she nodded. "Okay. Thank you. Yes."

"Great," Gary said. "A refill?" He reached for her glass with a lopsided grin.

Even though she was feeling the effects of the wine, and an additional glass wasn't the most responsible course of action, Grace nodded. "Thank you."

When she watched his retreating figure in his jeans and off-white sweater, she grinned. She, Grace Harrison, was having a fantastic evening!

~

Their relationship progressed smoothly from there on. Gary had walked Grace back to her dormitory the night of Dana's party and said goodbye at the door. He called her the following day, and they'd made a date for the next weekend. Gary suggested the dinner venue, and Grace had easily agreed. She didn't care where they ate, didn't care about much in the way of details. She just wanted to be with Gary, to get to know him better.

Weeks passed then months, and Grace found herself in cap and gown. She would have to further her education and get her teacher's certification in order to secure a job in the state of Massachusetts. She'd do so directly upon graduation while she worked at a daycare center that had recently hired her to begin in June. Gary had already asked her to move in with him and his two roommates, and Grace had readily agreed.

Her life was slipping into place.

Grace moved in with Gary and his two roommates and was happy there for the duration of the summer, even if it was more boisterous than she was used to and despite the fact that she was in the city, a place that continuously put her at unease. Gary's roommates grew on her, and in time, she found a level of comfort in their presence.

Summer waned, and autumn began. Leaves changed color, their vibrant orange, yellow, and red hues aiding in Grace's enjoyment of the season and in her happy state of affairs, for she *was* happy. Blissfully so. She was in love with a man who treated her well, who was attractive and attentive. She was in love with a man whose manner of speech was succinct when they were around other people. Grace often retreated to the shadows, where she felt more at ease

26

and where she could revel in the pleasure of watching her partner, listening to him argue a case, or merely enjoying the show of Gary's various facial expressions when in good company—merriment, shock, intrigue.

Gary's proposal was anticlimactic, though Grace didn't mind. It was enough for her that she was with him in the first place. He proposed while the couple was walking along the Charles River. They had stopped to rest on a metal bench overlooking the water, and Gary had turned to Grace. When his lips lifted in a grin of amusement, Grace furrowed her brow inquisitively.

"What is it?" she asked.

"Nothing," Gary replied, though his grin widened.

"Seriously, Gary," Grace protested. "What is it?"

"What would you say if I asked you to marry me?"

Grace was completely caught off guard and was left open-mouthed and astonished.

Gary laughed.

Grace didn't take her eyes off Gary and eventually managed a meek, "What?"

Gary laughed again and repeated, "What would you say if I asked you to marry me?"

"Are you... do you really mean it?" Grace asked.

"Would I be sitting here asking you if I didn't mean it?" Gary retorted playfully.

"I... well, I guess not. But, Gary..."

"Mmm?" Gary raised his brows, his smile still wide, exuding a sense of confidence.

"Where did this come from?"

"I've been thinking about it for some time now," Gary said.

"You... you have?" Grace asked.

"Sure have," Gary confirmed. "The timing's right,

don't you think? You're finishing up with the daycare, and you'll be starting at the new school soon. The apartment is getting cramped with all four of us living there. Don't you want a place of our own?"

"Well, yes," Grace said. "Sure I do. I mean, yes, I'd love to have a home with you. But, Gary, we can get a home even if we're not married."

"I know that," Gary said. "But I figured it was time. What? You don't want to marry me?" He gave Grace a sly smirk.

"That's not it at all," Grace said, her voice raised and her eyes wide. "I do want to marry you!"

"Oh, you do, yeah?" Gary wrapped his arm around her shoulders and pulled her closer to his chest. "So that's a yes?"

Grace lifted her head and looked into his deep brown eyes, so dark they almost appeared black. She swam in them. She dove. Lost herself completely.

She relaxed into his embrace and put her head on his chest. "It's a yes," she whispered. "A definite yes."

"Thought so," Gary replied before kissing her forehead and leaning back on the bench, his body entirely relaxed as they watched the water of the river ripple under the sun. Crowds of people passed them by, though there was no indication whatsoever that something truly momentous had just transpired between the tall, brown-haired man in a gray woolen sweater and jeans and the brunette by his side, her hair tucked under a knitted orange hat.

CHAPTER 2

*G*race remembered the day she and Gary went furniture shopping for their new home. They had found a cute place just outside the city in a quiet neighborhood and had moved in a few months after their July wedding, when Grace had just turned twenty-three. They didn't have many material possessions to transfer to their new house from the small apartment they shared with their two roommates in Boston, so they set a date for a Saturday morning to explore their options. Gary had taken Grace to a local furniture shop in town, and Grace had been giddy with excitement. She had a new husband, a new home. Soon, they'd have their very own new furniture to fill the space they were fortunate to call theirs.

Gary and Grace.

The future was looking bright.

Grace had fallen in love with a brown plush sofa set, and although Gary feigned indifference, she could see that he wasn't as attached to the set as she was. But—since no other option seemed to catch his eye—he capitulated. They had kept the bed Gary had acquired in his college days, but he wanted to replace his old desk, as it was showing its age. The desk he chose felt rather ostentatious to Grace, with its thick mahogany top and large drawers. It was much larger than he needed, really, but it was what Gary chose, and Grace didn't feel she had any say in the matter. It was his desk, after all. It was Gary who would be using it to complete projects when he was home or to peruse his computer for personal enjoyment.

At a store down the street from the place in which they procured their new furniture, Grace and Gary purchased kitchen gadgets too—a slow cooker, utensils, a rather expensive knife set that had caught Gary's attention, and pots and pans, among other necessities. Although Grace knew she'd be the one utilizing these items—Gary didn't like to cook—she let Gary make the choices. She didn't care what they got. She was just thrilled to be married to him, to come home—to *their* home—and wait for him to arrive from work. It fulfilled her, made her happy. It flooded her with a sense of purpose.

She was Mrs. Clarke.

They arrived back home on that summer Saturday morning from shopping with Gary's new car loaded to the roof and the promise of delivery from the furniture store. Grace had set about washing the kitchenware and enjoying every moment of deciding where things would be kept. In her very own kitchen. The kitchen she shared with her husband.

Gary was indifferent as to where the knickknacks would go throughout the house—a large lamp, a decorative koala, a globe, a wicker basket for storage. Grace held each item in her hands and looked down at it with a smile before making a decision that she was sure she'd retract later when she'd happen upon an even better place for display. She knew not a lot of people would see these items, but it wasn't about other people for Grace. It was about her and how she felt. It was about making this space theirs, a place that she was happy to come home to, a space where, when she opened the front door and stepped over the threshold, she'd find her body immediately relax, her shoulders droop in ease, her stress melt away.

Yes, she remembered that day well.

Perhaps it had been the beginning of the end.

Gary worked late hours at the office, but this did not come as a surprise to Grace once they were married. Grace had known early on in their relationship that Gary worked sometimes in excess of seventy hours a week. Although she didn't fully understand what it was he did, even though he had attempted explanations time and time again, she knew it was important work. She knew her husband was an asset to his company, and this filled her with a sense of pride. She was okay with it: the late hours, constantly returning home to a quiet, empty house. When the bell rang out to sound the end of the day at her elementary school, she'd run errands if needed then drive home to clean or simply relax.

Then she would prepare dinner and wait for her husband. Often, he'd call to let her know that he wouldn't make it home in time, but she didn't mind. It was expected. She ate alone with classical music playing in the background or while watching the television set in the living room on their plush brown sofa. And on the days she knew in advance that Gary wouldn't be home, she'd invite Bethany over to the house.

Bethany was the wife of a man that Gary worked with —Jordan—and both she and her husband had been constant companions to Gary and Grace. Although Grace and Bethany hadn't shared much in the way of intimate details about their lives, either past or present, and conversations tended to remain superficial, Grace enjoyed Bethany's company and was pleased to call her a friend. In fact, Bethany was one of Grace's only friends. Sure, she had Dana, but Dana was a busy woman due to her extroverted nature and wasn't often free. Grace also lacked the ability to easily invite people over to her home or to a local coffee shop for a drink, no matter how much the desire presented itself.

But with Bethany, it was different. Gary was close to Jordan, and somehow, that made it easier for Grace. Plus, Grace now had a cell phone. They certainly made communication easier, didn't they? Grace didn't have to pick up her home phone, didn't have to talk into the receiver. She could plan out her words before she made a call, or she could simply text. She did love that.

A year into Grace's marriage, Bethany came over to the house for dinner while Gary was working late into a Friday evening. The timing was good, as Bethany's husband had made plans to head out for the night with some buddies of his, and Bethany didn't like to be alone.

The doorbell chimed, announcing Bethany's arrival. Grace smiled, removed the large stainless steel spoon from the simmering pasta sauce, and placed it on the granite countertop. She hastened to the door, turned the knob, and flung the door open.

"Hello!" Grace exclaimed.

"You're in a happy mood," Bethany remarked.

"I guess I am."

"Why? What's up?" Bethany stepped inside, and Grace closed the door behind her.

"Nothing's up, really. I'm just glad you're here."

"Okay." Bethany smirked. "Wish I could muster up some of your enthusiasm."

"What?" Grace asked playfully. "You're not happy to be here with me?"

"Course I am," Bethany replied. "But it's been a long day."

"Then come in and have a seat. The spaghetti's cooking right now and should be done soon. Sit on the couch and relax while I finish up in the kitchen. Make yourself comfortable. Want a glass of wine or something? Gary keeps beer in the fridge, as you know. I'm happy to get you one if you'd prefer that."

"Wine's good. Could use one right about now," Bethany said.

"Then wine it is," Grace replied. "I've got red and white. Any preference?"

"How about a red tonight? Might go well with the pasta. And speaking of which, I can smell that sauce. Yum!"

"I know, right?" Grace grinned. She had to admit that she did make some really fantastic homemade pasta sauce, and since pasta dishes weren't Gary's favorite, Grace often saved them for Bethany's visits.

Bethany situated herself on the living room sofa while Grace headed to the kitchen to stir the sauce, check on the spaghetti, and pour two generous glasses of wine. When she returned to the living room, she handed Bethany's glass off and sat next to her friend.

Grace took a small sip and then asked, "Why was your day so tough today?"

Bethany lifted her brows. She took a large gulp of her

wine, rested the glass on her lap, then looked at Grace. She sighed audibly. "Just work stuff," she said. "I don't really want to go into details right now. I just want to forget about it. It's the weekend. I don't have work. I can shove it to the back of my head."

"I understand," Grace said with a nod. "Of course. We don't have to talk about it."

"I'm telling you though," Bethany said. "Once we have a baby, I'm done. Done with it all. I don't make a crap ton of money anyway. Jordan's salary will do it for us. I'll stay home with the baby, Jordan can work, and I can quit that awful place. Good riddance. I'll be happy if I never have to step foot inside it ever again. Ever!"

Grace nodded again and took another sip of her wine. She knew that Bethany and Jordan had been trying for a baby for several months now, and she knew, too, that Bethany wasn't happy with her current place of employment. They had had this conversation before. On several occasions, in fact. Bethany felt pushed around, taken advantage of. She didn't like her boss or her coworkers, and she didn't find the work to be satisfying.

Grace felt, not for the first time, incredibly fortunate that she was welcomed, wanted, and appreciated at her elementary school. She didn't know the other teachers and staff well and only spoke to them about work matters, but they had all been very kind to her. She forewent lunch in the common area, instead choosing to eat at her desk in her classroom and get some extra work done while the children were eating lunch themselves and then out at recess. She spoke to her coworkers when needed—during staff meetings, when a teacher in either of the rooms that adjoined hers required a reprieve for a minute or two while class was in session, or when the entire first grade was working on the same curriculum and came together for projects and experiments.

She found she did well under these circumstances. When there was an agenda on the table, she could contribute without preamble. It was when someone attempted to speak to her about her personal life that she found she muted up and lacked the mental capacity to continue the conversation. For Grace, speaking about herself instead of work or the children in her care was something she continuously struggled with, even after all this time. Though she had to admit that she was proud of herself. Immensely proud. Through the years, she had gotten better and had found the slightest bit more ease when approaching people or when they approached her.

She was hopeful for the future.

"I really do hope it happens for you soon, Bethany. This baby, I mean."

"I know," Bethany sighed. "I hope so too. Can you imagine me as a mom?"

She smiled behind her glass of wine, half gone now.

"I really can," Grace said wholeheartedly. "I think you're going to be a fantastic mother."

"I still can't believe you don't want kids. We'd be so good together, you know, pushing the strollers around the city, going to the park. But you probably wouldn't want to quit your job, huh? And I don't want to get all friendly with your nanny. It wouldn't be the same."

"None of that is going to happen," Grace said. "And you're right. If it did, if Gary and I did have a baby, then I wouldn't want to leave work. I love it too much. And somehow, I'd feel like I was letting my children down."

"But they wouldn't even know. They'd be in the next grade or something, right?"

"True, but... I just can't explain it. I've known for a while that teaching is what I was meant to do, but a mother? I think that just takes everything to the next level. I know myself too well. I'd have trouble as a mom. Not with loving the child. I know I'd love them so much, but with everything else that comes with having children, especially as they age. I'm not good with people, Bethany. If I had to fight for my child for whatever reason, if I had to speak to others... can you imagine me in a PTA?"

Bethany snorted. "Nope. Definitely not."

"That's what I mean. I'm really happy with my life as it is right now. I love Gary. I love my job. And I knew very early on in our relationship that Gary didn't want children. He told me that maybe within the first couple of months we were dating. And when he told me... I was actually okay with it. I remember being completely fine. It didn't affect me like maybe I thought something like that would. I can't really explain it. I can't seem to put it into words. It's just... I'm happy. Right now. Right as I am. With my job and with Gary. I don't need anything else.

Plus, if I did change my mind and told Gary that I wanted children, I'm not sure how he'd take that. He made it pretty clear to me a while back that he wasn't interested, that he just wanted it to be us. He works so much. He wouldn't be able to help me if we had a baby. And he likes his freedom. He likes being able to head out the door on the spur of the moment on a weekend. And honestly, I like that too. I just like being with him. Goodness knows he works so much that I'm hardly with him during the week now as it is. Could you imagine if we brought a baby into the equation?"

"Yep," Bethany said. "He'd totally learn to love it."

"I'm sure he would," Grace agreed. "And so would I.

Very much. But I don't think it's in the cards for us, and I'm completely okay with that."

Bethany shook her head. "To each their own, I suppose. But I'd still love to trot down the road with our babies in their strollers."

Grace laughed at an image that her mind conjured of Bethany shaking her hips as she pushed a posh stroller down the cobblestoned streets of Boston, designer jeans on her legs and heels clicking on the ground.

"What's so funny?" Bethany asked.

"I'm just thinking about you, that's all."

"And I'm funny to you?" Bethany smirked.

"No, that's not it. It's just that… I can see you, Bethany. I can see you happy with a child. I can see you with your stroller and at the playground. But I know you also have lots of other friends. I bet some of them have babies, right? You're older than me, some of your friends have to be as well. Maybe in the same stage of life as you are now?"

"Yeah," Bethany said. "I've got other friends with kids and a few that are expecting right now. But it would be fun to add you in."

Grace smiled and took a sip of her wine. "Sorry to burst your bubble."

"Ah." Bethany flicked her hand. "That's okay. You can be my babysitter."

Grace chuckled. "Your babysitter, huh? That's what I am to you now?"

"Sure are." Bethany smirked.

"Well, all joking aside, I'd love to be a babysitter for you," Grace admitted.

"And you'll be a great one."

Grace smiled a bit shyly. "I think I would be," she said.

Grace felt rather tired that night, so she headed to bed before Gary got home from work in the city. She woke with the sun the following morning. She had always been a morning person. When Gary awoke a couple of hours later, Grace offered to make them both some scrambled eggs and toast for breakfast. Gary rubbed the sleep from his eyes, his brown hair a disheveled mess, his boxer briefs tight on his thighs and his chest bare.

"Yeah. That would be nice," he said.

Grace got to work making their breakfast, and then she and Gary sat at the dining room table to eat. They made small talk for a few minutes, Grace pondering how she'd broach the subject she had been thinking about since Bethany had left her home the night prior.

"Hey, Gary?"

"Mmm?" Gary's mouth was full of eggs.

"You know that Bethany came over last night."

"Yeah," Gary mumbled in response.

"And you know that she and Jordan have been trying for a while now to have a baby."

Gary swallowed and looked up at his wife. "Yes," he said slowly.

"I just… I wonder sometimes… well…"

"Spit it out, Grace. What's on your mind?"

"I've felt pretty confident all this time that we've been happy, that… that you've been happy with me."

Gary looked at her with his piercing dark eyes.

Grace paused and then eventually said, "With only me."

"Yeah?"

"And I guess I just wonder… well… do you still feel that

way? With others that you work with, with so many of your friends having kids these days, well… are you still happy with it just being the two of us?"

"Of course."

"Really? I mean… truly?"

"Yeah. Why? What is this all about, Grace?"

"Nothing, really. I just wanted to be sure, that's all."

"You haven't changed your mind, have you?" Gary asked with a trace of annoyance lining his voice. "When I told you I didn't want kids, you were always fine with it. Are you fine? Are you changing your mind now that Bethany's trying? Don't tell me you're changing your mind…"

"No, no," Grace assured him, "that's not it at all. I haven't changed my mind. I am so happy with it just being the two of us, Gary. Truly, I am. I'm not lying to you. I just thought I'd ask if your feelings had changed."

Gary lifted his fork to his mouth, full of eggs, and his shoulders relaxed. "I haven't changed my mind," he said. "I like the way things are."

"So do I," Grace assured him. "I really do."

"Scared me for a minute there, Grace." Gary smiled through his mouthful of food.

"I'm sorry. I didn't mean to scare you. I just thought I'd ask. I thought I'd be sure."

"Nope," Gary said, a bit of egg peeking through his lips. "Haven't changed my mind. I don't want kids."

Grace picked up her slice of toast and took a small bite.

CHAPTER 3

*B*ethany announced her pregnancy the following month, and she and Grace enjoyed a celebratory dinner at a restaurant.

"Have two glasses of wine tonight," Bethany told Grace. "One for you and one for me, since I won't be drinking for a while now." Her smile was enormous, radiating off her face. So large, in fact, that her happiness was contagious as she sat across the table, eating. The friends spoke animatedly together, but as soon as they parted ways, Grace couldn't help but wonder if everything would change for them now.

And change it did.

But not because of Bethany's baby.

It was because of Gary's.

Time passed until Grace and Gary had been married for twelve years. The time passed quickly and pleasantly for Grace. She was happy with Gary, fulfilled by the life they had built with each other.

True to her word, Grace babysat for Bethany and

Jordan. Often, in fact, as their friends enjoyed nights in the city—dinner, dancing, drinking, shows. Bethany didn't slow down much after the birth of her first daughter, didn't slow down after the birth of their son three years after that, either, and Grace was always happy to help in any way she could. That often consisted of watching the children while Bethany and Jordan went out. Grace spent more time with the kids than she did with Bethany.

Grace loved babysitting for Bethany. She'd often do it in her home and had amassed her own collection of toys—blocks and musical instruments when the kids were younger and coloring books and crayons, puzzles, and books as they grew. She loved her time with the kids, and they adored Grace in return. She felt more like a beloved aunt than she did a family friend. And the children kept her busy during those nights in which Gary worked late or went out for a beer with his friends. They even had their own room at Grace's house, adorned with bunk beds and paintings on the walls.

Twelve years. Grace was often stunned that she and Gary had been married for twelve years now. The number seemed so large to her, and yet the time had gone by so swiftly. She was now thirty-five years old, Gary forty-three. Their life had truly fallen into place.

Or so Grace had thought.

It was a Saturday morning when Gary slowly walked through the front door of their home. He had called Grace the evening prior to say he'd be spending the night at a friend's house in the city. The telephone had woken her up. She always kept her cell on and charging atop her bedside table in case of emergencies or in case Gary just needed to get in touch with her. Nobody else really called. Bethany sometimes, yes, and Dana on those rare occasions when she checked in. Grace's father didn't often keep in touch; it was always Grace that made the overtures when she felt compelled to do so. And her mother...

Well, her mother was another story.

Grace had groggily answered the telephone, listening as Gary told her he had had too much to drink and would be crashing at his friend's place. As this happened often, Grace wasn't surprised in the least, and she didn't mind, either. She always acquiesced, letting her husband have his fun.

She just hadn't been aware of the true nature of her husband's engagements. Had she been, she wouldn't have been so indifferent.

Grace knew immediately that something was wrong with Gary when he stepped through the door that Saturday morning. She had been married to him for twelve years, after all. For twelve years, he had been the most important person in her life. For twelve years, she had doted on him.

She could read him well.

Gary told her to sit down. She should have known then. Gary had never begun a conversation by telling Grace to sit down. She acquiesced and sat on the soft brown sofa that they had purchased together when they'd first moved into this house, the house that they had made into a home, the house that had brought Grace so much joy.

Then Gary began to talk. He averted his eyes, twiddled his thumbs. And once the truth hit her, Grace's mind shut down, protective measures taking hold. She heard only bits and pieces from there on in. Fragments. Shattered. Disjoined.

Stephanie. Four years. Baby.

Leaving.

Leaving her. Leaving Grace.

Grace sat utterly stupefied on the couch, tears coursing

down her cheeks and wetting her stringy hair, plastering it to her skin. Gary packed a suitcase. Said goodbye. Walked out the door.

The house was eerily quiet. Quieter than it had ever been before. Grace was deaf to the ticking of the clock on the wall and the soft buzzing of the refrigerator in the distance.

She didn't know how long she sat on the couch, but the sun was setting when she eventually extricated herself. Her legs felt weak. She stumbled. She fell to the rug on the hardwood floor, catching herself with her hand and twisting her wrist.

She didn't care. She lay on her side, tears dripping from the corners of her eyes, plopping from the bridge of her nose and her temple to wet the rug below. She moaned. She closed her lids. Fell asleep.

When Grace finally stood, it was morning. The sun's vibrancy taunted her. The trees along the sidewalk burst in a riot of autumn colors, singing, swaying with a soft breeze.

She left her windows closed.

Grace didn't want to eat and didn't think she'd be able to keep anything down if she tried. Instead, she slowly made her way to the bedroom she shared with Gary.

Had shared.

Past tense.

Moving unsteadily and by rote, Grace made it to the bedroom. She climbed into bed, scooted under the thick comforter, and closed her eyes.

She slept.

She slept the entire weekend. By Sunday, she still hadn't eaten, and she hadn't received any phone calls either. Nobody knew what she was enduring. Not her father, not Dana. But Bethany? Perhaps Bethany knew. But no... if she knew, then she would have called Grace. Had she known, she undoubtedly would have ensured her friend was all right.

By Sunday evening, Grace's stomach was hollow. She vacillated between getting up and eating and staying in bed to wallow. Eventually, she sat up and pushed the comforter off her legs. She stood and slowly made her way to the kitchen. She'd have to find her phone at some point too. She needed to call into work. She couldn't see the smiling faces of her children, couldn't acknowledge the joyful greetings of her coworkers, and pretend that nothing was amiss.

Her husband had just left her. He had left her for another woman. A woman that he had been having an affair with for the past four years.

A woman that was pregnant with his baby, the baby that Gary had adamantly claimed he didn't want.

At least, not with Grace.

She was broken, a shell of her former self.

She wasn't whole.

Not without Gary.

But Gary didn't want her, didn't love her. He was with another woman now, a woman Grace knew nothing about, and it was tormenting her to the core.

Who was this woman? What did she look like? Was she married too? How had they met? Had she always wanted a child? When had she convinced Gary to have a baby with her? Had they even been trying, and if so, for how long? Was she attractive? Was she younger than Grace? Older? Was she accomplished, refined? Was she an extrovert, the opposite of Grace's inherent personality? Was that why Gary had fallen for her? Four years? Had they truly been together for four years? Did this woman know that Gary was a married man? Had he taken off his ring every time he was with her? How often were they together? Every day? Every week? Once a month? How had this begun? Why? Why had it begun?

Why, why, why…?

Stephanie.

She envisioned the woman in her mind: beautiful, slim. She saw her smile. She saw her white teeth, perfect and straight. She saw breasts beneath a fitted sweater and then hands—Gary's hands—grabbing her waist, pulling him toward her.

Grace wrapped her arms around her chest and hunched over. She left the refrigerator door ajar as she slid down the wall and to the floor. Her mouth was open, but not a sound emerged. Tears coursed from her eyes, blurring her vision. Saliva trickled down her wet lips as her stomach flipped, protesting more and more, until she could no longer hold it in. She leaped from her seated position and hovered over the empty kitchen sink. She heaved. Once, twice. Bile rose to her throat, but nothing emerged. There were no contents in her stomach to purge. She slipped back down to the hard floor below and lost herself to her misery.

Grace called out of work for the entire week, not explaining on the voicemail why she'd be absent for that extended amount of time. But she knew she'd lose her job if she continued to miss work in excess of that week with no explanation, relying on the school to find a substitute for her room even though Grace had no plans in place for a lengthy absence.

And yet she couldn't muster up the heart to care. Her life had just been considerably altered. The happy, contented life she had known had been a lie, a farce. The husband she had known, the husband she had been so utterly in love with, didn't love her in return and hadn't loved her for years.

Bethany hadn't called Grace to check in. Perhaps she didn't know what had transpired. Even though Jordan and Gary were tight, she mustn't know. Surely she would have made sure Grace was all right if she did.

By Friday, Grace had managed to eat a few small meals. She hadn't stepped on the scale, but the pants she'd lacked the motivation to change out of for the past six days were now loose on her waist. She paid no mind.

Grace lifted her cell and clicked on the appropriate icon. She slowly typed a message out to Bethany. *Did you hear what happened?*

Grace didn't hear back from Bethany that day, nor did she hear from her on Saturday. By Sunday, she was perplexed. And hurt. She typed another message to her friend. *I hope you got my last text. Gary left me. He's been having an affair. He got her pregnant. He moved out.*

Bethany didn't write back, which pushed Grace over the precipice. Her husband had left her for another woman that he was starting a family with, and now it appeared that her only friend had betrayed her.

She desperately hoped this wasn't the case, that there was some sort of explanation, but Grace felt alone.

So utterly alone.

She took a shower on Monday morning, the first shower she had taken since Gary had left. The water pounded on her back and cascaded down her legs. She turned and lifted her face to meet the hot liquid with her eyes closed and her mouth open. She felt large, warm hands on her shoulders, and her skin reacted as those hands made their way down her arms. She felt morning stubble tickle her cheek as she was snuggled from behind.

But Grace knew they were only memories that her mind conjured to torment her even further.

Nobody was with her now.

Gary's hands were holding tight to another woman.

Grace knew she shouldn't perseverate on this other woman, the woman that had stolen her husband's affections. The woman that was carrying his child.

Gary had always claimed he didn't want to be a father. He'd been adamant about that fact. He was happy with it just being him and Grace in the house, and he liked his freedom. That was what he had claimed time and time again. That was the conversation they had had when one and then another friend had had a child.

And Grace had always agreed. She loved kids, adored them, really. But she was content with the children she taught at the elementary school. Would she have been a good mother if she and Gary had decided to start a family? Yes… yes, she had to admit that in a way, she would have been. She knew she would have loved that child unconditionally. Knew it.

But they had been happy as they were. So happy.

She had truly believed so.

What was it about this woman that had changed Gary's mind? What was it about this woman that convinced him to turn on a heel and do a complete one-eighty?

Intentional or not, he was going to be a father. Gary was going to be a father. He'd hold a newborn baby in his large hands, look down upon their face with their tiny nose and angelic lips. That baby would open its eyes and see Gary. Their father. And when Gary turned to the baby's mother, perhaps with glistening eyes, it wasn't Grace he'd find.

Tears commingled with hot water as Grace wept. She absentmindedly ran a bar of soap over her skin. She forgot to wash her hair.

When she turned the knob and the water shut off, Grace climbed out of the shower. Silence greeted her. No Gary. They didn't even own a cat, for goodness sake.

Grace dressed in a pair of jeans and a light sweater. She left her hair wet as she stepped into a pair of brown boots that were on a mat at the front entryway to the house. The sun was shining, and Grace wanted nothing more than to pull the blinds and go back to bed. She didn't want to drive her little car to the school. She didn't want to encounter all the smiling faces of her coworkers or the children that would inevitably ask her where she had been and tell her that they had missed her. On any typical day, this would have pleased Grace greatly.

But not today. Today was anything but normal.

Grace walked to her car and realized that she had forgotten her purse. She turned and walked back indoors. She grabbed her purse from a hook on the wall then closed the front door behind her, forgetting entirely to lock it when she left.

She stepped inside her car. She turned the key in the ignition, the hum of the engine playing in her ears. Grace breathed in deeply then exhaled. She allowed herself a moment to compose her roiling thoughts, her quaking, empty stomach, and her aching body. Then she looked behind her and backed out of the small driveway and into the road, steeling herself for the day to come.

She was sitting behind her desk in her classroom half an hour later. The children were playing outside on the playground as parents and bus drivers continued to drop them off at school, assuming that it would be a good day for all involved, taking for granted that this was just another gorgeous fall morning in New England. She could hear the children's gleeful laughter pour through her open windows, and the sun shone down on the ABC rug at the center of the room.

Grace rested her elbows on her desk and rubbed her red, puffy eyes. She had been accosted the very moment she walked through the main doors of the building, but she had attempted to politely brush off the well wishes, coworkers supposing that Grace had been out due to illness for the past week. She'd let them think whatever they wished. They didn't need to know the truth. And anyway, it *was* an illness, wasn't it? Grace was convinced that her heart was about to give out at any moment, that it would cease to beat, and thus she would perish. That was how she felt, anyway.

Dead.

The bell rang, indicating the beginning of the school day. Children screamed from the playground, their little feet pounding on the pavement as they ran to line up at the outside door. Grace clenched her fists then slowly stood from her desk and walked to the entryway of her classroom to greet her children. This was where she always stood at the beginning of the day as the children poured into the hallway from the outdoors, and she knew they'd expect nothing different from her now. She must not let her emotions betray her, or she knew she'd be in for an even more difficult day than she anticipated.

Grace plastered a smile on her face, a facade of joy. She bit her lower lip and released it only once she tasted blood. Her eyes began to water, and she forced the tears to retreat.

She would not cry. She would not!

49

Children came bounding down the hallway, continuously reminded by teachers and monitors to use their walking feet. Some paid heed and slowed, others did not. One very exuberant child was showing her friend her newfound skipping skills as her pigtails bobbed up and down.

Grace's first student approached the door, all smiles, with her backpack slung over one shoulder. "Mrs. Clarke, you're here!" she exclaimed.

Mrs. Clarke.

Grace cringed, and her forced smile waned. "Yes... yes, I'm here."

"Where were you?" the little girl asked. "We missed you. Mr. Davis was here instead of you."

"I... I..." Grace had obviously not thought this out well enough. She wasn't entirely sure how to answer.

"Mrs. Clarke!" A boy sidled up next to the girl in the doorway and looked up at Grace.

"Hi, Elias," Grace said.

"Well?" the little girl persisted.

"Well?" Grace mimicked, a bit confused. Her mind was addled.

"Where were you?"

Another girl entered the conversation. "Yeah," she said, "where were you? You were gone."

"I... I wasn't well," Grace replied.

"Oh, you were sick?" the first girl asked.

"Yes, Sara," Grace said. "I was sick."

"You were sick for a really long time," Sara said.

Grace nodded. "I was."

"But you're better now?"

"I... I will be," Grace said, not believing her own words.

"Oh no," Elias chimed in. "You're not supposed to be at school if you're still sick. Once, I got sick at school. I puked all over the floor. Remember that, Sara? It was last year, in kindergarten."

"Ew…" Sara crinkled her nose in disgust. "Yeah!"

"I had to go home, and my mom had to get out of work, and then she let me watch TV all the rest of the day, and even at night. And then I felt better. I wanted to go back to school in the morning 'cause I wanted to see my friends, but my mom said that I couldn't. She said that I wasn't allowed. Some sort of rule or something."

"Well," Grace said slowly, "this is different. I'm not sick like that, Elias."

Elias lifted his brows. "Oh, good," he said then slipped past Grace and into the classroom without further care.

"I'm glad you're back, Mrs. Clarke," Sara said. "And that you're not sick anymore."

Grace held back a sob. "Thank you, Sara." She motioned for Sara and her friend to head into the room.

The day progressed. Slowly. Ever so slowly. Grace wanted to be at home. She didn't want to be there in the school. She didn't want to be in her classroom, surrounded by the smiling faces of little children who knew nothing of her pain.

When the lunch bell rang out the children either buoyantly ran to their cubbies to grab their lunch boxes, or they scooted off to the door and formed a line. When all her first graders were set, Grace led the way to the cafeteria, where she ensured every child was secure, and then walked back to her classroom, her head down and her eyes trained on the floor.

It wasn't until Grace sat at her desk that she realized she had forgotten her lunch, and she lacked any motivation to walk to the staff room, where they kept a vending machine and various baskets of snack bars and fruits. She didn't want to be forced into polite conversation with anyone, and so she rested her arms on her desk, put her head down, and closed her eyes. She'd eat later.

Maybe.

Grace drove home in a stupor at the end of the school day. She was exhausted. Utterly exhausted.

How was she going to make it through this?

CHAPTER 4

$\mathcal{N}$ ot only had Gary served her with divorce papers, but he had also snuck into the house while Grace was at work just days after she had returned to her children. He took the brown sofa set they had acquired at the furniture store almost thirteen years prior when they had just bought and moved into the house. He took lamps and decorations. He took a few wall hangings, and Grace noticed some of the kitchen utensils were missing as well. He took the large, heavy wooden desk that Grace had never liked.

But he left the bed, the one thing Grace would have preferred to do without, the bed that they had slept in together, in which they had been intimate. The bed in which Grace had stared for hours into her husband's mesmerizing dark eyes.

Grace led her life on autopilot in those early days, waking in the morning, getting ready for work, spending the day with her children, eating lunch alone in her classroom, and returning home when the bell rang through the building and the school day was over. She shopped for food about once every week and a half and only did so because she was in desperate need. She always waited until there was barely a crumb left in the pantry and the fruit bowl on the kitchen counter was empty.

They still owed on the house, and a hefty mortgage it was. Fortunately for Grace, the mortgage was in Gary's name. There was no way she'd have been able to afford the financial strain of that property on her measly teacher's salary.

Once the divorce was finalized, Grace didn't know what would become of her. Gary had already taken everything that Grace loved: the furniture, himself. Would he take the house as well? Surely he wouldn't do that to her. Surely he still had some semblance of affection for the woman he had spent well over a decade with.

And now it had been six months.

Six months since Gary had left her. Six months of torture.

It was spring. The birds were out and chirping their melodies. The leaves were growing back on the trees, green and vibrant. The beauty of the season only served to heighten Grace's depression.

Grace spent the one-year anniversary of Gary's departure at a playground in the city. She didn't fully comprehend why she wanted to be there; perhaps she thought she'd run into the man himself; perhaps she figured she'd finally see his new wife. Maybe she'd see a small child in a stroller and instinctively know it was Gary's child—loved, wanted, adored.

She knew she was just torturing herself, but she was beyond caring. This was where her feet had led her. This was where she wanted to be, needed to be somehow. She felt it to the core.

The divorce had proceeded without any complications. Grace hadn't protested. What did she have to protest, anyway? Her husband had left her. She knew he wouldn't be back. So he had taken those household items because he had moved into the city. Whatever. Take them. So he had moved into close proximity to one of the best private elementary schools in Boston. So be it.

So he would be marrying this woman—Stephanie— once the divorce was finalized. Grace wasn't surprised. She had gleaned through conversation at the lawyer's office during the divorce proceedings that Stephanie was a rather well-sought-out attorney in Boston. An attorney. One of the many professions that Grace knew she'd fail terribly at if she ever had an inkling to try. Grace was anxious, timid. She was far from being the aggressive, assertive kind of woman who could litigate. She also knew through conversation between Gary's lawyer and him in that stuffy office that Gary knew his then-unborn child was a boy.

His son.

She lost the house. Gary didn't take it after all, but he might as well have. Grace could stay in the home that they had found together as long as she paid Gary half of the appraised cost. She couldn't afford it. And so the house had been emptied—not that there was much to pack up, anyway, after Gary had taken what he wanted to start his new life, his new family—and put on the market. Grace and Gary split the proceeds, and the money Grace had been able to bank helped pay the down payment on a small townhouse on the other end of town, a bit closer to her elementary school.

Grace now sat on the metal bench at the playground, watching the children swoosh down the slide, gleeful bouts of laughter leaving their lips. Her eyes turned to two children playing in the sandbox and then a child persevering on the monkey bars. She couldn't believe it had been a year. In one way, this year had gone by very quickly. In another, it had crept along, slothlike, her days monotonous and empty.

After her first meeting with Gary after he had left, Grace had phoned Bethany. Bethany hadn't returned a single text Grace had sent. When Bethany didn't pick up the phone, Grace mustered up the courage to take the T into the city and knock on Bethany's door. She wasn't sure if anyone was home, but she figured she had to give it a try and was compelled to know why Bethany had left her too. She'd thought they were friends. She'd thought their relationship was one of substance. And in leaving Grace, Bethany had also ripped her children away from Grace's loving care, which further tore at Grace's heart.

Bethany hadn't answered the door, but Jordan had. When Grace asked to speak with Bethany, Jordan claimed she wasn't home.

"Can... I mean... when will she be home?" Grace asked.

"I don't expect her anytime soon," Jordan answered rather briskly.

"Oh. Okay. I... Jordan?" Grace chanced a look up and held his eyes.

"What?"

"I don't understand. I thought we were friends. I mean... why hasn't she returned any of my texts? Why is she doing this? We were close. I miss her. I miss the kids."

Jordan sighed, and his hand slipped from the door to his thigh. "You have to understand," he said. "Gary and I are close. Bethany and I are a couple. We see Gary and Stephanie all the time…"

"So then Stephanie has replaced me?"

Jordan grimaced, but he didn't look hurt or ashamed. Rather, he looked offended and put off. "It's not like that."

"Then what's it like?" Grace asked. "I really don't understand, Jordan. I haven't done anything to Bethany. I don't deserve this."

"It would be weird for Bethany if she still hung out with you."

"It would be weird for her? What does that even mean? Jordan, we were friends. Really close friends. Just because Gary has left me doesn't mean that Bethany has to as well."

"You just don't get it," Jordan said. He looked down at Grace from his perch on the upper step of his apartment with pity. "Friends come and go, Grace. I'm sure you have other girls you're close to. Bethany just isn't comfortable seeing you anymore."

Grace steeled herself and clenched her fists at her sides. She ground her jaw in an attempt to stave off the tears that threatened to drip from her eyes. She would not give Jordan —or Bethany, for that matter—the satisfaction of seeing her left emotionally hurt and affected. She would not!

Grace turned and began walking down the steps without another word. When she heard the door close behind her, she looked in its direction. As she turned onto the sidewalk, she could have sworn she saw Bethany behind a curtain in the large front window.

Other girlfriends to lean on? Jordan had been far from right. Grace had no other girlfriends. Bethany had been it. She spoke to Dana, but rarely, and her anxious personality had holed her up in her classroom too often to accept any overtures her coworkers had offered. They had since ceased to occur.

Grace sat on the bench at the playground and brought her knees to her chest, wrapping her arms around her shins and resting her sneakered feet on the seat. A tear trickled slowly down her cheek, warm and uninvited.

Grace was suddenly interrupted from her misery by a loud plonk and an exasperated sigh.

"It never gets easier."

Grace looked beside her and saw a woman had seated herself. In tight neon-pink athletic pants and a tie-dyed tank, the woman was sweaty despite the crisp autumn air and had clearly been exercising. Her hair was short, shorn on the sides and spiky at the top, just a couple inches in length. It was blond, though the shade was clearly not the woman's natural color. She smirked, her chest heaving, as she turned blue eyes to look into Grace's brown ones.

Grace didn't reply, but the woman continued. "I always tell myself, I say, 'Ally, what the hell are you thinking? You know you're not a runner. You've tried this before, girl. Sit your butt down or get your damn bike out. It's a good day for a ride.' And then my stupid mind takes over and I convince myself that I can give running another chance. This is Boston, after all—not the best city for cycling, but damn, is it a good one for those that run. And then here we go. Again. I've proven myself right. I am not a runner!" She ran the back of her hand against her forehead, wiping away droplets of sweat. "You a runner?"

Grace shook her head.

"Good for you. Running sucks."

Grace was so taken aback by the woman's cordiality and gusto that she found her lips lifting slightly.

"Cycling is great though," Ally said. "Even in the city, though people here are crazy, I tell you. Just crazy. You don't want to know the amount of times I've been honked at. But I'm good at steering with just one hand. My left hand here, yeah... it's got a choice finger that has seen a lot of action when those people don't have the patience."

Grace's lips lifted even farther.

"I'm Ally." The woman held out her hand, looked at it, then thought otherwise, retracting it to her thigh. "Yeah, I'm sweaty. If I were you, I wouldn't shake it."

"I'm Grace."

"Nice to meet you. You got a kid here somewhere?"

Grace shook her head. "No. I was just... going for a walk."

"But not running. Good girl." Ally smirked, and Grace smiled in return. Ally looked at her surroundings then said with a frown, "Now I'm stuck."

"What do you mean?"

"I pushed myself, and now I'm several miles from home. I don't mind walking back though. It's a nice day."

"It is," Grace agreed.

"You live around here?"

Grace shook her head. "I don't. I live just outside the city. I took the T in. I guess I just felt like I wanted to be here for some reason." Grace wasn't about to divulge personal details to this stranger, no matter how friendly she appeared.

"I get it. I get notions all the time. Mostly I follow them, too, as long as I'm able. Just the other day, I was walking in to work when I ended up taking a different way. Don't know why. One minute, I was walking my regular route, and the next, there I was on a completely different road. And don't you know, that's when I ran into a friend I haven't seen in over a year! A year! Can you imagine not seeing someone in over a year and then, *bam*, there they are right in front of you? On my way to work, too. I was so damn happy I ended up talking to her for twenty minutes with a promise to have coffee soon. I was late for work, but luckily, I have the best boss ever. He just looked at me with his eyebrows all squinted and his hands on his hips. But I won him over with my smile. Yep. I have that effect on him." Ally placed her elbows on the back of the bench and grinned.

Grace could clearly tell she was joking, and it made her smile even wider.

"Well, now I want a smoothie," Ally announced quite out of the blue.

"A smoothie?"

"That's what I said. A smoothie. Just all of a sudden." She slapped her palms on her thighs and stood. "It was really nice to meet you, Grace. I hope you have a great day."

"Thanks, Ally. It was nice to meet you too."

It was only after Ally had left and Grace saw her off in the distance that she came to the surprising realization that she hadn't been uncomfortable with Ally at all. Quite the opposite, actually. Ally might have been a complete stranger, but Grace felt like she had been in the company of a long-lost friend.

On a Saturday morning two weeks later, Grace awoke to the sun's rays shining through her bedroom window. The maple tree outside swayed with a slight breeze, and an orange leaf slowly floated to the ground. She closed her eyes once again, thinking that perhaps she'd fall back asleep, but to no avail. She was awake.

Grace lifted the comforter off her legs and stood. She slowly made her way to the kitchen, where she spooned coffee grinds into a filter, poured water into the machine, and turned it on. She inhaled the coffee's aroma as it began to brew.

When Grace sat down on her small couch—one that she had acquired on her own when she bought her townhouse—and took her first sip from her mug, she realized that she didn't want this coffee. In fact, she didn't want to be home at all. It was a foreign sensation, really, but she obliged her yearnings. She poured the liquid down the sink, unplugged the coffee maker, slipped on her boots, grabbed her purse, and walked out the door.

Grace stopped momentarily on the stoop outside. She closed her eyes, lifted her head, and breathed in deeply. She felt the sun's rays upon her face as the soft autumn breeze blew her hair and caressed her skin.

Grace decided to walk. She had seen a coffee shop just down the street from her townhouse and figured it was a nice morning to get outside. There wouldn't be many more mornings like this one in Massachusetts. Soon, the snow would hit, and the air would be so icy that it would numb her nose and sting her cheeks.

Grace slung her purse over her shoulder and walked. She passed a few other pedestrians on the sidewalks. She came upon restaurants and a small empty shopping mall that hadn't yet opened for the day, and then she halted in front of the double doors of her desired destination. She didn't know what she was doing there, but she supposed she had a book in her purse to read so she could lower her head and avoid the gazes of curious patrons acquiring their morning caffeine or sugary pastries.

Grace stepped forward, and just as she reached out a hand to open the door, a woman emerged.

Ally! Grace recognized her spiky blond hair and blue eyes immediately. Grace was surprised to notice that Ally was shorter than anticipated, several inches shorter than Grace, in fact, but she supposed that she had been sitting down on the bench when they first met, which had made it more difficult to gauge Ally's height. Instead of neon-pink athletic pants and a tie-dyed tank top, she was wearing a pair of frayed jeans and a short mustard-yellow sweater that touched the tip of her pants. A smile of recognition immediately played on her face.

"Grace, right?" Ally asked.

"Yes. Ally?"

"That's me. I got stood up. Can you believe that? I was supposed to meet a friend here this morning, and she didn't show. Been waiting for forty-five minutes. Oh, well… guess that happens sometimes, doesn't it?"

"I'm sorry," was all Grace was able to manage. Had Grace been the one waiting for a friend to show up and realized they weren't coming, she wasn't sure she'd take it as well as Ally appeared to be doing.

"Not a problem," Ally replied. "Hey, are you meeting someone?"

Grace looked down at the ground and shook her head ever so slightly. "No." Her voice was barely audible.

"Then how about I ditch going home, and you and I grab some coffee and chat?"

Grace smiled. "I'd like that."

"Great. Let's do it." Ally held the door open, and Grace

walked inside. Together, they made their way to the counter.

"Already got myself two cups of coffee while I was waiting, but what's one more?" Ally said. She turned to the attendant. "Coffee for here, please. Room for cream. And oh, one of those monstrous blueberry muffins you've got. Those things are great."

"And you?" The attendant looked at Grace.

"Oh," Grace said, a bit flustered. "We're not together. I mean... we are. I mean, we're going to sit together, but... I'll pay for myself."

"I'm happy to pay," Ally said. "My treat. Hey, I got stood up then found you here. That's something pretty awesome right there, wouldn't you say? What would you like?"

Grace was touched. "Thank you," she said.

"You're welcome." Ally smiled genuinely.

Grace turned to the attendant. "A cup of coffee, please. Also for here. Also room for cream."

"Anything to eat?"

"No... no, I'm good."

"You've got to try one of their muffins," Ally insisted. "Have you ever had one before?"

Grace shook her head. "I've never actually been here before."

"Oh, wow," Ally said. "I live in the city, so I don't get here often, but my friend doesn't live all that far away. That's why we chose this place. And they have the best darn muffins in the universe. Seriously. You should try one. No pressure, but..." Ally lifted her brows and smirked.

Grace laughed. "Okay." Then, to the attendant, she said, "I'll take a muffin, too."

"What kind?"

"I guess I'll also have a blueberry," Grace said, although it sounded more like a question.

The attendant rang them up, and Ally handed over cash. "Sweet," she said. "I almost never carry cash on me. I've seriously paid for a dollar candy bar before with my card. But look at me now... simple pleasures."

Grace smiled. Ally seemed to have that effect on her.

Grace and Ally were handed their mugs and small white plates with the most enormous muffins Grace had ever seen. Large granules of sugar sparkled on their raised tops under the ceiling's lights.

"Now that's what I'm talking about," Ally said enthusiastically. "I was waiting on my friend to get one of these things, but I should have gotten one anyway. I definitely could have tried to fit another."

"I'm not even sure I'll be able to eat this one, let alone two," Grace replied.

"Just wait until you taste it. You can taste the butter. And I'm a huge blueberry fan."

"It does look really good," Grace agreed.

The ladies walked to a small counter with various milks and sugars, cinnamon and nutmeg. Grace splashed a small amount of cream into her cup and one packet of sugar. Ally put as much cream into her cup as was possible without it overflowing and then scooped up a handful of sugar packets. She looked around the room. "Want to head outside? Maybe there's a free table out there. Plus it's too nice a day to be cooped indoors."

"That would be nice," Grace said.

Much to Grace's delight, there was one unoccupied table. Ally hastened over and scooted into a metal seat, spilling some of her coffee onto her hand. "Ouch!" she exclaimed. "I'm so damn clumsy sometimes, and that was hot stuff."

Grace laughed. "I don't think your mug could have been any fuller," she teased. And then she realized just how comfortable she was with this woman, a woman she still knew next to nothing about.

"Yep. You've got that right. They make these mugs way too small."

Grace chuckled. "I think they're actually pretty big."

"Maybe for a normal person, but I'm far from normal." Ally smirked then bit into the very top of her muffin. "Mmm," she moaned. "I'm telling you. These are just fantastic. And the tops? The best!"

"You know, I've heard of some places just selling the muffin tops, not the bottoms at all. I think they cut them off because there are people that prefer the tops."

"That's just a huge waste," Ally said, her mouth full. "I seriously love eating the entire thing. I just love the sugar. And the crunch. And I… well, darn… I just love everything about these things."

Grace laughed again. "It appears that way."

Grace gently pulled at the wrapper, exposing a portion at the side of the muffin. The pastry was so large she wasn't sure she'd be able to bite into it without making a fool of herself, so she used her fingers to pry a small piece off. She set it on her tongue, and immediately, the flavors seeped through. Grace's eyes opened wide, and she began to chew. "Oh my goodness," she said. "You weren't kidding, were you?"

"Nope," Ally said, apparently knowing exactly what Grace was suggesting. "Told you."

"How have I never known about this place before?"

"Got me," Ally replied. "But now you'll be coming here more often, huh?"

"I think I might just have to."

"You live close by?"

"I do," Grace said, swallowing her bite. "Only a few blocks away."

"Well, that's convenient. Lucky you."

"In this sense, I have to agree," Grace said.

"Wish I lived closer by. Well, no. That's a lie. I wish this place was closer to me. I love where I live."

"In the city?"

"Yep," Ally confirmed, taking another large bite of her muffin. "Live with my best friend. Yeah, I know what you're thinking. Here I am, thirty-three, and living with Chase. But Boston is pricey, and even though I like my job, it doesn't pay the best. Plus, I don't think I could ever live alone. I'd get bored."

Grace lowered her head. "I don't think it's strange to live with your friend."

"I love it," Ally admitted. "Works out perfectly for the both of us. Plus, when Chase brings a girl home, he looks to me right away for my opinion. I'm a pretty good judge of character."

"Does he date often?"

"Yep. Even the ones I like don't last long. Chase has a bit of a commitment issue."

"And... the two of you have never dated?"

Ally laughed, careful to keep her chewed muffin in her mouth. "Me and Chase? Oh gosh, no! I love Chase, don't get me wrong. But he's like a brother to me. I could never date Chase."

"Oh, okay," Grace said quietly.

"How about you?" Ally asked. "You live with anyone?"

Grace toyed with her finger, unadorned because she had placed both her wedding and engagement rings in a small jewelry box in her bedroom. They had been a constant reminder of a life turned upside down. "No," she said. "I…" She paused and then blurted, "I'm divorced."

Ally nodded nonchalantly as if divorce were one of life's most common occurrences, as if the word itself didn't warrant a look of pity or a slightly raised eyebrow. Then again, Grace supposed, perhaps for some people it was and it didn't. But for Grace, it was just a reminder of her failure and of her hurt and angst. She had never in her wildest imaginings thought she'd be a divorcée.

"Definitely happens," Ally said as she took another bite of her blueberry muffin. "Sucks if it wasn't mutual though. Was it? Mutual, I mean."

Grace was taken aback by Ally's forthrightness. Grace herself had never been one to immediately divulge whatever was on her mind, and typically, she wouldn't answer such a blunt question from one she didn't know well, but with Ally… with Ally things just somehow seemed different. Grace couldn't exactly decipher why this was so, but it was intuited. Ally didn't appear to be a person that would jump to conclusions, to judge harshly.

Grace hoped her intuition was correct. Taking a deep breath she said, "No, it wasn't mutual. Far from it."

Ally's brows rose. "Oh? Now you have me intrigued."

"I…" Grace looked at her muffin, averting her eyes from Ally's blue stare. "He left me. He came home in the morning after he told me he was spending the night at a friend's house in the city because he had too much to drink the night before. I think that was all a lie. I'm pretty sure he was with her…"

"Her?" Ally asked. "Uh oh…"

Grace looked up and into Ally's eyes. "Yes," she said. "Her. Stephanie."

"Doesn't sound good to me," Ally replied. "And who is this Stephanie?"

"The woman my husband…" And then Grace stopped herself, retracted. "I mean my ex-husband—Stephanie is the woman he left me for. Apparently, they were having an affair for four years that I knew nothing about. Gary—that's my ex—told me that she was pregnant."

"Shiiit," Ally said as she picked at the remains of her muffin.

"Yes, I guess that's a good word to use. She's had the baby, although I know next to nothing about what Gary has been up to. But he's a father now. A father even though he always told me he never wanted any children."

"So you and he don't have any kids together?"

Grace shook her head. "We don't."

"And you don't have any from another relationship?"

"No."

Ally plonked the last of the crumbs onto her tongue. "Crazy that you never knew he was having an affair. I guess some guys are super sneaky, though, huh?"

"I truly never knew what was going on," Grace admitted. "Gary had always worked really hard. I think that's one of the things that attracted me to him when we were first dating, how hard he worked. A great work ethic, really. I think… when I was growing up…"

"Yeah?"

"Oh, nothing. It's just something that I really liked about Gary. And I didn't mind at all that he worked really long hours. Truly, I didn't. I was happy with the way things were. *Just* as they were. When he didn't make it home when he said he would, I never thought anything about it. He'd

68

always call. It was how it had always been with his job. But I suppose he just found the time to be with... or maybe... maybe he always did have the time? I don't know. I've thought about this over and over in my head for the past year, and I just can't figure it out. I guess I never will. We don't talk, Gary and I. We don't have any communication with each other at all."

"I'd want to know all the little details," Ally said. "I'd seriously be that crazy stalker lady that follows him after work to see where he ends up. I'd be that cuckoo with the camera, snapping away at this Stephanie chick and that baby of theirs too. I mean, what the hell?"

Grace merely shook her head.

"No, seriously. I'm probably scaring the crap out of you." Ally laughed. "I wouldn't do anything like that, promise. But..." She smirked. "I'd want to."

Grace smiled. "It's crossed my mind," she admitted. "But I can't be that person. It's been a struggle enough to get over him, to get over *this*. I think if I did something like that, I'd be stooping to his level in a way. At least, that's what I think in my head. I just want to find a way to move on, to feel well again."

"You're not?"

"Feeling well?" Grace asked for clarification.

"Right."

"Not so much, no," Grace admitted. "It's been over a year, and I'm still having a tough time."

"I get it," Ally said. "Ultimate betrayal."

"Yes," Grace said. "That's how I feel."

"How long were you married to the guy?"

"Twelve years."

Ally rolled her eyes. "Ass," she said.

Grace smiled. "Yes," she said. "My exact thought."

"I've never been married," Ally said, "Don't think I could do it."

Grace cocked her head. "Really?" she asked.

"Yep," Ally confirmed. "Not for me. I've been in relationships. Plenty, actually. I just don't think I'm the type of person that can be weighed down in a relationship as serious as marriage is. Don't get me wrong, I love having a companion, but that's about it. I'm super independent, and I like my life that way. Hate being told what to do and when to do it. Hate feeling like I need to dote on another human being. I don't people. And before you ask, it's totally a thing. I. Don't. People."

Grace laughed. "What does that even mean?"

"You know those T-Shirts out there that say things like *I like dogs more than I like people* and other things that just ring true for a lot of us?"

Grace nodded and laughed. "Yes, I've seen those around. But—and I know that I've just met you—but you really seem like a people person to me, Ally. You're very outgoing, and really, well… you just seem so upbeat."

Ally laughed. "Upbeat? Yeah, okay. I get that. And I kind of am. I'm definitely an extrovert, I really like being around people. But here's the thing: I like being around people that aren't jerks, and that narrows things down in the city."

"But you said you like the city."

"Love it," Ally said. "Love the city."

Grace offered Ally a look of confusion.

"A contradiction, huh?" Ally asked.

"Well… yes," Grace agreed. "I think it is."

"Not at all," Ally offered. "I like people. I like being around them. I like surrounding myself with others. I like being in the middle of a crowd. Being around people is where I'm most comfortable. It's where I'm most like myself. But I have very little tolerance for jerks. I just don't surround myself with them in my social life. The greatest thing about Boston is that you can walk down the street and come across hundreds of people in a single day, and although you might not know any of them, you feel like you're still somehow in good company, that you're not alone. And when I do want to be alone, which isn't often, then I just go back to my place. I've got a room if I want it, but mostly, I hang with Chase."

"I think maybe you and I are really different people," Grace said. "I like to be alone. People make me nervous."

"Oh yeah? How so?"

"I just… it's… well, they always have. I have a really hard time talking to people, and I don't like being forced into uncomfortable situations. And honestly, most situations are uncomfortable for me if they involve other people. I'm always watching what I say and what I do. It was much worse when I was younger, when I was a kid. It was even terribly bad when I was in college and when I first met Gary. I've gotten better since then. But people still make me nervous. Very much so. When someone looks at me in a specific way, my mind runs in all sorts of different directions, playing out various scenarios, wondering what the person is thinking. And they might not even be thinking a single thing. They might not even be looking *at* me. But it still makes me nervous. And I hate confrontation."

Ally laughed, though not unkindly. "You could have fooled me," she said. "Here you are, sitting with me at this table, eating the best dang muffin in New England, and talking away. You don't look uncomfortable."

"I… well, I'm not," Grace said, and as the words left

71

her mouth, she realized how true they rang. She wasn't uncomfortable. Not with Ally. And the notion boggled her.

"It's just my charm," Ally said as she smirked playfully. "I've wiggled my way into your life. And hey, you can't be all that uncomfortable in social situations if you made your way over here in the first place, huh?"

"I don't even know why I came here, to be honest. I don't often leave my house. Not unless I'm going to work. I'm comfortable at home, and I like my own company."

"Yep, the universe obviously knew we had to meet today, just like it knew we had to meet at the park after my failure of a run a couple of weeks ago," Ally teased. "See? You need to get out more often, and I needed to meet another woman who isn't a total jerk and a half."

"A jerk and a half?" Grace smiled.

"Yep. Just thought of that one. How do you like it?"

"I think it sounds a bit silly."

"Then it's perfect for me," Ally said.

Grace laughed. "I'm beginning to think that maybe you're right."

Now it was Ally that laughed, merry and bright, the sound melodious and welcoming. Grace felt comforted, at ease. She felt at home.

Renewed.

Alive.

～

Grace and Ally sat at the table for another hour and a half. They both refilled their coffee mugs, and Ally ordered a chocolate croissant.

"You do have a healthy appetite," Grace observed.

"That's your polite Gracey way of saying that I'm a pig and eat way too much," Ally quipped.

Grace laughed. "Gracey? And no, I'm not saying you're a pig."

"Yeah, Gracey. Hope you don't mind. That one just kind of slipped out. And it's seriously okay if you call me a pig. I am one! I'm telling you, I could eat everything on the menu here if I had enough cash to do it."

"I'm surprised your stomach can fit any more food. I'm really full from the muffin. It was huge!"

"I've always had the most ginormous appetite."

"I'm not sure where it goes," Grace said as she looked at her petite new friend, for a friend she was. Grace was sure of it. Even after just two chance meetings, she felt more comfortable in Ally's presence than she ever had with Bethany, and it had taken Grace an immense amount of time to begin opening up to Bethany about herself, about her past and her life, about her thoughts and her passions. And even once she had, Grace and Bethany's conversations often ran superficial.

Bethany's betrayal hurt anew. It washed over Grace as she looked at the smiling woman in front of her. Grace forced the thoughts to the back of her head. She would not let Bethany ruin the amazing time she was having with Ally. She would not let her fear of another heart-wrenching betrayal hinder her from furthering this new friendship.

"Don't know where it goes?" Ally said with a sly smirk. "I didn't really think I needed to talk to you about anatomy, Grace." She lifted her coffee mug to her lips and took a sip of the creamy, steaming liquid.

Grace arched her brows. "That's kind of gross," she said.

Ally laughed. "You lined that one up for me."

73

"I suppose I did," Grace said. "I just meant that you're a rather small woman, but I can see you have an appetite."

"Yep," Ally said. "I've always been on the smaller side. Genetics, I guess. My mom is small. Hey, speaking of which, how about you? You close to your folks?"

Grace looked down at her hand and began to strum her fingers gently on the table. "Um... I..."

"Looks like I've made you uncomfortable," Ally said. "That sucks. Sorry about that one, Grace."

"It's okay," Grace replied, and then she lifted her gaze. "Maybe we can leave that conversation for another time though?"

"Yep," Ally agreed. "Sounds good. But you're assuming we'll get together again."

"I... I..." Grace felt suddenly flustered, extremely embarrassed, and hurt all within the matter of a fraction of a second.

"Holy crap, Grace," Ally chuckled. "I was seriously joking. Of course we'll see each other again. Why would you think otherwise after we've been sitting here all morning, chatting away? I obviously like you, and I'm guessing you like me, too."

Grace nodded. "I do."

"Then let's make a date." Ally extended her hand over the table, palm up.

Grace gave her a quizzical look. "Um..."

"Your phone, silly," Ally said.

"Oh. Okay. But why do you want my phone?"

"So I can add my number," Ally replied.

"Oh. Yes. All right." Grace reached into her purse and took out her phone, handing it off to Ally.

"Ah, nope," Ally said. "Can you punch in your passcode for me?" She turned the screen so it was facing Grace.

"Oh, yes, of course." Grace punched in her passcode, and Ally brought the phone close to her chest, tapping on the screen. Grace noticed that Ally's tongue peeked out of her mouth ever so slightly, touching the corner of her upper lip.

Ally handed the phone back to Grace. "You've got my number now, and I sent myself a text so I can save your number, too. How about I text you so we can make a date?"

"That would be very nice. Thank you."

"Great," Ally said. "You mentioned work, so I'm guessing you work during the week?"

"I do, yes."

"Typical working hours?"

"That's right," Ally confirmed.

"What do you do?"

"I'm an elementary school teacher," Ally replied.

Ally smiled. "I can seriously see you doing that. Kids don't make you nervous though?"

Grace shook her head. "They don't, no. Children never have. Just adults. And teenagers. I know teenagers are still kids, but they make me nervous."

"But not elementary school kids?"

"No, not my students. I teach first grade."

"You have a soft voice, and you sound kind of soothing," Ally said. "I bet your kids love you."

Grace smiled. "I hope they do," she said. "But I think so, yes. Well, not every child, I'm sure. But my students are often happy to see me, and we have lots of smiles in the classroom."

"I could never be a teacher," Ally said as she leaned back in her metal chair. "Don't have the patience for it. One or two at a time is okay, but a whole group of kids screaming and running around and whining? No, thanks."

Grace laughed. "It's not really like that."

"Oh yeah? You've got fifteen, twenty, twenty-five kids in a classroom at one time. That's more than I can handle. I do better in a crowded room of total strangers or at a concert where people are constantly bumping into me."

"Oh, no," Grace said. "I couldn't do that. I think I'd have an anxiety attack."

"Ever had one?"

"A concert?"

Ally laughed. "No. An anxiety attack."

"I don't think so?"

"That sounds convincing," Ally said with a lopsided grin. She lifted her mug and finished off the remnants of her coffee.

"I'm really not sure," Grace said. "I deal with anxiety all the time in some shape or form. Pretty much every day. But I'm not sure if I've ever had a full-fledged attack, one that would be diagnosed by a psychiatrist as such, anyway. Does that make sense?"

"Yep," Ally said. "Sure does."

"Do you… are you…" Grace paused and then asked, "Do you ever have trouble? I mean, do you ever get nervous about things?"

Ally's voice lowered as she said, "I don't. Not really." She reached out and placed her palm on the top of Grace's hand. "But I can see how it would be rough going. Must suck to feel that way all the time."

Grace gazed into Ally's face, at her delicate pixie-like features. "Thank you," she whispered. "That means a lot."

Ally squeezed Grace's hand, and for a moment, the two women sat and smiled at each other. No further words were needed. All was understood.

Ally was the one to ignite their next topic of conversation, and after twenty minutes, she looked at her watch and gasped. "Oh, crap! I'm gonna be late!"

"Oh," Grace said. She instinctively pushed her chair back on the patio as if it was she that had a pressing appointment to attend.

"I've got to go," Ally said. "I'll text you, Grace. Promise. I had so much fun with you today. Super glad I ran into you. Obviously! We've been here way longer than I thought." She laughed and then stood. "I'll see you soon."

"I'd like that," Grace said.

"Are you a hugger?"

"What?"

Ally smiled. "Are you a hugger?" she repeated.

"I… sure?"

Ally laughed again, her zest obvious in the countenance displayed, unhindered, unabashed. She extended her arms outward, and Grace stood. Ally took a step forward and embraced Grace heartily. When she released her hold, she was still smiling.

Ally began walking away quickly, her short legs working overtime. She turned and looked behind. "I'll text," she called.

Grace waved goodbye then sat back down. She looked at her empty coffee mug then over at the mug Ally had left on the table.

And she smiled.

CHAPTER 5

*T*rue to her word, Ally texted Grace.

Grace had gone directly home from the coffee shop that splendid morning she had run into Ally and made herself lunch. She was amazed at the amount of time she and Ally had spent together, sitting outdoors at the shop's metal table, sipping coffee, and eating their muffins. It had been glorious, rejuvenating.

It had been exactly what Grace's heart needed.

In her text, Ally had invited Grace to join her for an after-dinner drink at a bar near her apartment that she frequented. She explained to Grace that the location had always appealed to her, as she could simply walk the few blocks home if she felt she had had too much to drink instead of leaving impaired and getting behind the wheel of her car or even on the T, possibly placing herself in a precarious position.

Grace admitted to her new friend that she wasn't entirely sure a bar would be conducive to her enjoyment.

Wouldn't a bar be noisy and hinder them from any promise of engaging conversation?

Ally assured Grace that this bar was upscale, was not boisterous, and would offer plenty of opportunities for them to speak with each other. She knew the weeknight bartender and coaxed Grace with the promise of a delicious drink in a modish atmosphere.

Grace honestly wasn't thinking about the atmosphere, whether new or old, stylish or dank and dreary, and she didn't care about the drinks either. She was most comfortable, most herself, when she was at home, and she would have preferred to have Ally over at her townhouse, where they could sit on the living room sofa or at the kitchen table, or even in the two chairs that she had placed just outside her sliding glass back door, and enjoy a glass of wine or coffee with no noise and no interruptions, but she obliged Ally's wishes. Ally did seem eager, through her texts, to take Grace to her favorite after-dinner bar.

So Grace mustered up her courage, took the T into the city, and met Ally at the decided venue the following Wednesday evening.

Grace triple-checked the street sign, the number above the wooden door, and the establishment's name to ensure she was in the correct place before she took a deep breath, exhaled, and turned the knob. Typically, Grace wasn't tardy to her appointments, whether business or social, but she feared she'd walk into the bar, look around, and find that Ally hadn't yet shown up. The last thing she wanted to do was to sit at the bar or at a musty, sticky table and have eyes wander her way, surmising that she was alone. She didn't want to draw attention, and she most definitely didn't want a stranger to approach her and attempt to strike up a conversation, so Grace had purposefully left her house on the later side, hoping that she'd arrive after the agreed-upon time, and Ally would already be waiting for her.

The moment Grace stepped inside, she was taken aback. Was she truly in a bar? Grace had expected people. She had expected noise and the pungent aroma of hard liquor or beer. Instead, what she found made her eyes widen with pleasure. Grace stood at the threshold of a small venue. Lights hung from the ceiling over the bar and over small tables, their illumination dim but inviting. The wooden floor appeared clean, and the tables did too. Copious bottles of alcohol were stored in an orderly manner behind the bar, and the counter itself was spotless save for the few glasses resting on its surface in front of patrons. She saw men in suits, women in skirts and blouses, some in jeans. She heard laughter, but it wasn't the obnoxious, drunken laughter she had expected from her preconceived notion of what the inside of a bar entailed. Rather, it was light and flowy, gently bouncing off the tastefully decorated walls to her ears.

To say Grace was surprised would have been an understatement.

She glanced around the room and was displeased not to see Ally. And then a woman sitting with her back to Grace turned her head and looked over her shoulder. She was sitting at the end of the bar, perpendicular to the front window overlooking the dark sky and streetlamp-illuminated road.

Grace's eyes widened farther as her lips lifted.

Ally smiled joyfully and waved.

Grace made her way to the bar and paused at Ally's side. She looked down at her friend, at the smart pantsuit she was wearing and the blouse that was unbuttoned at the top. "I didn't know it was you," she said, sounding naive even to her own ears.

Ally laughed. "Yep, I clean up good, don't I?"

"I... I didn't mean..."

Ally laughed again. "Sit down, silly," she said. "You've only seen me in workout gear and jeans. I had a business dinner meeting after work, so I thought today would be the perfect time to meet you, since I was already going to be out. Might as well come here, huh? End the day on a good note."

"Okay," Grace said.

"Aren't you gonna sit down?" Ally smirked.

"Oh, yes," Grace said. "Sorry."

"What's your poison?" Ally asked.

"Excuse me?"

"Seriously?" Ally asked. "You've never heard that saying before?"

"No, I don't think so."

"What do you want to drink?"

"Oh... I guess a glass of wine?"

"Sure," Ally said, and then she leaned over the counter, sought out the bartender at the other end, and called, "Hey, Derrick, we're ready for your concoctions, you know."

"Hold up, Ally," Derrick called back. "Not always at your beck and call, believe it or not."

"Right," Ally teased. "You just keep telling yourself that." She smiled, and Derrick smirked back.

Derrick made his way toward the women a moment later, and Ally leaned back as Derrick placed his elbows on the bar and rested his stubbly chin in his palms. "You know I was helping another customer, right?" His brown eyes twinkled through their crinkled corners.

"Nah." Ally brushed off the notion playfully. "You were

81

done. Plus you know you love me. You wanted to come and chat with me anyway."

"Maybe I did," Derrick teased. "Or maybe I just pretend. You're a good tipper, you know."

"I sure am," Ally replied. "So you'd better remember that when you talk to me. You might want me to keep believing that you love me."

"Good point," Derrick said with a grin. "I'll have to remind myself of your pockets every time I see you walk through my front door."

"You know I come here just to see you, right?" Ally cocked her head.

"Oh, I know," Derrick said. "But you do know I'm gay, yeah? Sorry to disappoint you, Ally, but we have no future together."

Ally sighed audibly and crossed one leg over the other, the tip of her heeled shoe tapping against the wall of the bar. "That hurt, Derrick. Very much. You could have at least gone on pretending for my sake."

Derrick waggled his brows. "My boyfriend's coming in tonight, so the cat would have come out of the bag."

"Truth." Ally laughed.

Derrick grinned in return then pushed off the counter with his elbows, leaned even farther over, and kissed Ally's waiting cheek. "Love you. Even if you are an ass."

"I love you too," Ally said, then she reciprocated the affection onto Derrick's turned cheek. "Looking forward to seeing Mark."

"So am I," Derrick replied with a large grin.

"Hey," Ally said. "This is my friend, Grace. Grace, Derrick. You'll have to get used to this guy if you'll be coming here with me, and I do hope you'll be coming back after tonight."

"Hi, Grace." Derrick held out his hand, and Grace shook it.

"Hi, Derrick."

"Nice to meet you."

"And it's nice to meet you too."

"Haven't seen you in here before."

Grace shook her head. "No. No, I haven't ever been here before."

"Then let me start by getting you something to drink."

"And it's my treat," Ally said.

"Oh, no," Grace demurred. "You don't have to do that."

"I know I don't have to," Ally replied. "But I'd like to. Thanks for coming into the city tonight. I know it's not your favorite place to be."

Ally looked at her surroundings. "This place is actually really nice," she admitted. "There aren't a whole lot of people. It's... I have to admit it's really not what I was expecting."

"And what were you expecting?" Ally raised a brow.

"Um... I think..."

"Did you think you'd walk into a rave? What? Like a club and people would be drunk and dancing, shooting up in the bathrooms?" Ally smirked at Grace.

Grace blushed and looked down at the hands resting on her lap. "No... no, I didn't think that. I just... wasn't expecting it to be so nice."

"Have you seriously never been in a bar before?" Ally asked.

"I have been," Grace replied. "Not for a very long time though."

"How long?"

"Since…" Grace looked at Ally shyly. "Since college. Gary took me."

Ally grinned. "Yep. It's been a while for you. There are all different types of bars in the city," she said. "Just because a place's purpose is for someone to get a drink doesn't mean it has to be grungy."

Grace found the warmth spreading through her cheeks again. "No… I guess not. I'm…"

Derrick dismissively flicked his hand in the air. "Whatever," he said. "Not a big deal. Glad you've come to my bar, anyway."

"That's right," Ally agreed. "This is the place to be. Especially if you haven't been out much since…" Ally looked at Grace with widened, unbelieving eyes, "college," she finished. "For real, Grace? You haven't been out since college? At least that's what I'm assuming now. Didn't you tell me that you're, like, thirty-six or something?"

"Yes, that's right," Grace confirmed. "I'm thirty-six. But I'm most comfortable at home. I like to be home. I liked it even when I was married. And it's not like I never went out."

Ally offered her a sideways eye.

Grace smiled. "Okay, so I didn't go out often. But Gary and I went to restaurants. We'd eat out. I just… it was always Gary that went out with his friends after work."

"And you never met up with him?"

Grace shook her head. "He never asked."

Ally frowned. "You were married to the guy. He didn't have to ask."

"No, I know…" Grace said. "But I just… I guess I never wanted to meet him. He was with his friends. I never really knew what to say to them. I was happier at home. I liked being at home."

"All right then," Ally replied. "You're a homebody. But I'm seriously getting you out on the town, gonna show you places you'll actually like. I get that you're a homebody, but too much of it isn't good for you."

"I'm not sure I agree," Grace countered.

Ally looked at Grace knowingly. "By the time I'm done with you, you will."

Derrick chuckled then asked Grace what she'd like to drink.

"I'll just have a glass of Riesling, please."

Derrick smiled. "Got it." He turned his back on the women and walked away. Grace watched him leave then glanced back at Ally. "He didn't ask you what you wanted."

"He doesn't have to. Remember, I'm here all the time. Derrick's got me."

"Oh... yes. I suppose that's right."

Derrick returned with a glass of wine for Grace and a burnt-orange drink in a martini glass for Ally.

"Thanks, handsome," Ally said. "That's just what I've been looking for." The grin on Ally's face was expansive when she lifted her glass by the stem, took a sip, and rolled her eyes as she tilted her head back with pleasure. "Delicious. You make them just right."

"So I've been told," Derrick said. He winked at Ally then left to help a man who had just seated himself at the other end of the bar.

"What is it?" Grace asked.

"It's called a sidecar."

"I've never heard of a sidecar before."

"I don't think a whole ton of people have. But it's seriously the best drink ever."

"I'm not much of a drinker," Grace admitted. "I do like a glass of wine on occasion, but that's really it."

"Then you're missing out. Here," Ally extended her glass. "Try it."

Grace looked at her skeptically, and Ally laughed. "Seriously," Ally coaxed. "Give it a try."

Grace accepted the glass and slowly lifted the rim to her lips. She tasted the sugar first, then the liquid slowly trickled onto her tongue. She lowered the glass and swallowed.

Ally took the drink from Grace and looked at her questioningly. "Well?"

Grace scrunched her nose. "I think there's a reason I don't drink often."

Ally laughed. "It's my all-time favorite. You and I just have different tastes, I guess."

"I think we do," Grace agreed with a smile. "I'll stick to my Riesling."

"Are you hungry at all?" Ally asked.

"Not really. I ate before meeting you."

"Me too. Dinner meeting and all. But they've got some great eats here. They've got these little appetizer bite things. They're kind of known for them. Maybe you'll just have to meet me here again soon, and we'll come with empty stomachs."

"I think I'd like that," Grace replied. "Especially if there aren't many people."

"It gets busier in about an hour," Ally said. "But it's never super crazy. And the people are always really nice."

"So no jerks?" Grace remembered their conversation from the other day when Ally had said she "didn't people."

Ally laughed. "Oh, I'm sure there are some jerks. But mostly, the crowd is great. I've got a lot of friends that come here, so I'll often run into someone I know."

"I'm getting that impression. We're very different in that way."

"And opposites can still be amazing together," Ally offered. "I like to be around people; you don't. I like crowds; you don't. I like to get my butt out of the house; you don't. And yet we have a lot in common, Grace. I bet we can teach each other a thing or two, yeah? Life's about learning or I'm not lifing right."

"Lifing?"

"That's right. We're lifing."

Grace chuckled. "I like that."

"Thought you would." Ally smirked then took another sip of her drink. She swallowed, smacked her lips, then said, "Now that's what I'm talking about. Lifing at its best." She lifted her glass. "Hey, cheers?"

"Cheers," Grace said then clinked her glass to Ally's.

"So, why is it that you're so anxious all the time?"

Grace was taken aback once again by Ally's forthrightness, though she found she wasn't offended in the slightest as she might have been had anyone else asked her the exact same question. Ally was blunt, yes. But she also seemed genuine, kind. Grace didn't fully comprehend why she didn't have a difficult time speaking with Ally, why she wasn't nervously twiddling her fingers or constantly searching for an excuse to walk away, but her intuition spoke to her, soothed her. It assured her that Ally was one to be trusted, and Grace was beginning to embrace her intuition's guarantees.

"I... I think..." Grace began. She looked at the ceiling in an attempt to sort out her thoughts. "I think it's in my genes."

"In your genes?" Ally looked at her with a frown.

"Yes," Grace said. "My father... Ally, I haven't really told many people about my childhood. It's nothing to be

87

ashamed of, I know that now. But I guess I just… I think I'm a private person."

"You don't have to tell me a single thing that you don't want to. I know I ask a lot of questions. I'm seriously the type of person that lays it all on the table. You'll know everything there is to know about me by the end of next week." She laughed. "But I know that not everyone is of the same mindset as me. I get it. Seriously, Grace. Don't say anything to me that you're not comfortable saying. We'll get there, I'm sure. Or maybe not. Whatever. I just like talking to you. Change the subject if you want."

Grace took a moment to reflect on Ally's statement. She looked into Ally's blue eyes, darker on the perimeter, flecks of silver toward the pupil. "No," she eventually said. "I'm okay." She took a deep breath. "My parents met when they were in high school. My mother always told me they were drawn to each other somehow. She didn't know why, but they just were. I was extremely close to my nana—my mother's mother—when I was growing up and all the way until she passed away when I was a freshman in college. I wasn't all that close to my grandfather, but he was a nice enough man from what I remember. I just didn't see him all that often. My father's parents were just absent, I think. I didn't know them well when I was growing up. They're both gone now.

"I'm an only child, and when I was really small, I think I began to notice that my parents were different from other parents. I'd watch other kids get hugged by their mothers when they were getting picked up from school. My mother wasn't affectionate. I always thought she was kind of… well, I guess when I was really small, I thought she was out there, flighty. She wouldn't often look at me when we spoke; she always seemed to be somewhere else.

88

"My father wasn't affectionate either, but in a different way. He'd say things to me sometimes. I know now that they weren't typical things a father should say to his daughter, but I didn't know that then, especially when I was just four or five years old. And he'd say them so matter-of-factly, so I never thought what he was saying was wrong or harmful. Again, I know now that's not the case."

"What kind of things did he say to you?"

Grace bit her lower lip then said, "When I was a little girl, I always liked wearing my hair in two ponytails, and I really liked dresses. When I was in kindergarten, dresses were all I'd wear. I'd get up in the morning, and even then, I'd make my own breakfast. Nobody made it for me. I'd eat, brush my teeth, then get dressed. Sometimes it was Mom that would put my hair up, but other times, she wasn't home in the mornings, though I didn't know why back then, so I learned to do the ponytails myself. I'd walk downstairs, all proud and ready to start my day at school. I liked school even back then.

"My father would always be sitting at the kitchen table with his coffee in front of him—black—and he'd look up at me with what I know now was a disapproving expression. But it wasn't entirely obvious back then. He was always good at masking things. Or maybe 'masking' isn't the right word to use. It was more that he was so subtle when he did or said anything to me, and I hadn't really been over to many kids' homes, so I didn't know any different. He'd look at me and squint just a tiny bit, and then he'd say something like 'your hair is crooked' or 'your dress doesn't fit.' Something really minor, really, but it hurt just the same. I was only five years old, but I remember these moments well. I remember how I felt. I remember how deflated I was."

"He never helped you get ready for school in the morning?" Ally took another sip of her drink.

Grace shook her head. "No. Not that I can remember. When I think back on my childhood, he's always at the table and always with his black coffee in front of him. Sometimes my mom would be there, sometimes not, but I didn't think this was out of the ordinary back then either.

"As I grew, my father would say other things to me, and again, they were subtle. 'Makeup's messed up.' 'Jeans are too small.' 'Don't slump your shoulders.' 'You don't bring friends around—what, you ashamed of your old man?' I think over time, all his words sank in. I felt them. Deep inside.

"I was in middle school when my mom left for good, and it was only then that I learned she was a heroin addict. My father called her a no-good junkie from that day on, but I could tell her leaving affected him greatly. He taunted me more after she left. It almost seemed to me that he blamed me for her leaving, so that's what I internalized. I started to blame myself. I knew then that most mothers were caring. I knew then that most mothers loved their kids, would do anything for them. I didn't understand why she didn't love me. Or so that's what I thought back then. This is also the time that I clung onto my nana a bit more tightly."

"And your nana never did anything about the way your father was treating you?" Ally asked.

Grace shook her head. "I don't think she knew. I never spoke up to her about my father. I was too ashamed."

"Damn, that seriously sucks."

Grace nodded then continued. "In high school, I learned that my father was on meds for anxiety and depression. I don't know when he started taking the pills, I just know that's when I found out. In hindsight, I think he's always struggled with anxiety and depression. I just couldn't put a name on what I was seeing. I learned that his father, along with alcoholism, also had clinical anxiety. Things started to come together for me then. I started to understand. Or at least I tried.

"I'll never forget the day I came home from high school and my father looked at me. I felt his eyes all over, and it made me incredibly uncomfortable. 'You got your boobs,' he said. Just like that. No preamble. Just 'You got your boobs.' I ran up the stairs to my bedroom and cried. I stopped wearing makeup; my father told me it looked terrible anyway. I was also self-conscious about what I wore in the morning, always wondering what my father would say to me.

"I don't know... I think my father really loved my mother. Maybe they both loved each other. But the heroin won out, and she left. I think he needed a scapegoat, and I was there. I know now he had a whole slew of issues. When you hear things about yourself the way I heard them from an early age, from your first memories, you begin to believe them. It was hard for me. I've had years to look back on how things were with my parents, how things were growing up, but even now, I have a hard time with certain things. Crowds, people looking at me. I haven't worn makeup since high school, and I really have no desire to. When I'm alone, there's nobody there to tell me I'm doing things wrong, nobody there to criticize me. I can do things the way I want to do them.

"So yes, I think in part, I am the way I am because of my genes—my dad's anxiety and depression and my mom's propensity for addiction. But also because of the way things were when I was a child."

"Damn," Ally said breathily. "That sucks ass."

Grace's eyes widened. "Sucks ass?"

"You bet."

"You say the strangest things sometimes," Grace said with a chortle.

"Yep, I know," Ally said. "They just come out."

Grace looked at her new friend, and she felt that she was understood, appreciated even. She felt something inside her core that she had never experienced before, not with Gary, not with Bethany. Not after thirty-six years of life. Maybe not even with her nana. And not for the first time, Grace was floored that she had only just met this amazing woman beside her and had so readily felt comfortable in her presence. "I like what you say," she said.

"I'm glad you like what I say," Ally replied. "Because I don't intend on stopping anytime soon."

"Please don't. You make me smile."

"Glad I can do that," Ally said. "That's my mission in life, I suppose."

"To make people smile?"

"Hey, sure," Ally replied. "Why not? If that's my purpose, then I've got a pretty damn good purpose, don't I?"

"I guess yes… yes, you do."

"You see your dad still?"

Grace shook her head. "Not really. Maybe once every year or so. And every time I see him, it brings everything back. It brings it all to the surface. I can't stand it. It takes me a week or two to recover after we spend time together."

"Then why the hell do you even make the effort?"

"He's my father," Grace said as if that explained everything.

"So?"

"So?" Grace repeated. "He's my father."

"Yeah, okay," Ally said. "And he's an ass. He might have provided the sperm, but he doesn't sound like much of a father to me, Grace. You don't owe him anything."

"I... I think... I guess I've always thought that I do owe him. In a way. He's my father. I grew up with him. He provided for me. He's in my blood. He's inside of me."

"Too much of him is inside of you, and it's toxic. It's bringing you down. He might be your father, but you're an adult now. You have every right to rid yourself of the things in your life that weigh on you. Purge that shit."

Grace's eyes widened. "It's really hard for me to see it that way," she admitted.

"I get it," Ally said. "He wormed his way in. You do what you need to do, whatever that is. I'm glad you only see him once a year. I think that's plenty, and much more than he deserves by the sound of it."

Grace looked at her half-empty glass. She twisted the stem in her fingers. "I can't just let go..."

"Then don't," Ally replied. "But think about why you're holding on."

Grace pondered then looked up. She nodded.

Ally sighed. "Don't get me wrong. I get it. My parents suck, too."

"They... they do?" Grace asked, somewhat surprised.

"Yep. They never wanted kids. Made that mighty clear to me when I was growing up. I was an accident. And they used that word, too. 'Accident.' They even went so far as to say that I was an unwanted pregnancy. Unwanted. So yeah, Grace, I get it. I get having words thrown your way when you're young and impressionable. My mother was forty-three when she had me, my father forty-six. They never expected their lives to take such a turn. I seriously think they should have given me up for adoption. I bet I would have been so much happier, and I *know* they would have been, but nope. Not the Cummingses. What would people think if they gave away their kid, right? So yeah, Grace. I get it. But like I said, throw that toxic shit away!"

"Oh my goodness…" Grace said, her voice soft. "Do *you* still talk to your parents?"

"Not so much," Ally replied. "On very rare occasions, but they're happy going on their cruises or doing this thing and that. I'm not sure they think of me all that often, and I'm much happier where I am in my life right now without them to bring me down."

"Oh my goodness," Grace repeated.

Ally laughed. "On to a lighter conversation?"

"Yes, please."

"Dogs or cats?"

Grace laughed. "Really? Where did that come from?"

"What could be more light than the ever-present dog-versus-cat conversation?"

"I don't have either."

Ally swallowed a sip of her drink. "Don't have to," she said. "But everyone has a preference."

"I guess I'd have to say dogs."

"Sweet. Great minds think alike."

"Do you have one?" Grace asked.

"Hell no," Ally said with a grin.

Grace laughed, the conversation about her parents temporarily forgotten. "That was a very decisive answer."

"Darn right. I love dogs. Like cats too, honestly. But there's no way I could own one. I'm not home often enough. The poor thing would act out just to get my attention. It wouldn't be fair. For now, I'll just get my dog fix from friends. I've got plenty of friends that own them. A couple with cats, too. Cats can be little assholes though,

94

huh? I've got this one friend that has a cat that swats my ankles every time I go over. I look for the thing, don't see him, walk, then *thwack!* Claws on my ankles! Every damn time. He's this gray striped animal, super fat. So fat you'd think he wouldn't be able to move, but you'd be wrong. Move he can. Just to taunt me."

Grace laughed. "I haven't been around many cats, but I've heard these stories before."

"He's an ass," Ally said with a grin. "He's got it out for me. No clue why. I'm awesome." She offered Grace a playful grin and a wink before taking the last sip of her drink, a minute portion of orange remnants pooling at the bottom of the glass when she placed it on the countertop. "Damn, that was good."

"I'm glad you liked it."

Derrick reemerged then, gently placing another sidecar in front of Ally and removing her empty glass. "You are wonderful, my friend," Ally told him. "This is why I love you so much."

"Because of my drinks? I thought it was because of my charm."

"What charm?" Ally asked with a lopsided grin.

"You need to leave my bar," Derrick replied.

Ally gasped with mock incredulity. "Look who can't take a joke."

Derrick looked over Ally's shoulder. "And who's suddenly in a much better mood."

When Grace turned around, she saw a black-haired man walking their way, a huge grin on his attractive face. He sidled up next to Ally and kissed her exaggeratedly on the cheek.

"At least Mark loves me." Ally was looking at Mark, though her statement was clearly meant for his boyfriend.

"You need to leave this man and be with me. We can run off into the sunset…"

Mark rested his arm on Ally's shoulder. "Sounds like…"

"Paradise?" Ally suggested.

"Unnatural," Mark countered with a grin.

Ally swatted his chest.

Mark looked at Derrick behind the counter. "You didn't shave. You look like you just rolled out of bed."

Derrick lifted his brows suggestively, leaned over, and kissed Mark hello.

"Well, good to see you too," Mark said when they parted. "This girl giving you trouble?"

"Nothing I can't handle," Derrick promised.

"Keep on thinking that," Ally said.

"And who are you?" Mark turned to Grace with a smile.

"This is my friend, Grace," Ally offered. "We just met, and she's pretty wonderful. Don't tease her, now. You two have that tendency. I don't want her running out of here never to return."

"Nice to meet you, Grace," Mark said as he extended his hand. "Mark."

Grace felt her cheeks flush as she placed her palm in his. "Hi, Mark."

"New customers," Derrick announced. "Gotta go." He turned and walked toward two women who had just seated themselves at the bar.

"See you," Mark said to Ally.

"Leaving so soon?"

"Got myself two good-looking dates over there." Mark motioned with his chin toward a table near the back of the room, where two men were chatting animatedly.

"Have fun," Ally said with a wink.

"Nice to meet you, Grace," Mark said as he took his first step. "Hope you'll come again."

"I think I will," Grace said. "It was nice to meet you too."

"That was Mark," Ally said as she glanced back from his retreating figure.

Grace laughed. "Yes. I know."

Ally smirked in response. "They're great guys. Chase and I have them over to our place sometimes, but mostly I see them here."

"How often do you come here?" Grace asked. She was getting the impression that Ally was at the bar often.

"Usually a couple of times a week. It's a great place to be. Don't usually come on the weekend, but it's soothing to be here after dinner."

"I'm not sure I'd use the word 'soothing.'"

"It is to me," Ally replied.

"What other places do you like to go?" Grace asked.

"Oh, tons. There's another bar I frequent, but this one is my favorite. I love eating out, and I do that a lot on the weekends. Coffeehouses are a must in the mornings. I stop in on my way to work. Plenty around, for sure. Love the ones where I can sit outside when I have time. I might not people sometimes, but I'm a people watcher. You ever just sit there and watch people pass by? Look at their faces, wonder what they're thinking? Look at what they're wearing, look at the way they carry themselves?"

"I do sometimes, yes."

"I do it all the time. I make up stories as I go. This person just got out of work, this person had a crappy day, this person is going to meet their partner based on the smile on their face. Or maybe they're just super excited to get a muffin from the coffee shop down the street from you. That would put a silly smile on my face, right?"

Grace laughed. "Yes, I think it would."

"Let's do it again. This weekend?"

"Really?"

"Uh… yes! Hello! Blueberry muffin? Giant, delicious blueberry muffin with sugar and buttery goodness? Pair that with a cup of coffee—"

"A giant cup of coffee."

"Right. A giant cup of coffee, according to you—I still think they're small." Ally smirked. "Sounds like a good friend date to me. For the morning, anyway."

"And what's your idea of a good friend date in the evening?"

"Karaoke."

Grace started. "Karaoke?" she croaked. "Really?"

"Hell yeah. You ever been?"

"To karaoke?" Grace whispered.

"No… to outer space. Might as well be outer space with the way you're looking at me right now."

"I'm… I'm sorry," Grace managed to say. "I shouldn't be surprised. You seem like the type of person who would enjoy karaoke. It's just that… I think you know me well enough by now. I have never been to karaoke. Ever. I think it would send me over the edge. Something like that is way out of my comfort zone."

"Give me time," Ally said.

"For what?"

"Give me time, and I'll have you in a karaoke bar. Hell, I'll even have you up on that stage with me, singing your heart out."

"Absolutely not," Grace protested.

"We'll see…" Ally said with a grin.

Grace shook her head. "No," she said. "That's not something I can do."

"Well, why don't we start with coffee and a muffin, yeah?"

"That sounds good to me."

CHAPTER 6

*T*hey met for coffee that Saturday morning, exactly a week after they had run into each other at the coffee house, and spent time in the beautiful autumn sun, talking and greatly enjoying each other's company. This morning was no different. In fact, Grace thought her time with Ally was even more enjoyable as the two women spoke, drank several cups of coffee, and ate their muffins— Ally a blueberry muffin again and Grace trying a chocolate-chocolate chip variety, which she relished wholeheartedly.

"You have chocolate in your teeth." Ally laughed.

"Oh," Grace said bashfully as she closed her lips.

Ally took a big bite of her muffin, scrunched her nose, then opened her mouth to show a generous portion of chewed pastry.

"That's kind of gross," Grace said with a smile.

"But it did the trick. You're smiling."

"Yes," Grace agreed. "Thank you."

"You never have to feel embarrassed with me," Ally said. "Seriously."

"I know," Grace replied. "But as they say, 'old habits die hard.'"

"We'll have to work on that," Ally said.

Grace nodded and smiled into her mug.

They spent two hours at the coffee shop before saying their goodbyes. "I want to take you out next weekend," Ally said as she stood from the table. "Meet me at my house first? That way, I can introduce you to Chase. You'll hit it off. Everyone loves Chase."

Grace nodded. "I can do that, and I'd love to go out with you again. But Ally?"

"Mmm?"

"Nothing too intense, okay?"

"I promise," Ally said, a gleam in her eye when she turned to walk away.

Grace said goodbye to her first graders as the bell rang at school the following Friday afternoon, walked them down the hallway to their appropriate dismissal lines—one for pick-ups, another for buses—packed up her belongings, and left the building for home. On her way, she passed by the coffee shop she and Ally had since deemed their own, and she smiled with gratitude. She believed she had discovered a kindred soul in Ally, another woman in whom she could confide, with whom she felt, perhaps for the first time in her life, that she could truly be herself: flawed, raw, evolving.

She parked her car in her narrow driveway—large enough for only her one vehicle—fit the key into the front doorknob, and stepped inside. Her home was quiet save for the gentle hum of the refrigerator and an overhead fan in the living room that she had left on low to circulate the air in her absence. She wondered—not for the first time—if she should adopt a cat from the local animal shelter. Then she'd have a comforting presence to come home to. The notion made her mind immediately conjure an image of a fat, gray, striped cat that swatted at her ankles and ran amok, causing holy terror, and Grace smiled, thinking of Ally and the story she had relayed at the bar.

Grace was going to meet Ally for dinner that night, though she had promised to first stop off at Ally's apartment to meet her best friend, Chase. Grace had been quite pleased when Ally suggested they go out to dinner; she had been fearful of what Ally had in mind for their outing, and Grace had conjured up images of a karaoke bar, the space crowded, the pressure to perform. Eyes on her. People laughing at her expense.

But dinner she could do. With Ally as company, Grace knew that she wouldn't be discomfited by the other patrons, and she knew, too, that they'd engage in pleasant conversation. She enjoyed her time with Ally very much and found she often craved more once they parted.

She boarded the bustling Friday-evening T into Boston. As much as she loathed the T, the thought of driving in city traffic made her stomach quake; all the honking, impatient drivers, cars inches from her tail and on either side of her. She didn't think she could contend with the inevitable. At least with the T, someone else was doing the driving, and she merely had to sit or hold onto a pole for balance, clutching her purse close to her chest, her head down and eyes trained on her shoes while her nostrils breathed in the stagnant city air.

When she arrived at the stop that Ally had indicated was the one closest to her place, Grace deboarded and stepped onto the concrete platform that would take her to the stairs and up onto the lamp-illuminated street outside. She paused momentarily to read the lettering on the gray wall. She wanted to double-check that this was, indeed, her stop before she continued on her way. She pressed her fingers into her purse, still clutched against her chest. She looked around.

People.

There were so many people.

The fact that Ally loved the city made Grace shake her head as she took her first step forward, the sound of the T ringing in her ears, the whoosh of warm air blowing at her hair, her clothes as it sped past, inching closer to the next stop. Men and women, boys and girls would depart on their way to their desired Friday-night destinations. Perhaps a movie or the theatre. Perhaps a friend's house. Maybe someone was headed to a bar or a restaurant like she'd be going to with Ally tonight.

Grace climbed the stairs and exited onto the street, the air stale but cold. She pulled her nana's burnt-orange hat farther down over her ears.

Ally's place was close by, or so she had claimed. She had told Grace that she was to take a left out of the T station and walk two blocks, but Grace took out her phone and punched in her friend's address just to be sure. She didn't want to find herself wandering through unfamiliar territory. Alone. At night.

With phone in hand, the screen illuminated and marking her location, Grace walked. It took less than five minutes to arrive at Ally's doorstep. She lived in a three-story red building, the paint chipping off the sides. Grace opened the front door and stepped inside. Ally's door was the first one on the left and was marked with her last name,

Cummings, and Chase's as well, Hoffman, just below Ally's on a small gold placard adhered to the door.

Grace had found it without hindrance. She sighed, feeling quite relieved, and knocked.

It took only a moment for the door to open, and standing there in the threshold was a man Grace intuited to be Chase, Ally's best friend and roommate. A mass of loose brown curls sat atop his head, and light-brown eyes shone with pleasure as his lips lifted into a smile, revealing straight white teeth. He wasn't much taller than Grace at five foot six, maybe a couple of inches at most. He wore a pair of Adidas track pants and a gray hooded sweatshirt.

"You're Grace," he said matter-of-factly. "Come on in. Ally's getting ready, but she should be out in just a minute."

"Thank you," Grace said, her voice just barely above a whisper. Chase appeared genuine enough, but he was still a stranger to Grace, and strangers made her nervous. Especially men. Even when he was Ally's best friend.

"Can I get you something to drink? Glass of water maybe?"

"No, but thank you. I'm all set."

Chase nodded. "Got it. Sit down if you'd like." He motioned to the couch.

"Thank you." Grace stepped forward and sat down. Chase made himself comfortable on an oversized cushioned chair opposite her.

"Ally's been talking about you a whole lot," Chase said. "You two just met?"

"Yes, that's right. Not long ago. I think… just a few weeks."

Chase's nod indicated to Grace that his question had been rhetorical. "Ally's good like that. You meet her, you're hooked."

104

Grace smiled. "She's very easy to talk to."

"That she is," Chase said.

"When... when did you two meet?" Grace asked.

"We met in college. Both went to BU. It was freshman year, same bio class. We were paired up for a project, and the rest is history. Hung out all the time after that, and when we were set to graduate, she needed a place to live. I was headed to grad school and was living here with a buddy of mine. He was a year ahead of me and was moving in with his girlfriend, so I found myself in need of a roommate. The timing was perfect. Ally moved in, and we've been here ever since."

"That worked out really well."

"Sure did," Chase agreed. "Not the most glamorous place to live, but it's near everything we need, it's safe, and it does the trick. We don't need anything else, so we've stuck with it."

Grace smiled. "Then I'm glad you were able to find it in the first place."

"Lucked out with that one. My old roommate had the place, and I moved in. I was just lucky enough to keep it when he left."

"And Ally moved in."

"You've got it." Chase grinned. After a moment's lull, he said, "Ally says you're a teacher."

Grace nodded. "Yes. I teach first grade."

"I bet that's a tough job."

"No," Grace replied. "Not really. I have rough days sometimes, and there are difficult situations with some of the children, but I would say the toughest part of the job isn't the children at all. It's the parents."

"What do you mean?"

"Well," Grace continued, "I can't say too much because

of privacy, but I find some of the parents to be difficult to deal with. I've gotten many phone calls from upset mothers and fathers or grandparents or some other form of caregiver, stating that I'm not treating their child well, that a grade they've gotten wasn't warranted, or it wasn't fair that I didn't let their child sit next to their best friend. Things like that."

Chase looked at her with a perplexed expression. "Wait a minute. I thought you just said you taught the first grade."

Grace nodded. "Yes, that's right. I do."

"Whoa. So you're telling me that you've gotten complaints about fairness and whatnot in the first grade? First? About grades? Do you even give grades that young?"

Grace laughed. "Not entirely, no. When a child does an assignment in the classroom, I often try to write something on their paper before they put it in their folder to take home. Some of the children do really well, and I see that most of them are trying their best. But some of the children don't seem to care for the work they're doing and would prefer to fool around. I'll write something like 'So and so, I've seen you do this work, and I know you've got it down. You can do it!' I always try to be encouraging, but I also believe that parents and caregivers should know what's going on in school."

Grace paused and looked at Chase. She hadn't taken a breath since she began her explanation, and she realized that she had just spoken to Chase as if he was Ally. Despite her initial misgivings, she was suddenly comfortable, unabashed. It was a powerful feeling indeed.

"First frickin' grade. Damn!" Chase enthused.

"You'd be surprised," Grace said. "I've had a couple of parents call me in the past about their children, wondering why our progress reports only state whether their children understand the material presented or not. These parents want grades. They want to know where their child stands in their class. I think they want to know if their child has a superior understanding of the material, and that makes me fearful."

"How so?"

"Well," Grace went on, "it makes me wonder how that parent will react when their child is in high school, when they're taking more standardized tests and have the ability to take AP classes and see GPAs and have letter grades. I think... I guess I've just begun to believe that... I think... well, I think a first grader should be a first grader. Yes, I do believe that in first grade, there are certain things that they should know, but I also believe that all children learn at different levels and at different times in their development. I don't believe six- and seven-year-olds should be worried about how they are doing compared to their peers. I mean... I guess I should say... if a child is truly behind, that should be addressed. But if a child is just not grasping something as quickly as their peers, but I can tell they'll get it soon, that they're trying and making an effort, well then, I'm not worried. I feel we put too much pressure on our young children today. I want to see my kids go outside and play. I want to see them exploring their environment and learning how to connect with each other. They don't need to know long division and times tables."

Chase's eyes widened. "Do you really teach that in the first grade?"

Grace laughed. "No, not at all. I'm just trying to make a point."

"Ah. Gotcha. Makes sense."

"As they get older, I understand that more is expected of them. But a child is only a child once. And these children are young. I love to see smiles, and I love to see kids who are happy to come to my classroom each morning. I love to see how they interact with each other. And I love to see them enjoying the materials I bring out. Sadly, I'm seeing those smiles go away, and at an earlier and earlier age. It makes me... well, it makes me sad. I don't think young children should feel pressured. I think they should feel loved and understood. And seen and heard."

"Wow," Chase said. "You really feel passionately about this."

Grace blushed profusely and bowed her head.

Chase leaned forward, his elbows on his thighs. "No," he said. "It's cool. It's really great to see a teacher feel this way about her students. And I got you. We do pressure our kids. I was pressured, and first grade for me was a long time ago. But I still remember it. Seems like things are getting even worse these days."

"Not for all the children," Grace said, her voice low, the warmth in her cheeks still evident. "I think I feel a bit more for the kids that are pressured because I know how it is to be... to be let down. I know how it is to hear words that aren't kind."

"It sucks," Chase said.

"It does."

Ally bounded into the room. "I'm so sorry!" she shouted. Grace looked up and saw her friend's enormous smile. Ally's shorn hair was growing out on the sides, the blond tendrils at the top of her head still spiky and disheveled. She grabbed Chase from behind, threw her arms around his neck, and kissed his cheek. "I see you've met Chase."

"I have," Grace said.

"Grace and I were just chatting," Chase said.

"About?" Ally asked.

"About her work." Chase looked at Grace. "It appears that you've developed a friendship with one of the most caring teachers out there."

Grace lowered her eyes, feeling incredibly self-conscious. She fiddled with her fingers on her lap, and just as she had sensed her blush dissipate, Chase's statement sent her into a new flurry of embarrassment, her cheeks burning. She wanted to lift her fingers to touch them, to feel how hot they must be, but she refrained. She was already unsettled enough. She didn't need to place attention on something she was sure Chase was already attuned to.

"Oh yeah, I know," Ally said joyfully. She released Chase and hopped over to Grace. She sat down beside her on the couch and flung her arms around Grace's back and chest, pulling her in for an embrace. "I'm learning all sorts of new and wonderful things about my new friend Grace here."

Grace felt the burning wane as she looked into Ally's blue eyes, but she still sensed Chase's presence. She was flummoxed that she had gone from feeling so comfortable when they spoke to feeling like a leper, his eyes on her, engaging, seeking.

It wasn't a new sensation; she often felt like this when around new people. And yet... it was somehow a different sensation altogether.

And she didn't know what to make of it.

"I made reservations," Ally announced. "It's a great place, Grace. You'll love it. I hope so, anyway."

"I'm sure I will."

"We should get going, though. I wanted you and Chase to get to know each other a bit more, but I flaked out when making the reservations. I should have made them a bit later, but oh well. It is what it is."

"That's okay," Grace said.

"We'll have plenty of time to see each other again, I'm sure," Chase added.

"You bet," Ally agreed. She stood from the couch, ran her palms down her stonewashed jeans, and made for the door. "Chase, you going out tonight?"

"Yeah. With Missy."

Ally grimaced in response.

Chase chuckled. "I know you don't like her, but you don't have to be so obvious."

"Don't I?" Ally asked innocently. "Isn't it the job of a best friend to let you know when you're dating a snobby ass?"

"Snobby ass, eh?" Chase laughed. "Good one, Ally."

"So not sorry," Ally said. "I love you, Chase, but sometimes you make terrible decisions."

"And you don't know her as well as I do."

"I know enough," Ally said with a frown.

"All right," Chase said. He flicked his hand toward the door. "Out you go. Have fun, you two."

Grace slowly walked forward and met up with Ally as Ally grabbed her bag from an end table and turned the doorknob.

"Nice to meet you, Grace," Chase said.

Grace turned. "It was nice to meet you, too."

"Have fun tonight."

"Thank you," Grace said. "You too." Then she followed Ally out the door.

∾

The restaurant was within walking distance, but Grace was still pleased that she had possessed the foresight to wear comfortable shoes. She enjoyed walking, but since she drove in to work each day, she didn't walk extensively. Ally was wearing heeled maroon suede boots. It was a wonder to Grace that Ally could walk at all, let alone walk down the streets of Boston a good quarter of a mile away from her apartment.

"I know you didn't get to talk with Chase for long, but I'm glad you met him. He's seriously a great guy."

"Yes," Grace said. "He seems to be."

"I'm sure you'll get to know him more."

"Okay."

"Okay?" Grace laughed.

"I didn't know what else to say."

"Well then… okay," Ally said with a playful grin.

They arrived at the restaurant, and Ally held the door open for Grace to enter first. Grace stepped foot inside and looked around. It was busy. Very busy.

A smartly dressed man was standing at a small booth just to the side of the doorway. "Do you have a reservation?" he asked Grace.

"I… um… we…"

"Yep," Ally said as she closed the door and sidled up next to Grace. "Under Cummings."

The man looked down. "Ah, yes. I have you here. Table for two?"

"That's us," Ally said.

"Right this way." He grabbed two menus from the side of the booth and led the way, Ally following in his footsteps, with Grace just behind her.

"Here you are," the man said. He placed the menus on the table and offered a closed-lipped smile. "Enjoy."

"Thanks a bunch," Ally said merrily. She slid into a chair, and Grace took the seat opposite her. "You ever been here before?" Ally asked.

"I haven't."

"A little too posh for my liking, so I don't come here often, but I'm telling you, the food is freaking fabulous. I seriously had a craving for pasta tonight. Hope you don't mind. Darn. I should have asked you before choosing the place. I don't even know if you like Italian."

"I like pretty much anything," Grace replied. "I don't mind that you made the reservation. I'm glad you did."

A young woman approached their table and placed a small wicker basket of rolls at its center along with a white plate of what appeared to be a butter-and-herb concoction. "Can I get you anything to drink tonight?" she asked.

"I'd love a glass of wine. Anything red. You pick," Ally said.

"All right. And you?" The woman turned to Grace.

"I'll have the same."

Ally looked up at the woman. "Might as well just bring us a bottle to share, yeah?"

"I can do that," the woman replied.

"That okay with you, Grace?"

"It is," Grace said.

Ally nodded at the woman. "Sweet." She smirked.

The woman turned and left the table. "You've got to try some of this bread," Ally said. "It's one of the best things about this place. And don't forget the butter. I have no clue what they put in it, but it's awesome." She picked up a roll and spread butter on the top. She took a large bite. "I'm telling you…"

Grace chuckled. When she reached into the basket, she was pleasantly surprised to find that the rolls were warm to the touch, and when she spread some butter on one, it began to melt, the yellow substance glittering in the light provided by a hanging chandelier placed strategically over the table. Grace took a bite, and her eyebrows rose.

"Told you," Ally said.

"How do you know about all of these places?" Grace asked. "I mean, you had me try a muffin at the café, and it was wonderful. You brought me to your favorite bar. And now here we are. And you were right. This roll is really very good."

"It's more than good."

Grace laughed. "Okay," she agreed. "It's more than good."

"I get out a lot, remember? And I've lived in the city for a while now. Plus, I like to try new things. Add that all up, and I know where to go."

Grace nodded. "Yes. That makes sense. Thanks for bringing me here tonight. If these rolls are any indication about how dinner will taste, then I'm sure I'll love it."

"I'm getting the butternut squash ravioli. I don't even need to look at the menu. It's freaking fantastic. It's seasonal right now, and just like this damn butter, I have no clue what they put into their ravioli, but I'm seriously hooked."

"I think I'll look at the menu, but that sounds wonderful."

Grace did, indeed, peruse the menu, but like Ally, she ordered the butternut squash ravioli, and when she took her first bite, the flavors bursting on her tongue, she was certain she lacked the ability to recreate anything even remotely as tasty as what they had done in the restaurant.

"It's award worthy, yeah?" Ally asked.

"Oh my goodness…" was all Grace managed in reply.

After a pause during which both women savored second

113

bites of their dinner, Ally said, "Tell me something I don't know about you."

"What do you mean?"

"We haven't known each other all that long, but it feels like it's been longer."

"I feel the same way," Grace said.

"So tell me something I don't know. It can be anything. I don't care. Something heavy or something super light. I don't even know what your favorite color is."

"Burnt orange."

"Ah… like your hat."

Grace looked over at her purse hanging on the side of her chair, her nana's woven hat stuffed inside. "Yes," she said. "Like my hat."

"Did you make it?"

Grace shook her head. "I didn't. My nana made it."

"Ah, yes. The nana you spoke about when you were telling me about your parents. Your mother's mom, right?"

"That's right," Grace replied.

"And she died?"

"Yes. She died."

"What of?" Ally cut a ravioli with the edge of her fork, pressed the tines into it, and lifted the piece to her mouth.

"She wasn't well. She had a whole slew of health issues: asthma and allergies, GI troubles, hypothyroidism. She landed in the hospital with pneumonia and didn't make it out." Grace fiddled with the stem of her fork, her eyes trained on her plate as the painful memories began to flood her mind.

"That sucks."

Grace nodded. "She was my best friend." Her voice was low, her words spoken slowly.

"When did she die? I think you told me, but I forgot."

"When I was a freshman in college."

"Sorry to hear."

"Thank you," Grace said.

"And she made you that hat? Your nana?"

"Yes. She made it for me the year before she passed away. She said she knew it was my favorite color, and nanas should knit. I remember laughing at her, at the stereotype. My nana never knitted, not for as long as I knew her. Not until that year. I remember being really surprised that she could even find the yarn at the craft store." Grace chuckled. "You… you kind of remind me of her, of my nana."

"Yeah?"

"Yes. Nana was outgoing. She loved people. She loved being around them. She loved doing things and going places. When my mom left, my nana was always there. She was really the only person I felt I could go to when I needed something. She was the only person I could talk to. I felt like she was the only person that understood me, even though we were so different."

"And your mom's an addict?"

"Yes."

"How did your nana feel about that?"

"She was torn up," Grace said. "I'm not sure if she ever told me all of what she was feeling, but I knew it affected her greatly. My nana was such a wonderful person. My mother grew up in a stable home, and Nana never understood why she tried heroin in the first place. I think she blamed herself. I think she felt like she failed as a mother."

"Can't be a good feeling."

"No," Grace agreed. "Not at all. But I think it proves that drugs can affect anyone. They can take anyone. Fully and unconditionally. They can alter the lives of people from stable homes just as much as they alter the lives of those growing up in dysfunctional families."

"Truth," Ally said.

"What's your favorite color?" Grace asked.

"Hot pink."

Grace laughed. "I can see that."

"I dyed my hair hot pink last year. I should do it again."

"Did you really?"

"Oh, yeah," Ally said. "It looked awesome. My boss wasn't thrilled, but there was nothing he could do about it." Ally gave a sly grin.

It took Grace and Ally a while to finish their meals—they made no effort to slow their chatter. After the conversation about Grace's grandmother, they spoke mostly of superficial things: their favorite season and holiday, jobs they had held in high school, their favorite foods.

When Grace stood from the table, she felt lighthearted and carefree. Satiated.

"Off to my place?" Ally suggested. "I can make some coffee."

"I'd like that. Thank you."

The women left the restaurant and made their way down the sidewalk of the busy Boston street and back to Ally's apartment. Ally fit her key in the doorknob, pushed the door open, and walked through. She halted just inside, forcing Grace to stagger abruptly so she didn't bump into Ally's backside. "What are you doing home? I thought you were going out with Missy."

Ally made her way farther into the room. Grace closed the door behind them and watched her friend approach Chase, who was sitting on the couch, his feet propped up on an ottoman, his phone in hand.

"Don't even ask," Chase mumbled.

"That good, huh?"

"That good," Chase confirmed.

"Aw, Chasey," Ally said playfully. "Wish I could say I felt sorry for you. Ha! Chasey and Gracey. That's cute."

Chase offered Ally a grimace, brows furrowed, while Grace felt herself blush. Again.

"Not cool," Chase said.

"Yeah, I know it's silly. Just trying to make you smile."

"By telling me you don't feel sorry for me?" Chase asked, though a slight smirk was visible on his lips.

"That's right," Ally said with a grin. She wrapped her arms around Chase's shoulders, leaned in, and squeezed him in a hug. "I love you, you know."

"I know," Chase said.

"Okay." Ally stood erect. "Grace, you want anything?"

"Maybe that coffee you were talking about?"

"Coming right up," Ally said then made her way to the kitchen.

Grace sat down in the chair opposite Chase. Eventually, she said, "I'm sorry you didn't have a good night."

"It's not a big deal," Chase replied. "I was only seeing Missy for a couple of months. Things happen."

"Yes," Grace said. "I suppose they do."

"Did you and Ally have a good dinner?"

Grace smiled. "We did, yes. Ally seems to know so many places, doesn't she? The dinner was delicious."

"Yep. Leave it to Ally."

They sat in silence—Grace twiddling her thumbs and looking around the room awkwardly and Chase skimming through his phone—until Ally returned a minute later and sat beside Chase on the couch. "It's brewing," she said. "My favorite decaf. It's some sort of fall maple blend, and it's delicious even though it's decaffeinated. Figured I shouldn't send you home all spiked up."

"Spiked up?" Grace laughed.

"That's what I said. 'Spiked up.' Like, hyped up on caffeine."

"I understood what you meant," Grace said. "I just think it's a funny saying."

While Ally chuckled, Grace stole a glance at Chase, at the waves of brown curls, at his relaxed posture in his Adidas pants and hoodie. And before she turned her gaze back on Ally, she didn't miss the amused grin on Chase's lips, his eyes still trained on the screen of his phone.

It made Grace's stomach flutter.

"So, Grace," Ally said.

"So, Ally."

"I want you to come cycling with me tomorrow."

"I… um…" Grace frowned. "What?"

"Cycling. You and me."

"Not gonna get out of this one," Chase interjected. "When it comes to Ally and her bike, she'll convince you. No one is immune to the Ally charm."

"I… cycling?" Grace said, flustered.

"It's one of the greatest things ever. I've given up on running. You saw me that day we met on the bench. Running is so not my thing. But cycling? Let's do it! I know the best routes."

"In the city?" Grace could feel her insides plummet. The noise, the cars, the honking, the impatience. The possibility of getting hit.

"Yep. Right here. Or I can take you near your place if you want. I know a couple of routes there that are pretty good. There's one around a lake not too far from the coffee shop. Want to do that one?"

"Yes," Grace croaked then cleared her throat. "Yes, please. I think riding in the city would make me nervous. But… I don't have a bike."

"Already thought of that. I'm borrowing one from a friend. She and I ride together sometimes, and she said she's not going out tomorrow."

"And she doesn't mind that I use her bike?" Grace asked.

Ally shook her head. "It's all good. So how about it? I'll pick the bike up from her place in the morning and then head on over to you. We can ride from there."

"I… I guess… okay."

"Sweet," Ally said enthusiastically. "I hope you love it."

"I really don't know about that," Grace admitted. "But I'm willing to try."

The coffee maker beeped, and Ally stood from the couch. "Be right back," she announced, clasping her hands.

There was a bounce to her gait as she left the room.

"See?" Chase said. "She has a way of hooking you. You're in for it now."

Grace, though nervous about what she'd agreed to do, couldn't help but smile.

CHAPTER 7

*S*aturday morning dawned. The sun splayed on the concrete of Grace's narrow driveway, on the dewy grass in her diminutive front lawn, and seeped through the cracks of the blind on her bedroom window.

Grace rolled over in bed and stretched her legs. Gosh, did it feel good. She rubbed the sleep from her partially closed eyes, breathed in deeply, and clumsily put a foot down on her carpeted floor.

Coffee. She could use some coffee.

This morning, she was meeting Ally for a bike ride through town. Grace couldn't remember the last time she had ridden a bike—childhood, perhaps? Even then, she hadn't ridden often. Would she even remember how to ride, or would she find herself struggling for purchase, the tires teetering precariously, and Grace herself tumbling off the seat onto the hard ground below?

And the people. There would be a good number of people around, she was sure. People watching her ride, people instinctively understanding that she wasn't a natural cyclist by the way she clutched the handlebars, by the way she tensed her shoulders. People attempting to go here and there on foot or in their vehicles, hurried movements, feet on gas pedals, swerving so as not to hit her.

Or would they fail to swerve? Would they fail to obey the rules of the road, impatient enough to arrive at their destination, annoyed at the two women who were taking up a portion of the road otherwise used for motorized vehicles, zooming by mere inches from where she'd be pedaling?

Surely, she and Ally wouldn't be the only ones out there this morning. There would be other cyclists, yes?

Grace trudged to the kitchen, shaking her head and running her fingers through her hair. *Get a grip, Grace*, she thought to herself. *It's only a bike ride, and you're being ridiculous. Calm your nerves. Ally would never do anything to put you in harm's way.*

Grace set the coffee maker to brew then made her way to the living room, where she sat on the couch and looked out the front bay window to the circular street of the townhouse complex. Two children were already fully awake and kicking around a soccer ball. A woman in athletic gear was bending over, apparently stretching her limbs, perhaps readying herself for a morning run. A man in a green sweater was looking at his reflection in the driver's-side mirror of his sedan, running his tongue over his teeth. He unlocked his car and stepped inside.

When the coffee maker beeped, Grace walked to the kitchen. She pulled down her favorite mug from the cabinet over the countertop—white with a centered depiction of a freckled girl with pigtails—and poured the dark, steaming liquid inside. She added a splash of cream and a small amount of sugar, stirred, and took her first welcome sip.

Grace closed her eyes, inhaled the aroma of the coffee as she swallowed, then walked back to the couch.

Ally would be here soon, Grace knew. She had stated that she wanted to get an early start, even though it was well into fall and quite chilly outdoors. She had instructed Grace to bundle up, since there were some portions of the ride in which they'd be coursing downhill, and the wind produced from their speed would inevitably be intense.

Grace wasn't looking forward to the experience.

She lifted a book from the end table, still clutching her mug of coffee, and opened it to the page she had last read. The book was middle-grade fiction, Grace's favorite to read, though she didn't merely read books, she devoured them. One of her favorite times of the day with her school-children was when she read aloud to them, always after they came back from lunch and recess. She found it was the perfect way to calm their excited bodies, and she was good at reading aloud, she had to admit. She manufactured different voices for characters in a book, with varying tones and timbres, and the children took to it well. They'd smile, they'd laugh. All eyes were on her. Had they been adults, their attention might have placed Grace in a state of unease, but her children? Yes, she greatly enjoyed this time with her students and they with her.

Grace had read several pages of her book when she lifted her mug to her lips and found she had finished her coffee. She set the book back down and took the mug to the empty sink. She wasn't much of a breakfast person but knew she'd need substance since she was headed out with Ally. She didn't know where Ally was taking her, and she didn't know how long they'd be out. She'd have to ask Ally if she should pack a lunch, maybe sling a small backpack over her shoulders for the day.

Grace was just finishing her scrambled eggs when the doorbell rang.

"Hello, hello," Ally said joyfully when Grace opened the front door.

"You're very happy," Grace observed.

"I am. I like mornings."

"Ugh," Grace moaned. "I used to be a morning person too."

Ally laughed. "Plus, we're going to have a good day. I don't have to go to work, it's gorgeous, and I've got two bikes on my rack calling our names."

Grace frowned.

Ally's tongue peeked from her lips as she snorted. "Buzzkill."

"Sorry," Grace said. "I'm just... it's been a really long time."

"You've got this," Ally assured her. "And if you don't like it, we won't go again. But you're seriously gonna like it."

"You seem sure."

"That's because I am." Ally lifted her brows and smirked.

"Come in," Grace offered as she extended her arm.

Ally walked inside. "So this is your abode, yeah? Cute place."

"I know I don't have a lot of decorations up," Ally said by way of apology for her sparse accommodations. "I just... haven't had much of a desire."

"I get it. It's still cute."

"Thank you."

"Do you like living here?" Ally asked.

"I do. It's pretty quiet."

"And I know you like being alone."

Grace nodded. "I do."

"Well." Ally clasped her hands together and grinned wildly. "You ready?"

"Now?"

"We can hang out for a bit if you want, but yeah. Now. I've been looking forward to this. Wait till you feel the thrill."

Grace looked at her friend skeptically. "Okay. We can go. I'm as ready as I'll ever be."

Ally laughed. "You've got this."

"Do I need to pack anything?"

"Nope."

Ally led the way out the door, and Grace locked it behind her. She pocketed her key inside her windbreaker. She had a nagging desire to grab her nana's orange hat but knew she wouldn't be able to wear it under a bike helmet.

"Okay, here we go," Ally said as she unfastened a bike from the rack at the back of her compact car and plonked it down onto the concrete. She extended it toward Grace and said, "This one's for you. I hope it's a good fit, but I'm pretty sure it will be."

Grace grasped the handlebar hesitantly.

Next, Ally removed her own bike from the rack and rested it against the side of her car so she could grab the two helmets from the backseat. "For you." Ally handed a bright-blue helmet off to Grace, who fastened it on, clicking the buckle into place under her chin. "Does it fit?"

Grace nodded.

"Sweet."

Ally put her helmet on—neon pink—and smirked at Grace before swinging her leg over the middle bar of her bike and resting her bottom on the seat. "Ready to go?"

"Um... yeah. Okay. I think so. Do I just follow you?"

"Yep, just follow me. I've got a great route. You're going to see things through different eyes today, Grace, I guarantee it. But first…" Ally reached into the pocket of her riding jacket and handed a pair of cycling glasses to Grace. "You're going to need these, trust me. It's chilly, and the wind will make your eyes water. Plus, you don't want any little bugs swooping in, yeah?"

"I hadn't thought of that."

"Neither had I when I first started riding. I went without glasses and could barely see that first time, my eyes were watering so much. And I caught a bug in my mouth. And one in my eye. Had to blink that one out and eventually stop the damn bike because I couldn't see."

"And you didn't give up on riding?"

"No way. It was awesome!"

Grace sighed. "Okay. I'm ready." She put the sunglasses on.

Ally put her glasses on as well and set off.

Grace inhaled sharply, put one foot in the stirrup, and pushed off the ground with the other. She wobbled profusely but caught herself before she fell. She stopped the bike and tried again.

Ally looked back over her shoulder and shouted, "You've got this, Grace!"

Grace placed her foot back into the stirrup, grasped the handlebars tightly, and bore down with her free sneaker. She managed to get her bottom onto the narrow, hard seat and was pleasantly surprised to find that she also succeeded in fitting her free foot into the opposite stirrup.

"Whoo!" Ally yelled. "Look at you!"

Grace smiled as she began to pedal, her bike inching slowly toward Ally.

"Okay," Ally called. "I'm going faster now to get us

125

going. Let me know if I'm going too fast or if you need to stop or whatever. 'Kay?"

"Yes," Grace said. "Okay." She clutched the handlebars more tightly, her knuckles turning white.

Grace followed Ally to the stop sign at the beginning of the townhouse complex. Luckily, the street wasn't often busy, which gave Grace a modicum of comfort if they had to cross, but Ally didn't stop. She moved her bike to the right and merged onto the road. Grace followed, her front wheel wobbling as she turned.

Ally looked over her shoulder. "You good?"

"Yes... yes. Okay."

"I'm speeding up."

"Oh, goodness," Grace said. "Okay."

Ally smiled, turned back to face front, and pedaled harder. Grace heightened her momentum, her wheels spinning faster, her knees bobbing up and down. She was relieved to find that she was able to keep herself straight, that she didn't seem in any danger of falling or losing control.

They pedaled down the road for about half a mile, and then Ally looked behind her, moved into the middle of the lane, and extended her left arm to the side.

Oh, my goodness, Grace thought to herself. *She wants me in the middle of the road? Oh, gosh... we're turning? With cars?*

Grace moved behind Ally, her jaw clenched. Ally slowed down but didn't stop entirely. A car passed them in the opposite direction, and then Ally stood on her pedals and began to pedal again.

Grace followed Ally as she turned left and merged onto another road. She sighed with relief when they had safely made it across. Perhaps she should have suggested they bike on a path, one devoid of vehicles, with very little foot traffic. That would have more likely placed her mind at ease.

Another mile passed by before Ally turned right, and Grace found they were following the perimeter of a small lake. Grace was pleased with the direction Ally had taken them, for she knew this road to be one that wasn't well traveled. She breathed more easily now as she pedaled. Ally sped up, and Grace moved in tune. She turned her head to look at the water, glistening in the morning sun's rays. She glanced at the vibrantly colored leaves still left on the trees as they swayed and at the leaves scattering the ground. She felt the raw wind tickle her face. She lifted a finger to wipe her slightly running nose and found her hands were cold.

Perhaps she'd wear a pair of thin gloves the next time they rode.

The next time. Grace was surprised to find she was even thinking of there being a next time. And it was only when a piece of fuzz from a tree landed on her lower lip that Grace realized she was smiling.

"Okay, Grace," Ally shouted behind her. "We're going downhill. You ready?"

Grace steeled herself but didn't verbally reply. She found she couldn't. So far, all had been well and good, but downhill? Goodness!

And then she saw it. She had completely forgotten this hill was here. Or perhaps she just hadn't paid attention to it before now. When one was in a car, hills didn't matter much, did they?

Grace felt the change as her bike began to descend. Faster and faster her wheels went. The force of the wind swept her hair off her shoulders, and she felt it seep between the open space of her glasses at her nose. Her windbreaker flapped profusely, and Grace gritted her teeth.

She was moving so rapidly! Holy shit, she was going too fast!

Ally whooped in front of her, loud and clear even through the deafening sound of the wind in Grace's ears.

Grace was clutching the handlebars tightly. Ever so tightly. But her bike didn't teeter. She seemed in control. She had stopped pedaling. She didn't think her legs would be able to move that fast anyway.

Grace lifted her head and momentarily closed her eyes.

She allowed herself to feel, to be.

To feel the wind.

To feel the pedals under her feet.

To smell the crisp air in all its autumnal glory.

Grace opened her eyes and found they were watering, though she didn't believe it was from the wind. She pushed up from the handlebars and lifted her chest.

And then Grace was giggling.

She was giggling like a little girl.

She was giggling like one of her first graders after a tickling match with a friend.

And it was then that Grace realized she didn't know when she had last laughed like this.

When she had last truly let herself go.

The hill came to an end, and Grace began to pedal again. The exhilaration was over, though she still found she enjoyed the ride. Her legs were aching. She wasn't used to this type of exercise, so much exertion. She assumed she had been using muscles that otherwise weren't relied upon.

And it felt good.

A few more miles of riding, and Ally stopped in front of a bakery. When Grace sidled up next to her, Ally said, "Thought we could use a treat. What do you say?"

"I didn't bring any money. I'm sorry. I didn't know I'd need it."

"I told you not to," Ally said. "My treat."

"No, I—"

"My treat," Ally interjected.

Grace smiled. "Okay then."

Ally took off her glasses and unclasped her helmet. "So, what did you think?"

Grace sighed. "It was actually... I wasn't sure at first, but I kind of liked it."

"Kind of?" Ally tilted her head.

"Once I got used to it, I really liked it," Grace admitted.

"Ha! I told you! But no, seriously... I'm so glad you liked it. We'll have to go out again before it gets too cold."

"I'd like that," Grace said.

They strung their helmets over the handlebars and propped their bikes up against the side of the bakery.

"You don't think... nobody will steal them?" Grace asked hesitantly.

"Nah," Ally flicked her hand. "Plus we can see them when we're inside. I'll run out like a damn banshee if anyone even thinks of touching my bike."

Grace laughed. "I can actually see you doing that."

"Damn straight."

Grace and Ally went indoors and ordered—Ally a smoothie and Grace a hot apple cider—then Ally paid.

"Thank you," Grace said.

"Of course. I love to treat."

They found an open table next to their bicycles and sat down. They sipped their drinks and chatted amicably.

After forty-five minutes, Ally suggested they make their way back to Grace's townhouse.

"I think I'm ready," Grace said, but as she stood, she

wobbled. "Oh, my goodness," she said. "My legs feel like jelly."

Ally laughed. "Yep. That'll do it. Especially if you're not used to riding."

"Will I even be able to get back on the bike?"

"Of course, silly," Ally assured her. "With a couple strokes, your legs will get used to it again. I'm gonna take us on a different route back to your place. That way, we won't have to climb that big hill."

"Oh," Grace said. "I hadn't even thought about that. Good thinking. I'm not sure I can do hills."

"You can," Ally said matter-of-factly. "And we'll have to climb a few to get back, but they won't be as big as the one we came down. Wasn't that great though?"

"Wasn't what great?"

"The hill." Ally was grinning widely.

"It really was," Grace said. "I was nervous at first, but then... then I just wasn't. I couldn't believe how fast we were going."

"Yep," Ally said. "One of my favorite things to do in the whole entire universe."

"In the universe?" Grace chuckled.

"That's what I said." Ally smiled. "In the universe."

Grace found the ride home to be challenging, but with Ally's encouraging words and zestful attitude, she was able to make it up the hills. When she rolled into her driveway, she staggered off the bike and plonked herself on her bottom on the grass. "I am so tired," she said with a sigh.

"Great," Ally replied. "That just means we had an awesome ride."

"Oh, is that what this means?"

"You bet." Ally sat next to Grace and picked an orange leaf off the ground. She looked down, crumbling the leaf in her fingers, scattering the remnants onto the thighs of her cycling pants.

"Hey," Ally said. "Have I ever told you that I've got some mighty awesome intuition?"

"Yes," Grace smiled. "You've told me."

"Well, it's telling me that I think you're absolutely incredible and are turning into an amazing friend."

Grace started, her eyes widening.

"Really? Where did that come from? And Ally, we haven't known each other long. There's still so much you don't know about me."

"And I've known some people for years and years and feel like I know more about you than I do about them." She paused then said, "I don't think it's about how long you've known someone. Not really. I think it's about the feeling you get inside, how you feel when you're around them. How they make you feel about yourself." She looked into Grace's brown eyes, at her slightly rounded face. "And you make me feel pretty damn good about myself, Grace."

Grace felt a trickling of liquid behind her eyelids, and she blinked.

"The universe brought us together, you know," Ally said.

"The universe again?" Grace smiled.

Ally nodded. "The universe. It's always got a plan. And it planned on me meeting you that day in the park, on that bench. I got out to run for a reason, and we both know it wasn't because I'm a freakin' awesome runner."

Grace pondered for a moment then said, "If that's what you believe, then I think that the universe planned on me meeting you, too," she said. "I have never opened up to someone like this in my entire life, Ally. That friend Bethany I was telling you about? We never talked the way you and I do. And... I don't think you'd ever just stop talking to me like she did."

Ally shook her head vigorously.

"I think... even with Gary... I think about him a lot still. And I think of how I was with him. I think... I guess... between how I am inside sometimes and how I was when I was around him... I think... I think that he didn't let me be the person I feel like I am when I'm with you. I'm different when I'm with you. I'm more the person I want to be."

Ally offered a soft, contemplative smile. "What do you mean?"

"I was closed up with Gary. I was so happy to be with him. I really loved him, Ally."

"I know you did."

"But if I wanted something, but he wanted something else, I usually just gave in. I wanted to see him happy and didn't really care about the way I felt about it. I think... I think that his happiness always came first to me. And with all the time I've had to think about things, I think that a relationship—especially a marriage—should be about compromise sometimes. There wasn't much of that with me and Gary. I mostly just gave in to him. And then when I think about Stephanie, the woman he left me for, I know that she's a lawyer. That makes me think that she has a very different personality than me."

"How so?"

"From what I know about lawyers, they have to be around people a lot, they have to work with people. They have clients that they talk to and fight for, whatever that fight might be. I don't know what type of lawyer she was, but I got the impression that she was successful, and it's just always made me think that while I'm shy and reserved and always nervous about things, when I could never seem to make up my mind or I just let him do whatever he wanted, Stephanie was probably more assertive, right? That's what I assume. When I think of her, I just think of someone that's not like me. Not like me at all. And I've always wondered... I wonder if that's what drew Gary to her in the first place, the fact that she's so different. I wonder if that's what he needed, what he wanted all along. And..." Grace choked.

"What is it?" Ally asked gently.

"I still wonder if he really wanted kids but just never... never wanted them with me."

"Oh, Grace, you can't think that."

"But can you blame me?"

Ally looked away, sighed, then said, "No. I don't blame you. I probably would have thought the same thing. But Grace, how do you feel? Did you ever truly want kids? Or do you think you convinced yourself that you didn't want them because Gary didn't?"

Grace picked up a dead leaf from the ground and felt its wrinkled skin between her fingertips. Eventually, she said, "I don't know. One part of me thinks I'd be a really good mom. I get children. I do really well with children. Another part of me is anxious about parenthood. I get all quakey inside even thinking about it, and that can't be normal, can it?"

"What's normal, anyway?"

"I guess, but... Ally, you're pretty much the only person I'm truly comfortable with. I had a terrible childhood. I'm... I think I'm scared to be a mom. Plus I'm not even married anymore. And I'm getting older."

"Pfft," Ally said. "You don't have to be married to be a mom, and who cares if you're getting older? You're not even thirty-seven yet. I know plenty of women in their forties these days that are having kids."

"If I were ever to have a child, I'd like to have a partner to co-parent with," Grace said. "I don't think it's something I'd ever, ever be able to do alone."

"Of course you could," Ally insisted.

Grace shook her head. "No, I really don't think so... but I'd also not *want* to. I'd want to be with someone. Ally?"

"Yeah?"

"Don't you... do you ever feel lonely?"

"Hell no," Ally said vehemently.

Grace laughed. "I suppose I should have known you'd answer like that. But you have Chase, and you have all sorts of friends. I know you date a bit, too. I... I feel lonely sometimes. Even though I like to be alone, I'm still lonely."

Ally's eyes bored into hers. "You have me," Ally said. "I promise, Grace. You will always have me. I'm not going anywhere. You don't need to be in a relationship. Who the hell needs a man? Not when we've got each other."

Grace smiled, and she felt her shoulders relax. Ally was right: they might not have known each other for long, but intuition was strong. It was reliable.

And Grace knew already that Ally was the best friend she had ever known.

CHAPTER 8

*A*utumn leaves fell from the trees until the decaying grass was hidden and Grace's boots crunched beneath her. The first snow fell to blanket the ground in its frosty white sheen. Another showering of snow then another, until Grace found herself inhabiting the depths of winter. She and Ally met up often—after work during the week and almost every weekend for coffee or a frosty jaunt in the city. Ally had even convinced Grace to go sledding at a ski resort in Massachusetts, and much to Grace's delight, she had enjoyed herself greatly despite the frigid air that reddened her nose and cheeks and left her fingers aching in their gloves.

The winter snow melted, and spring arrived, buds forming on the trees, the air fragrant with renewed life.

On a Saturday morning in May, Grace found herself catching the T to Ally's apartment. Ally said there was something she needed to impart to Grace, and Grace, curious as ever, hadn't hesitated when Ally asked if she'd make the trip over.

It was Chase who answered the door when Grace knocked. "Hi, Chase."

"Hey, Grace. Come on in." He held the door open, but Grace hesitated. Something was off with his smile, something forged, forced.

Grace cocked her head questioningly as she looked at Chase.

Chase merely shook his head and averted his eyes. "Ally will tell you," was all he said.

Grace's stomach plummeted. It suddenly felt like a hollow cavern, devoid of substance. She held her fingers over her lips, and walked inside.

Ally emerged from the kitchen. Her hair had grown out since last fall when Grace had first met her. It was still short, but it now covered her ears when she didn't tuck her blond tendrils behind them. It wasn't spiky any longer; rather, it was wavy, layered. She wore a pair of loose-fitting sweat-pants and a hoodie that was so large Grace assumed it belonged to Chase.

"What's going on?" Grace managed to say, her voice merely a whisper. She felt a pull in her chest, and she feared she was going to be sick.

Ally shook her head. "Don't worry," she said. "It's all good." But Grace could see the wary expression on Ally's face.

Chase slowly made his way to the couch and sat down. He looked at Grace and patted the seat next to him. Grace turned to Ally, and when Ally nodded, Grace obliged her friends and sat down.

"Ally, you're really scaring me. I never see you like this."

Ally offered Grace a meager smile. "I'll really be okay, Grace," she said. "I promise."

"Then what is it? What's going on?"

Ally sat on the oversized chair opposite Grace and Chase. "Remember that guy I told you I met at the bar about a month ago? That guy that said he was here on business from—well, I don't remember where he said he was from. I think I was tuning that detail out."

"Yes," Grace said slowly. "I remember."

"I brought him back here. Chase was out."

"Yes," Grace repeated. "I remember."

"We were protected, but someone... Grace, I'm pregnant."

Grace gasped. "What?"

Ally nodded.

"Are you sure?"

Ally lifted her lips with amusement and offered a low chuckle in response to Grace's question. "I'm sure."

"How... what..."

And that was when Ally laughed outright. Grace couldn't believe it. The laugh was hearty. Light and clear and free. A contradiction to what Grace had detected on Ally's countenance just moments before.

Chase grinned at Grace's side.

"How... how can you be laughing about this?"

"Because of course," Ally said, throwing her hands into the air, "of course this would happen. The universe has a warped sense of humor, huh? But it's all good, Grace. I'm still shocked, but everything will be okay. I've had time to think this over. And Chase has been great."

"But... how can you be so sure? Ally, you work. You didn't plan on a baby, the father... oh my gosh, Ally! The father! Do you even know where he is?"

"Nope," Ally said. "We both knew what we wanted that night, and it certainly wasn't a relationship, and it certainly wasn't this." She looked down at her flat stomach.

"I… I… what are you going to do?"

"Damned if I know. I've thought about this scenario in the past, played it out in my head a bit. I mean, a single woman having sex? Yeah… protected or not, I knew there was a chance. I've already made the decision not to abort. Adoption? Probably not. I might have had a better childhood with adoptive parents instead of my own, and I might lead a crazy lifestyle right now, but I've got a stable job, and I know I can provide for a baby." Ally widened her eyes. "Even though I knew this could happen, it still sucks. I'm not prepared. But who ever is?" Ally shrugged. "I think I'm keeping it. The baby." She sighed. "My life has officially been flipped upside down. But… I can do this."

A tear trickled down Grace's cheek. "I don't know how you can be so calm right now. Unless… are you freaking out inside but trying to stay calm for me? Oh my gosh, Ally? Is it me? Are you afraid… well, are you afraid I'll react exactly like I'm reacting right now?"

Ally laughed. "I love you, Grace. Lots. You and Chase are going to be this baby's unofficial aunt and uncle. Damn straight. This baby is one lucky boy or girl." She sighed again. "And yes, I'm scared. But life throws you curveballs. You've gotta catch them and throw them right back. Don't let them hit you. Don't let them hurt."

"I wish I could think the way you do."

Ally smiled. "Then you wouldn't be Grace. See? We always complement each other."

"Ally?"

"Grace?" Ally smirked.

"I… um…"

"Spit it out."

"Are you… are you sure it was that guy?"

Chase erupted beside Grace, droplets of spittle flying

138

out of his mouth, a few landing on his lower lip that he wiped off with the collar of his shirt.

"That was seriously disgusting, Chase," Ally said.

"Caught me off guard there," Chase said as he looked at Grace. "Wasn't expecting that."

Grace felt her cheeks flush, and she looked down at her lap. "I'm sorry, Ally. I really hope I haven't hurt your feelings."

Ally laughed. "Not at all. And yes. I'm one hundred percent positive it's the bar guy."

"Bar guy," Grace said softly. "What are you going to tell the baby?"

"We'll figure that out when we get there," Ally replied. "For now, I'll take this day by day. But Grace?"

"Yes?"

"I need a night out. It's been one hell of a morning."

"I imagine so," Grace said. "If I'm feeling the way I'm feeling right now, I can't even imagine how I'd feel if I were in your shoes."

Grace laughed again. "No drinks for me, I suppose. But you're totally doing karaoke."

"What?" Grace said, her eyes large, her lips parted.

"You heard me," Ally said. "I've wanted to take you for a while now, and you've always said no. I've understood. But tonight, Gracey? Tonight, I need a good time. Tonight I need to fool around with you and Chase—"

"Whoa, you want me there?" Chase asked, as he sat more erect.

"You bet," Ally said. "You know you love it."

"You've been before?" Ally asked him.

"Yeah, I've been a bunch of times," Chase mumbled. "And I can't sing."

"But you're awesome," Ally said. "You can help me show Grace the ropes. We'll have a great time!"

"But…" Grace began, but when she saw the look in Ally's blue eyes, when she saw the eager expression on her face, Grace relented. "Okay. I'm in."

Ally flew out of the chair and raised her fists. "That's what I'm talking about! Chase?"

"Yeah," he muttered. "I'm there."

"Oh, this is going to be awesome!"

Grace wasn't so sure, but she'd give it a try. Right now, she'd do just about anything for Ally, for her best friend.

Chase made them all a late lunch, and while Ally ate with relish, Grace merely picked at her food. She was still trying to process the information imparted to her that morning. She was still in shock, still flummoxed that Ally was pregnant, that she was going to be a mother in less than nine months' time. In all of their conversations together, Grace and Ally had not spoken about Ally and the possibility of motherhood. With Ally's free lifestyle, her habitual casual dating, Grace had just assumed that Ally had no intention of becoming a mother. And the more Grace thought about it, the more surprised she was that she and Ally hadn't spoken about Ally's plans for her future. They had certainly spoken a lot, hours upon hours, in fact. And they had touched on deeper subjects as well: Grace's—and Ally's—childhood, her mother's drug habit, her father's verbal abuse, and her ex-husband, but Ally hadn't confided in Grace her utmost wishes for the days to come. Grace had learned that Ally was a personality that lived for the present, whatever inhabited that moment in time for her, and she accepted it, grasped it wholeheartedly. Grace wasn't sure Ally pondered much about her future, really. Ally thought more about what was happening to her right now.

And right now, she was pregnant.

Right now, she would *have* to think about her future, plan for this inevitable addition to her life.

Plan for the baby that would rely on her for sustenance, for survival. For love and emotional nourishment.

Grace bit into her sandwich, the cold turkey unpalatable on her tongue, the mayonnaise slimy, the tomato soft and slithery. She forced herself to swallow.

The afternoon began to wane. Ally, Chase, and Grace took a walk around the neighborhood, the spring city air heavy on Grace's skin. Vehicles amassed around them on the streets. Cigarette smoke billowed from the mouth of a woman walking in front of Grace and wafted her way, making Grace cough slightly. She scrunched her nose in disgust and turned her head away.

And then she thought about Ally walking beside her. Ally, who was now gestating a new life. Would that smoke affect her? Would the air in the city, the exhaust fumes, the smog—would it all affect the growing fetus within? These weren't thoughts that had crossed Grace's mind before. But now they crept their way to the forefront.

Grace saw Ally in a different manner now. The Ally who was walking beside her wasn't fully the Ally she had come to know this past year. The Ally beside her was a new, fresh version of herself. The Ally walking beside her now, with her blond hair, blue eyes, and spunky attitude, was going to be a mother.

A new role. A new label. A new existence.

And Grace wondered how much it would affect their relationship.

They made their way back to the apartment, where they played several games of Uno. Grace sipped a cup of coffee, while Ally and Chase filled themselves from a platter of cheese, crackers, and grapes. Ally and Chase laughed, teased. Their smiles were wide, genuine, happy. Grace smiled along, grinned when it was expected, but at times, it was a facade. She loved Ally. Loved her with her entire being. And although Ally had promised that all would be well, Grace was worried for her friend.

"I'm done with being at home," Ally announced around four-thirty that afternoon. "Let's go out to dinner before karaoke."

"You don't want to get food there?" Chase asked.

"Nope. I want Mexican! Oh, you know what? I'm seriously gonna pull out the pregnancy card from now on, tell you both that I've got cravings and such, and you'll need to cave in, let me get what I want. Because, you know… baby and all. The baby gets its way."

Chase laughed. "You've always gotten your way. Now you're just trying to use an excuse."

Ally grinned mischievously. "I don't always get my way."

Chase scoffed, though his expression when he looked at Ally was playful and filled with adoration. "You do so always get your way."

"Well…" Ally admitted. "Maybe I get my way sometimes."

"Sure," Chase chuckled.

"But pregnancy cravings are a real thing."

"And you just found out you're expecting this morning," Chase countered. "But I'm good with Mexican if Grace is."

"Grace?" Ally looked at her expectantly.

Grace nodded. "Yes," she said. "I'm okay with Mexican food. I don't really care what we have to eat."

"You haven't eaten much today," Ally said. "We've got to get some good food into that body of yours. Oh, yum! Now I'm thinking about tacos. Or maybe I want a burrito. I don't know... but we seriously have to get some chips and guac. Chase, you know the best place to get chips and guac, right?"

Chase smirked. "That I do."

"Let's go!" Ally said.

They arrived at their destination, a diminutive Mexican restaurant with a wooden door and only two small front-facing windows. Grace was certain she would have missed it if she were on her own. Ally opened the door and stepped inside, a large grin on her face. Grace followed behind and immediately smelled savory spices.

"You're going to love this place, Grace," Ally said as she turned to look over her shoulder.

"I'm surprised we haven't been here before if you like it so much."

"Yeah, but I like lots of places, and there are just too many to hit up all the time. But this place definitely has the best chips and guac, and the chips are always warm like they've just come out of the fryer, and they've got salt on them, too. Love that."

"They do sound good," Grace replied.

"They're good," Chase assured her. "This is a night for Ally, but this is a place I would have chosen for myself. Gotta try a quesadilla. They're always great."

Grace followed her friends to the small counter, looking around the room as she stepped. The place was so small that it only held four tables, each with two chairs, which led

Grace to the assumption that customers often called in an order to bring home with them instead of chancing that a table would be free. As luck would have it, one table was unoccupied, though Grace didn't know how that would suffice with the lack of a third chair.

"Hey there," Ally greeted the employee behind the counter, a young man with scraggly brown hair and a goatee.

"What can I get you?"

"Large chips and large guac," Ally said. "Actually, make that two. And I'll get—crap, do I want a taco or a burrito?"

"Both?" Chase chuckled.

"I guess I could always have leftovers."

"Or maybe not with your appetite," Chase quipped.

"Oh, funny man," Ally said. "But you're not wrong. I'll take a chicken burrito, rice, black beans, hot salsa and plenty of it, cheese, lettuce, guac."

"More guacamole?" Chase laughed.

"You bet."

"Anything to drink?" the young man asked.

Ally looked beside her at the cooler against the wall. She walked over to it, reached within, and pulled out a plastic bottle of lemonade. "This," she said.

"Lemonade with a burrito?" Chase lifted his brows.

"Yep," Ally said. "Sounds good to me."

"Yuck," Grace chimed in.

Chase laughed. "She's right," he told Ally.

"Now you're both just poops."

"Poops?" Chase sniggered playfully.

"That's what I said, isn't it? Poops. You're both poops. Two giant turds in my lemonade."

"Ally, that's just really gross," Grace said.

"I've got an unpleasant mental picture," Chase agreed.

Ally shook her head. "Whatever," she said and turned back to the employee. "Forget them. They just don't know what's good for them."

"And neither do you," the young man said with a smirk. "Lemonade with a burrito, guac, and chips?"

Ally laughed. "Hey, now," she said. "Watch yourself. Customer's always right, yeah?"

"Not this time." The young man smiled.

Ally nodded. "I like you."

"Lemonade it is," he replied. He turned to Chase. "For you?"

"Yeah… and I'll pay for the three of us."

"Nope," Ally retorted. "Not gonna happen."

"Sure it is," Chase said. "It's your night, isn't it? My treat. We'll fill ourselves with food and sugary drinks then head off and make fools of ourselves."

"You might make a fool of yourself," Ally said, "but I sure won't."

"We'll see about that," Chase said.

Ally swatted his arm.

"I will," Grace said softly.

Ally turned to look at her. "Will what?"

"Make a fool of myself," Grace replied.

"Nah." Ally brushed the notion off. "You've got this. I'm telling you, you're gonna love it."

"So?" the young man said as he looked at Chase. "What you want?"

"Cheese, chicken, and veggie quesadilla."

"Drink?"

"Not for me, thanks."

"He'll just steal my lemonade," Ally said. "Just you wait and see."

"Right," the young man said then looked at Grace. "And for you?"

Grace glanced at the wall above the man, at the scratchy chalk-like writing on a black background. "I think I'm actually going to try the spicy shrimp wrap, please."

"Oh, yeah," Ally said. "That's a good one. It's the sauce."

"And to drink?" the employee asked.

"I think…" Grace looked over at the cooler. "Just a water for me, please."

"Got it. Is that all?"

"Yes, sir," Ally said merrily.

The young man rang them up. Chase reached into his back pocket to extract his wallet and handed his credit card over the counter.

"Thanks for the treat," Ally said.

"Not a problem."

"Yes," Grace said. "Thank you very much, Chase. You didn't need to pay for me."

"My pleasure," Chase replied.

"Well, it was very nice of you to do."

"That's because Chase is a nice guy," Ally said. "We need more Chases in the world."

Chase flung his arm around Ally's shoulder, leaned down, and kissed her forehead.

"There's a table," Ally said. "Want to sit?"

"There are only two chairs," Grace replied.

"Ah," Chase said. "They have these." He walked over to the side of the counter, and Grace watched as he lifted a folding chair and brought it over to the table. "Problem solved."

"Oh," Grace said. "I didn't realize they had those."

"Tiny place but worth it. And when you don't get a

table, you just go and eat outside."

"Where?" Grace asked. "There were no tables."

"Ally and I just sit against the wall."

"You mean... on the ground?"

Chase laughed. "Yes, on the ground."

"That's... really dirty," Grace scrunched her nose.

"I'm not sure it's much dirtier than these chairs are."

"That's a really gross thing to think about," Grace said.

"Not sure they clean them."

"Oh, goodness..." Grace said, and she turned to find Ally stifling a giggle at her expense.

Grace sat in a chair, imagining the thousands of germs that were probably inhabiting the surface. She touched the top of the wooden table with a fingertip and mentally instructed herself to keep a bottle of hand sanitizer in her purse from then on in.

It only took the young man a few minutes to approach their table with two large baskets of corn chips as well as two bowls of guacamole.

"Now that's what I'm talking about!" Ally exclaimed. She lifted a chip and dipped it into the guacamole.

"Oh, my goodness," Grace said. "That's a lot of guacamole."

Ally grinned enormously. "It's the best!"

"Ally thinks you should have a chip with your guac, not the other way around."

"Mmm-hmm..." Ally mumbled as she stuffed the chip into her mouth. The sound of crunching filled the space around the table. "Oh my God," she said through a mouthful.

Grace smiled. Ally certainly did love her chips and guac.

Grace reached for a chip, dipped it gently into the bowl

of guacamole, and brought it to her lips. She bit into the chip, and despite her efforts to catch the crumbs that fell, she failed miserably and made a slight mess on the table.

"So?" Ally asked.

Grace nodded. "It's pretty good."

"That's it?"

Grace laughed. "I think it's good, but I also think I don't like guacamole as much as you do."

Ally took a sip of her lemonade. "You're crazy."

Grace blushed slightly, and Chase nudged her with his shoulder. "Not everyone is as nuts as you, Al," he said. "I think you're the crazy one."

Grace found herself blushing even further and trained her gaze on the tabletop. Her stomach flopped, and she placed a clammy hand to it as if it would help to quench her nerves.

"Got a point there," Ally said.

Their food came, and they struggled with where to place the plates on the small space provided. Grace's plate was pushed to the side, up against the wall, a portion of it hanging off the edge of the table. She lifted her wrap to her mouth, took a bite, and relished the strong flavors, her teeth catching a gummy shrimp and chomping through.

"I see that look," Ally said. "Was I right, or was I right? Good place to take you, yeah? Even if you aren't as crazy about the guac as I am."

Grace nodded as she swallowed. "Yes," she admitted. "This is very good."

"You're gonna give me a bite of that, right?" Ally asked Chase as he cut into his quesadilla.

"Of course. I know you." He pierced a small piece with the tines of his fork and brought it closer to Ally. She leaned in, took the bite into her mouth, and smiled.

"Don't know why I didn't get that," Ally said.

"Um… because you're a pig and already got a burrito *and* a taco."

"Oink." Ally laughed. "I couldn't decide."

"Obviously."

"Grace, you've gotta try Chase's quesadilla."

"Oh," Grace spluttered. "No… no, that's okay."

"It's no biggie," Chase said as he pierced another small piece of his food. "You can try it if you'd like."

Grace found her cheeks flush once again, the warmth spreading. Her insides roiled as she watched the fork move closer and closer to her mouth, Chase's light-brown eyes on hers as if his actions were of no consequence whatsoever. She awkwardly accepted the bite and chewed, her eyes focusing on a stray curl on Chase's forehead.

"Good, yeah?" Ally asked.

Grace nodded and looked at her plate so she didn't have to face Chase. "Yes," she managed to say.

Ally and Chase immediately dove into conversation as Grace poked at her wrap, lifted it, and chewed, breathing through her nose and desperately willing the warmth in her cheeks to dissipate.

Ally didn't finish her food.

"And you're just gonna carry that around with you while you sing?" Chase teased.

"That's exactly what I'll do," Ally replied. "Unless I get hungry and finish it before we get there."

Chase laughed. "And I wouldn't be surprised."

Once Ally got a box and a bag for her leftovers, they stood from the table, threw out their trash, and made their way to the door. Outside, Chase wrapped his arm around Ally's shoulder then looked over at Grace. He smiled amicably and reached for her, resting his palm on her upper arm and pulling her gently toward him. "Two great girls," he said. "I'm the envy of all of Boston."

"You've got that right," Ally said as Grace replied, "I'm not sure about that."

Chase laughed, and they walked down the street toward the T station, the sun making its nightly descent in the sky above.

They weren't on the T long before they disembarked and walked into the street on their way to the karaoke bar. Grace noticed Ally's steps quicken with a bounce in her gait, and she assumed they were getting ever closer to their target.

"This is it," Ally announced as Grace found herself standing in front of a large red door, bold and bright, seemingly staring her down.

Her pulse quickened as her anxiety emerged. Ally opened the door, and Grace was immediately bombarded by a cacophony of noise and the pungent aroma of beer. Ally led the way through a throng of people, and Grace found herself clenching her thighs as her shoulders tensed and her body went rigid.

Something touched her shoulder.

Grace turned her head and saw Chase just inches away, smiling comfortingly, his hand the reassuring sensation she had felt. And a minute portion of her anxiety melted away, left to float in the air behind her.

Ally sat down at an unoccupied table surrounded by a U-shaped, high-backed, cushioned bench. "Sweet," she said. "We scored a good spot."

Grace felt relief wash over her as she sat beside her friend and Chase scooted in next to her. The sensation of being cocooned between Ally and Chase comforted her greatly.

A waitress in a red T-shirt and a pair of frayed jeans approached their table a few minutes later. "Get you anythin'?" she asked.

"Beer—oh, crap," Ally said. "Never mind. A boring glass of water for me."

"I'll take a beer, whatever you've got on tap," Chase said as he smirked Ally's way.

"Jerk," she said, though Grace saw her lips lift slightly.

When the waitress turned to her, Grace said, "I'll have a… can I have a glass of wine?"

"No wine here," the waitress replied. "Just beer and the hard stuff."

"Oh," Grace said. "Then I think I'll have… I'll have a lychee martini. I haven't had one of those in quite some time. Are you able to make that?"

"Yep," the waitress said then turned on her heel and walked away.

"Oh," Grace said, rather surprised at her abrupt manner.

Ally only laughed. "That's Martha. She's like that. You'll get used to it."

Grace nodded, though she told herself that she wouldn't allow herself to get used to anything here, as she didn't think she'd be returning. This night was for Ally, and Grace was willing to be here for her best friend, but she wasn't about to make it a weekly ritual, that was for sure.

Grace looked around the room. The tables were packed with people, laughing, joyful, gay. One large booth boasted a bridal party, bride-to-be resplendent in a shimmering black dress, her soft brown curls cascading to the middle of her back and a tiara set strategically atop her head. A sash was wrapped around her chest announcing to all that she was to be married shortly. Her head whipped back as she laughed heartily at something a friend said at her side. A few men and women lined the walls, and there was a stage across the room from where Grace sat, lights shining upon the floor, a large television screen facing inward so the person or people about to sing could easily look at its screen. Large speakers sat facing away from the stage, and three microphone stands stood at the stage's edge, waiting for hungry singers to pick them up and belt out a tune to their heart's content.

Grace concentrated on her breathing.

The waitress returned five minutes later, carrying a tray with their drinks. She handed Grace's martini over to her, and Grace accepted it readily. The waitress then placed the water in front of Chase and the beer in front of Ally.

Ally laughed. She looked up at the waitress and said, "Hey, Martha, guess what?"

"Yeah?"

"This beer's not for me." Ally scooted the beer over to Chase and took hold of her water glass. "I'm pregnant."

Martha chuckled.

"That's funny to you?" Ally asked with a smile.

"Nah," Martha said. "Not funny. Just surprising. Baby's lucky, though."

"Thanks, Martha."

"Welcome, Ally." And off she went into the mass of people.

Ally took a sip of her water and grimaced. "Ugh. City water."

Chase lifted his glass of frosty amber beer and ran it under Ally's nose tauntingly. "Want some?" he asked.

Ally shot him an exasperated look and said, "Don't be an ass."

Chase laughed.

Ally looked at Grace's glass longingly. "How's your martini?"

"It's actually very good," Grace replied.

"I guess there are some things I'm really gonna have to get used to, huh?" Ally asked.

"Yep," Chase said then took a sip of beer. When he lowered it to rest on the table, froth lined his upper lip. Grace smiled behind her martini glass.

Music suddenly poured from the speakers on the stage, and Grace lifted her gaze to find a man in tight-fitting jeans and a thin sun-yellow sweater clutching a microphone.

"Whoo! Go, Gus! Get your song on!" Ally shouted through cupped hands.

Whistles sounded throughout the room, along with cheers of encouragement. Gus bowed dramatically and began to sing.

"Oh," Grace said. "He's good."

"Sure is," Ally agreed. "Gus is here all the time. Even more than me, I think. He's got talent."

"Not more than I do," Chase said.

"Aw, Chase," Ally said teasingly. "You'll just have to go next, won't you? Show him up?"

"Maybe," Chase said. "Or maybe you should go. Karaoke queen and all."

Grace sipped her martini as she watched Gus sing. She was mesmerized. This might be a karaoke bar, she might be surrounded by a crowd of strangers, but Gus had a presence about him on the stage, an aura, and it sucked Grace in.

When Gus finished his song and bowed enthusiastically, Grace found she was clapping heartily. "Wow," she said. "Are they all like that?"

Chase laughed. "Did you hear me earlier when I said I can't sing?"

"Oh," Grace said shyly. "Yes."

"Just you wait," Ally said. "Chase is gonna blow you away."

Grace smiled. She was looking forward to watching both Chase and Ally.

"Who's next, who's next?" A slight man had taken the stage and was talking into the microphone. "Any takers?"

Ally hopped up from the cushioned bench and waved her arms in the air furiously. "Me!" she shouted.

"Ah…" the announcer said. "It's our very own Ally Cummings."

Grace leaned into Chase. "They know her last name?"

"She's here a lot. Lots of regulars."

"I see," Grace said. "Goodness…"

Ally climbed the few stairs and stepped on the stage, happily accepting the microphone that was offered, and looked out into the audience. Grace felt awe sweep over her as she watched her best friend standing in front of her, the confidence she exuded, her carefree manner.

"Some of you I know, some of you I don't," Ally began. "But if you're here, then we can be friends."

The crowd laughed, clapped, and whistled.

"I have a tough act to follow, but here we go."

She lowered the mic and whispered into the announcer's ear. Grace watched as he grinned, walked to the edge of the stage, and began toying with various buttons on what Grace assumed was the mechanism that would play Ally's song.

Music sounded, loud and clear, and Grace smiled as she immediately recognized "Love Shack" by the B-52s. The beat was uplifting, catchy, and Grace found her hips gently swaying in her seat.

"Now, for this one, I need my two best people. Chase and Grace, get your asses up here!"

Chase chuckled as he shimmied out of the booth. "Of course she would," he said to Grace. He held out his hand, but Grace was too stunned to take it.

"I... I..." she stammered.

"Grace, you can *so* do this!" Ally shouted through the mic. "Come on, everyone! Let's show my girl that she's a rock star!"

The crowd boisterously shouted and clapped. Grace felt nauseous, but she slowly reached for Chase's hand, and when she placed her palm in his, he grasped it and helped her to stand. Hand in hand, Chase led the way, where he and Grace met a beaming Ally on the stage.

Since the music had been running and the singing should have begun, the announcer stopped it entirely. "Ready now?" he asked the three friends on the stage.

Chase had since let go of Grace's hand, but Ally took hold of it now and looked her friend intently in the eyes. She spoke without saying a word, and Grace nodded ever so slightly.

"We're ready!" Ally shouted to the announcer, not lifting her eyes from Grace's. Both Grace and Chase were handed a microphone.

Ally faced the audience, a spotlight illuminating her in its warm glow. She began to sing.

And then Grace's attention somehow zeroed in. Gone was the crowd, gone were the chants and the cheers. Her peripheral vision no longer existed in this moment. All she saw was her best friend. Ally, with Chase at her side. Ally with her enormous smile as her lips moved and she sang.

Ally with her ever-comforting presence, with her genuine kindness and her zest for life. Grace saw it all, felt it all.

And then she realized that Ally was nudging her, that Ally wanted her to sing.

Chase took center stage. He bobbed his head, acting much like a fool, basking in the attention, and when he sang his first tune, Grace had to stifle a laugh. He hadn't been kidding. He was terrible!

The crowd cheered even louder, egging Chase on, and Chase took the bait. He swung his hips exaggeratedly and continued to sing. Grace felt Ally gently push her from behind, and she took one meager step toward Chase. Then another. And before she knew it, she was standing next to Chase in the limelight. Chase looked over at her, and still singing, he smiled. His brown eyes shone. His body turned toward hers, and he moved it goofily, making Grace laugh out loud.

And then she did it.

Grace began to sing. Her voice, just barely a whisper at first, rose and rose until she was matching Chase's volume. Ally sashayed her way to Grace's free side, and the three friends sang and danced, Grace rather awkwardly but freely.

When the song ended, the crowd erupted in applause. Grace looked at Chase, at his mass of curly brown hair, at an almost imperceptible dimple lining his left cheek that she wasn't sure she had noticed until that moment. She turned to Ally. Ally, who had become her best friend. Ally, who accepted Grace for who she truly was, flaws and all.

Ally, who Grace loved with her entire being.

The best friend—the best person—she had ever known.

And Grace realized then, as she stood under the lights on the stage, that she was truly blessed.

CHAPTER 9

"*C*ome cycling with me." It was the following day—Sunday—and Grace had just answered the ringing of her cell phone to hear Ally on the other end.

"Are... can you do that?"

"What do you mean?"

"You're pregnant now. Can you ride your bike?" Grace asked.

"I haven't made an appointment with a doctor yet, so I guess I don't know. But there's a great trail I want to take you to that's flat and paved. If we take it easy, I bet it's safe. And if I can't cycle as this pregnancy progresses, then we seriously have to get it in while I can!"

"Okay then," Grace capitulated. "I'll go with you. But Ally?"

"Yeah?"

"I think it's time I buy my own bike."

"I know exactly where to go," Ally said.

Ally picked Grace up in her car later that morning, and the two set off for the next town over, where there was a specialty shop that supplied Ally with all her cycling needs. "I've been coming here for years," she said.

"Then you know your way around," Grace replied.

"Sure do."

Ally led the way through the door, and a bell chimed her presence. A middle-aged man looked up from some paperwork set upon the sales counter. "Can I help you?"

"Yep," Ally said. "You most definitely can. My friend here—she needs a bike."

"Well, you've come to the right place for that."

"Don't I know it," Ally said. "And while we're at it, let's get her a good helmet, too. Can't ride without that."

"What kind of bike are you looking for? Street, mountain…"

"Road bike," Ally replied.

"Right this way."

Ally looked at Grace and lifted her brows before tilting her head to the side and setting off in the employee's wake. Grace followed, tickled by Ally's enthusiasm.

Forty-five minutes later, Grace left the store with a new —and rather expensive—road bike, as well as a shiny cobalt-blue helmet, smiling gleefully. As she and Ally had cycled together on several occasions now and were bound to continue in the future, Grace deemed her money well spent.

Ally secured Grace's bicycle next to hers on the rack at the back of her small car, and the friends set off. A pleasant twenty minutes later, they arrived in the spacious parking lot of their destination.

"Let's do this!" Ally enthused.

Helmet secured snugly on her head, Grace placed the

ball of her sneakered foot in the stirrup, pushed off from the ground, and began to pedal. The soft spring breeze caressed her cheeks, and she closed her eyes, inhaling heavily through her nose. She held her breath momentarily and then slowly exhaled through her mouth, savoring the sweet, crisp sensation within her lungs.

"Race you!" Ally sped past, and Grace started.

"But… Ally!" she called. "You can't!"

Ally looked over her shoulder. "Just kidding." She laughed. "You should see the look on your face!"

"Oh, you…!"

"Me what?"

"You poop!" Grace said.

"Hey, that's my word," Ally protested with a smile.

"And it's rubbed off on me."

"Yuck," Ally teased.

"Ally!" Grace shouted. She pedaled faster and caught up to her friend. Together, Grace and Ally rode side by side, enjoying their morning excursion immensely.

About an hour into the ride, Ally said, "Hey, there's an ice cream stand when we have to cross the street in just a minute. Want to go?"

"I'd love to," Grace replied.

"They've got some great flavors, too."

"How do you know where everything is?" Grace asked. "You always know of little places that I've never heard of. Even out of Boston."

"Guess that's what happens when you can't sit still. You head out and explore. Plus, I like trying new things."

"Yes, you do," Grace said. "You're not held back at all. You're not shy."

"I can be shy," Ally insisted.

"When have you ever been shy?"

"Oh, well…" And then Ally laughed. "I guess I'm not really shy."

"How do you do it?"

"What?" Ally asked.

"Go through life the way you do. Hop from place to place with no inhibitions. Talk to people without any difficulty."

Ally shrugged as she held onto the handlebars of her bike. "Don't know. Guess it's just who I am. I've always been this way. I've always believed that life is what it is. It's gonna come at you, and you give it right back. I like meeting people, but it's seriously okay not to like everyone. If I did, then I wouldn't be human. I don't like jerks, as you know, and I don't want to be around them at all. But people will surprise you sometimes. You gotta give them a try. To be human is to love, to care, to experience… I just go with the flow. And I know everything works out in the end. It always works out one way or another."

"I wish I could see the world through your eyes for just one day."

"You do," Ally said as she looked at Grace. "Take cycling—you didn't want to go that first time, did you?"

Grace shook her head.

"And now look at you. You've got your own bike, and we're riding together. And we'll have plenty more days like this. I'll just have to get one of those things you put on the back of the bike that kids can sit in. Big flag and all. Oh, sweet! I'll sport a Pride flag during Pride month and a breast cancer awareness flag during Breast Cancer Awareness Month, and maybe a seriously awesome flag with a picture of a pink unicorn on it for all those regular months we've got."

Grace laughed. "A pink unicorn?"

"That's what I said. A pink unicorn. How awesome would that be?"

"You know," Grace said. "A pink unicorn kind of shouts 'Ally.'"

"You bet!"

The path came to a stop as it intersected with a road, and Grace and Ally halted their bikes for oncoming traffic. When all was clear, they set on their way again, the path running through the middle of a town square with various shops on both sides. Ally slowly pedaled then stopped, hopping off her bike and walking it to a sidewalk then to an adjacent crosswalk. "It's right over there." She motioned with her head, and Grace saw a large picture of an ice cream cone on the side of a wall.

Once the friends had crossed the road, Grace perused the various flavors written on a small billboard above the ordering window. "Oh, they have peppermint stick."

"One of my favorites," Ally replied. "But I think today, I'm gonna get chocolate. Just plain old chocolate."

"Really?"

"Yep. Really."

A girl who looked no older than fifteen or sixteen slid the window open and peeked her head outside. "Do you know what you want?" she asked.

"I'll take a small peppermint stick in a plain cone, please," Grace said.

"And me... I'll get a medium chocolate. Also in a cone. No, wait. I've changed my mind. I want that chocolate brownie ice cream you've got, the one with those huge chunks."

"Okay, will that be all?" the girl asked.

"Yep. No, wait," Ally said. "I think I want Snickers instead. But that's with vanilla ice cream, right?"

The girl nodded.

"Okay, then I'm switching back. I'll take the chocolate brownie. Medium in a cone."

The girl looked annoyed as she slid the window back into place.

"So much for plain old chocolate," Grace teased.

"A girl can change her mind once or twice," Ally said.

"Or three times."

"Or three times," Ally agreed. "But when it comes to ice cream, you really can't go wrong."

They found a patch of grass, sat down, and ate their treats, their bikes resting against a tree and their helmets slung over the handlebars.

"I'm really glad we're here," Grace said. "I'm glad you took me on this ride."

"Me too," Ally said with a smile. "Grace, can I tell you something?"

"Of course you can."

"You make me really happy."

Grace, about to lick her ice cream, stopped. She closed her mouth, and brought the cone to her lap. "Where did that come from?"

"When you feel something, you show it," Ally said. "If someone makes you happy, you tell them."

"I make you happy?" Grace felt her eyes well, and she willed the liquid away. Ally often affected her emotionally, but Grace still didn't want to tear up as often as she did.

"Yep. You do. You were meant to come into my life, you know. I've told you that before." Ally took a bite from the bottom of her cone. Droplets of melted chocolate ice cream dribbled out and onto her wrist.

"Can I tell *you* something?" Grace asked.

"Yep."

Grace's voice cracked. "You make me really happy too. I was a bit nervous when we first met. Nervous to let you in. I had been so hurt by Bethany, the friend that I had when I was with Gary. I didn't want to go through that again. But I shouldn't have been nervous. I think I knew early on that I could trust you."

"Two peas in a pod, you and I," Ally said.

Grace laughed. "Not so much. We're so different."

"Then we're two very distinguishable peas, but we live in the same pod. How about that?"

Grace laughed again. "I'll go with that. I'm happy to live in a pod with you, Ally."

"Me too," Ally said. "And in this pod, we have ice cream and coffee and Mexican food, and we have enough space for karaoke and our favorite bar for drinks, and of course, we need room for Chase."

"And this baby when he or she is born," Grace added.

Ally smiled. "Our pod is sounding pretty wonderful right about now. And full."

Grace couldn't have agreed more.

They were back in the parking lot of the bike trail about an hour and a half later.

"I'm beat," Grace said with a slump of her shoulders.

"That was a great ride. I'm seriously upset that it was probably my last one for a while."

"Especially now that the weather's only going to get warmer," Grace said.

Ally looked at Grace. "That's depressing."

"Sorry," Grace said with a chuckle.

"Guess I'll have to think of other things to do. Maybe you'll hike with me?"

"I'm not sure I'm much into hiking."

"You didn't think you'd be much into cycling either, and now look at you," Ally pointed out.

"I suppose there's truth to that," Grace agreed. "I'm willing to give it a try."

"Yep. And if you don't like it, then you don't have to do it again."

"But maybe I'll like it."

"That's the ticket. Maybe you will," Ally said. "Hey, want to head to our coffee shop? We could get some lunch."

"And a great-tasting drink," Grace said.

"You've got that right! Let's do it."

"Hi, Mrs. Clarke." It was Grace's young student, Penny, who spoke the following Monday morning at the door to Grace's first-grade classroom.

"Good morning, Penny," Grace replied. "How are you today?"

"Good. Mom let me have a brownie with my lunch."

"Oh, so she packed you a treat today."

"Ya huh, she did. A brownie treat. And it's a really big one."

"Well," Grace said. "That sounds very special for you."

Penny nodded her head feverishly. "Ya huh. Mom never lets me have junk food very much."

"I imagine she wants you to eat healthy food."

"That's what she says," Penny confirmed. "Want to see

my brownie?" She reached for the lunch sack slung over her shoulder.

"I'll tell you what, Penny. You go put your belongings in your cubby, and when it's snack time, you can show me your brownie, all right?"

Penny removed her fingers from the zipper of her lunch sack. "Okay," she said then entered the classroom and headed for her cubby.

Grace greeted the rest of her students as they approached the doorway. Smiling faces abounded, though a few students trekked along sluggishly, feet shuffling on the hard hallway floor.

The morning progressed swimmingly, and soon, the bell rang over the intercom, announcing the beginning of the lunch and recess period. Grace walked her students to the cafeteria, ensured they were set, then made her way back to the classroom, where she extracted her lunch bag from under her desk and set it before her. She sat down in her chair and reached for the zipper, but just as her fingers touched the cool metal, she pulled back. She thought about Ally and what she had said that past weekend. *People will surprise you sometimes. You gotta give them a try.*

Grace inhaled deeply. She let her breath out, grabbed her lunch sack, and slowly stood from the desk.

She wasn't going to eat alone today.

She'd go to the staff room instead.

CHAPTER 10

*G*race loved that she was fortunate enough to have the summers off from work. She knew that many of her coworkers taught summer classes at the high school level or acquired other part-time employment to ensure they had a steady stream of extra income for their families, but Grace wasn't financially in need of doing so. She adored her summers. In the past, she had found pleasure in walking around her neighborhood or simply having the ability to pick up a book on a sunny weekday morning with a cup of coffee instead of rushing off to work.

And this summer, she had Ally.

Granted, Ally was employed during the week, but they habitually came together on weeknights for dinner at either Grace's home or at Ally's, where Chase was often present if he wasn't out with the current woman he was dating. Grace didn't mind in the least when Chase was home. In fact, she enjoyed his company greatly and was always pleased when he was around. And she loved to be privy to his antics with

Ally, to watch their enjoyment of each other, their playful bantering.

Grace and Ally had spent every weekend together this summer, exploring various beaches, shopping in Boston, Newburyport, the Cape, and Portsmouth, New Hampshire. They went to the cinema together, out to lunch and dinner, and enjoyed plentiful hours at the coffee shop down the street from Grace's townhouse.

When Ally was working or when she wasn't available, Grace spent time with a woman from her school named Kathy, a fellow teacher, though Kathy taught the fourth grade and not the first. At twenty-nine, Kathy was younger than Grace, but through their conversations in the staff room, Grace had learned that she and Kathy had quite a lot in common, and when Kathy had asked Grace if she'd like to get together for a cup of coffee a few months ago, Grace had readily agreed. Like Grace, Kathy also had the summer months off of work, so the two women had found enjoyment in walking their town together and meeting for breakfast about once a week.

The months of June and July flew past for Grace, so fast that she had woken on the first of August, looked at the date on her phone while enjoying her morning cup of coffee on her living room sofa, and blinked with disbelief. She'd be going back to work in just a couple of weeks, and although she didn't mind that she'd be back to work soon—she was eager to welcome a new set of students to her classroom—she had had such an amazing, fun-filled summer that she wasn't yet ready for it to be over.

On an overcast morning in the second week of August, Grace met Ally at her apartment. Ally had taken the morning off of work so she could attend her first—and perhaps only—ultrasound appointment. Grace had been touched when Ally had asked her along.

"Of course I want you there," Ally had said when Grace had lightly protested.

"Isn't this something that... I guess... isn't it personal?"

"Who else am I gonna have there if not you or Chase? And Chase has to work. And you're my best friend too. Seriously, Grace. You're like this baby's other mom in a way." Ally laughed when Grace blinked back tears.

"Love ya," Ally said.

"I love you too," Grace replied.

Ally's OB-GYN's office was situated adjacent to the hospital in which she'd give birth, so instead of Ally driving her car, taking the T was more conducive to their transportive needs.

"I'm here to see Dr. Goshen," Ally told the receptionist upon their arrival. Her blond hair had grown out and rested against her jawline. She tucked a tendril behind her ear.

"Name?"

"Ally Cummings."

"Let's see here... yes, I have you. Nine o'clock?"

"That's right," Ally confirmed.

Grace and Ally found unoccupied chairs in the waiting room and sat down.

"I can't believe we're going to see your baby today," Grace said.

"I know," Ally replied. "The whole notion of me growing another human being is still foreign to me. Didn't think I'd be here for anything other than my yearly Pap."

"And here we are."

Ally nodded. "Here we are."

Ally's name was called fifteen minutes later by a nurse

in penguin-patterned scrubs. "Awesome," Ally said to her as she and Grace approached. "Love the pants."

The nurse smiled and looked down. "Thanks. They're my favorite. Even in summer."

"Who doesn't love penguins?" Ally asked.

Grace and Ally followed the nurse into a small examination room, where the OB-GYN met them an additional twenty minutes later. "Sorry," Dr. Goshen said. "I'm behind. It's been a crazy day."

"No biggie," Ally said. "I got off work for this, and I don't mind that one bit. I'm not in a rush to get back."

Ally and Grace were soon led down the hallway to an even smaller room in which the ultrasound equipment was erected and ready to go. Dr. Goshen introduced Ally to the young technician, who, in turn, met Grace's eyes and asked, "Is this your partner then?"

Ally laughed. "Might as well be," she said.

"Huh?"

"This is Grace," Ally explained. "My best friend. No father in the picture, but I've got two pretty awesome friends to help me out. Grace is one of them."

"Well," the technician said as she motioned for Ally to sit down on the examination chair, "it's nice to meet you, Grace."

"Thank you. It's nice to meet you, too."

"You can have a seat in that chair over there." She pointed to a small chair in the corner of the room that faced the ultrasound monitor. "Or you can stand. Whatever you want."

"Okay. Thank you."

Ally lay down on the examination chair and folded her arms behind her head. Grace chose to stand beside her.

"So, we're here to take a look at your baby then," the technician said.

"That's right," Ally replied. "I've been doing a little bit of research, and I think I'm at the point where this little one won't look so much like an alien."

The technician laughed. "No, they won't look like an alien at all," she said. "They'll look very much like a baby. Just smaller. And skeletal on the monitor."

"Skeletor," Ally said then turned to Grace. "Did you ever watch that show when you were younger? *He-Man and the Masters of the Universe?*"

"No."

"It came out before I was even born," Ally said. "But I saw an episode once a while back. Weird show. There's this creepy skeleton dude that has this really weird laugh that's probably supposed to sound sinister to little kids but makes you roll your eyes instead. Seriously strange show."

"Okay," Grace said with a smile. "But I'm sure you won't roll your eyes when this baby starts to laugh."

"Darn right," Ally said. "This baby's gonna have the best laugh ever."

The technician shook a small tube and then said to Ally," Can you lift up your shirt for me?"

"Oh, yeah," Ally replied. "I bet that would be helpful, huh?" Ally lifted her shirt then rested her hands just under her breasts. When the technician squirted a generous portion of the ultrasound gel onto Ally's lower abdomen, Ally said, "That feels so weird."

The technician smiled. "Don't I know it."

"You've had an ultrasound?" Ally asked.

"Several. I've got three kids, and my third had to be monitored, so I got to see him three times instead of just once."

"Bet that was pretty awesome."

"It was. And everything was just fine with him, which made things not so stressful."

"I'm glad to hear it," Ally said. "Three kids, huh? This is just my first. Don't know how I'd wrangle three."

The technician laughed. "You would figure it out. I think that's a lot of what motherhood is about: figuring things out. You just do what you need to do."

"I like your attitude," Ally said.

The technician placed the ultrasound wand on Ally's small protrusion and began moving it around. "You can look there," she said, motioning to the monitor with her chin.

"I have no clue what I'm looking for."

"I'll show you. See…" She held the wand with one hand while the other pointed at a black-and-white image on the screen. "That's your baby's spine."

"Hmm…" Ally said. "Grace, do you see it?"

"Yes," Grace said, her chest feeling heavy with burgeoning emotion. "I do."

"I still don't know what I'm looking at."

The technician chuckled. "I only do because I've been doing this for years now. Look here: this is your baby's skull, its forehead, it's eyes, its nose. And this is your baby's chin. Oops… baby's very active in there. Let me see…" She moved the wand over Ally's stomach. "There's a foot. Do you see the toes?"

Ally squinted her eyes. "Holy crap. Yeah! Grace," Ally turned, and then her lips lifted into a smile. "You're crying."

"I'm not crying," Grace said.

"Then what's that you're wiping off your cheek?"

"Allergies," Grace said, and then she and Ally exchanged a

look, and they both laughed. "It's just so… wonderful. It's truly wonderful. I've never seen an ultrasound before. I think… it's amazing to think that you've got a baby growing inside of you. And they're moving all around, Ally. Do you feel any of that?"

Ally shook her head. "Not very much. Sometimes, I can feel little flutters, almost like I've got a bit of gas, but that's about it."

"That's the baby," the technician confirmed. "You've just never been pregnant before, so you don't know what to expect."

"Weird," Ally said. "But it is moving a lot, isn't it? I mean, I think so, right? Am I seeing what I think I'm seeing?"

"You are," the technician said. "And yes, you have a very active baby. Maybe they enjoyed what you ate for breakfast." She smiled.

"That's such a strange thing to think about," Ally said as she placed her arms back behind her head. "This whole thing is strange. I never really thought much about motherhood, and now here I am… in this chair with this goo all over my stomach, looking at little Skeletor on a TV screen, knowing they're inside of me, but somehow still in denial a bit… Well, not denial. I know I'm pregnant. But I think things haven't fully sunk in."

"Just wait until your third trimester, when they're kicking you and rolling all around. I'd see a big bulge move from one side of my stomach to the other, probably an elbow or a foot."

"So weird," Ally said breathily.

"Weird, but wonderful," the technician replied. She went back to surveying the screen, pausing the image on occasion and tapping a few keys on her keyboard.

"What are you doing?" Ally asked.

"Taking measurements. Everything I'm doing is completely normal."

"Okay."

A few minutes later, the technician was moving her wand around when she paused the screen and announced, "This is your baby's bottom."

"Ha!" Ally said. "I don't really see it, but that's kind of funny."

"Would you like to know the sex?"

Ally's eyes widened. "I don't know… I…" she turned to Grace. "I seriously don't know what to think."

"It's up to you," Grace said.

"I know. I mean, I've thought about it, but do I want to know? Yeah, I think it would be pretty neat to know, but I also think it would be seriously neat not to know—keep it a surprise, right?"

Grace shook her head. "I'm not going to tell you what to do."

"Yeah, I'm not asking you to. Just thinking out loud."

"Some people ask me to write the sex down on a sheet of paper and seal it in an envelope," the technician said. "That way, if they choose to know, they can, and if they want to keep it a surprise, then they just don't open the envelope."

"Well, that's a tease," Ally said. "It's like this giant hovering secret, but you try to hold yourself back. But it's right there. In front of you. Taunting. No way I'd be able to have that in my house. But…" she looked at Grace. "You could."

"What?" Grace asked.

"You could take it," Ally said.

Grace shook her head and smiled. "I think that I'd want to open it, too."

"Ah, you know what?" Ally said. "What the hell? Just tell me."

"Are you sure?" The technician asked.

"No." Ally laughed. "I should have figured this out before today."

"It's all right," the technician said. "Why don't I write it down for you, and you can make your decision when you're ready."

"Yeah," Ally said. "Okay. I have a feeling I'm gonna rip right into it when I get out of here, but whatever."

The technician finished with her measurements then printed out a few photos for Ally to take along with her, small letters announcing the body part, with arrows pointing to what a particular photo showcased: head, foot, leg.

"Baby's measuring right on target," she said. "When's your actual due date? Must be at the beginning of January."

"January first," Ally said. "New year, new you, as the saying goes. In my case, though, it's a new year and a new baby."

Ally and Grace thanked the technician and then walked back to the waiting room, where Ally checked out. They then made their way to the door and to the warm summer air outside. The envelope with the baby's sex concealed inside was clutched in Ally's hand.

"Hey," Ally said. "I know I have to get back to work, but… I don't know why I did this." She held the envelope up. "What was I thinking? There's no way I can have this with me and not want to peek. Let's just open it."

"Right now?"

"Yep. Right now."

"But we're… around all these people," Grace said as she surveyed her surroundings. "Don't you want to wait until you get home?"

Ally shook her head. "Then I'd be alone, and even if Chase was home from work, you still wouldn't be there."

"Don't you want Chase to be there, though? If you open it now, you won't be sharing this moment with him."

"Yeah, I do. But I want to share this with you, too."

"You could call me."

"Nope," Ally said. "Not the same. At all."

"I'm afraid if you open it now, you'll be disappointed. I could be wrong, but it won't be special, Ally. We'd find out, but then you'd have to go right to work. We won't be able to talk about it."

"Yeah, you've got a point," Ally said. "Here—" She thrust the envelope toward Grace. "You take it."

"You want me to have it?" Grace's voice was wary.

"Yep. Just for now. Just so I don't go and open it at work and then get seriously bummed out that I did it without you. You keep it for now, and then you, Chase, and I can do it together."

"When?"

"Come over for dinner tonight."

Grace nodded but then said, "Actually… why don't you and Chase come to my house instead? I don't have to work, and I can make dinner and have it ready for you by the time you get there. And I can try to make it special for you."

"No need to make anything special."

"But I'd like to," Grace assured her. "I really would. I think it would be nice."

175

"Okay then," Ally agreed. "Your house. We can probably get there around seven. That okay?"

"Yes."

"I'll text Chase to see if he can make it. I'll let you know
if there's a problem."

"That sounds good," Grace said. Then she clasped her
hands in front of her. "Oh, this is wonderful, Ally. I'm
looking forward to it."

"Not much to look forward to if you don't take this
damn envelope," Ally said.

"Oh, yes..." Grace accepted the envelope, grasping
tightly with her fingers.

"Seven then?"

"Yes," Grace said. "Seven o'clock."

"See you then. I'm sorry I can't ride with you. We're
headed in opposite directions."

"I know, and that's all right," Grace said. "I'll see you
tonight." She held the envelope up. "Eek."

Ally laughed. "You're a dork."

"I know," Grace said.

"Love you, dork," Ally said. She turned on her heel and
walked away.

Grace arrived home just before noon. She turned her key in
the front door, pushed it open, and stepped inside.

Silence.

Typically, she relished the solitude of her home, but at
that moment, she suddenly felt disheartened. She had had
such a wonderful morning with Ally, and thrilling news
lingered within an envelope that was neatly folded and
resting in the pocket of her skirt. Grace knew that it didn't

matter in the least whether this baby was a boy or a girl, and she knew, too, that Ally was indifferent, but somehow... somehow, having information that only she and the ultrasound technician were privy to was exhilarating.

The entire way home, Grace toyed with several various ideas of how she could make tonight special for Ally. She had eventually settled on Mexican food. She'd attempt to emulate the restaurant that Ally and Chase had taken her to. She'd make her own chips and guacamole, and she'd try her hand at burritos. She had made plenty of wraps in the past, and she had thrown together what passed for a burrito, but never had she made anything like the food they had eaten at that tiny restaurant in the city.

Grace closed the door behind her, lifted the envelope from her pocket, and gently rested it on the kitchen countertop. She wanted so desperately to peek within but knew that wouldn't be right. The first person to learn about the sex of Ally's baby should be Ally herself. Still, it was difficult to control her excitement and not lift the envelope, bring it to the living room, and hold it up to the light seeping through the window. But Grace persevered and was determined to stay strong throughout the remainder of the day.

Grace walked to the dining room table and opened her charging laptop. She sat down and began typing, perusing the internet, attempting to find enticing, well-rated burrito, chips, and homemade guacamole recipes.

When Grace eventually closed her laptop, she had a list of foods and spices written out on a small sheet of paper. With a smile, she stood from the table, picked up her purse and car keys, and left her house.

At five o'clock that evening, Grace received a text message from Ally. *Can't wait to see u again. Have u ripped into the envelope? I seriously would have!*

No! Grace wrote back. *I've been good. See you soon?*

Yep. Chase is coming.

Great!

At almost exactly seven o'clock, the doorbell rang.

"Come on in," Grace called from the kitchen.

A muffled voice shouted back, "It's locked."

Grace wiped her hands on a small towel, walked to the door, and unlocked it. She turned the knob, and standing on her front stoop were both Ally and Chase.

"Don't really want us here, huh?" Ally said with a playful grin. "You never lock me out."

"Sorry about that. I don't know why I locked it."

"Habit," Chase suggested. "I always lock the door."

"We live in the middle of Boston," Ally said to him. "If we didn't lock our door, we'd be robbed. Even though our neighborhood is pretty safe for the city, it's not *that* safe!"

When Ally walked inside, she lifted her chin, sniffed, and said, "Holy crap, Grace. What are you making? It smells so good!"

Grace merely smirked. "You'll see. It's pretty much done. Why don't I meet you at the table?"

"Awesome!" Ally said. "I'm starving."

"Her appetite is increasing a bit," Chase said.

"How is that even possible?" Grace teased as she walked toward the kitchen. "She already eats a ton."

"Right? Don't know where she puts it all," Chase said, looking over at Ally. You'd think with how short she is, she'd grow outward, but she never does." He looked at Ally then sniggered.

"Hey," Ally swatted Chase's arm. "What was that for?"

"You're gonna get big." Chase chuckled. "Really big. Baby big."

"Great friend you are," Ally replied. She looked down

at her stomach, gently stroking the small bump that had formed. She laced her fingers together, and then her eyes shot up. "Oh, Jesus! If I ever get big enough where my hands don't come together, you'll have to help me off the floor, because I'll faint. Do women get that big? Nah. They can't, can they?"

Grace shot a glance at Chase from the kitchen, and he smirked her way.

"You haven't really paid attention to pregnant women, have you?" Chase asked.

"Nope," Ally said. "Not so much. Not unless I'm giving up a seat on the T or something. But even then, I don't stare down at their bellies. That would just be rude."

"You're short," Chase said. "With a small torso. Not much room for this baby to grow but out."

"Oh, ha," Ally said with a frown. "You're so funny."

"Not trying to be funny," Chase said with a grin. "Just realistic."

"You think I'm gonna get big then?"

"I think you're going to get huge." Chase snorted, and Ally swatted him again.

Grace came out of the kitchen area with a platter in hand. Ally stepped forward. "Whoa, Grace," she said. "What did you make?"

"What does it look like?" Grace asked.

"Oh, sweet! Guac! Burritos!"

Grace smiled shyly but proudly. "I looked up a recipe. I want everything to taste really good, like that restaurant we went to."

"Aw," Ally said. "You're pretty awesome, Grace. Thank you. My stomach's rumbling! Let's eat!"

The friends sat down at the table. Grace placed plates

in front of Ally, Chase, and herself, and they all dug in with relish.

"Holy crap!" Ally said through a mouthful of guacamole. "This is so darn good!"

"Oh, I'm glad," Grace said. "I wasn't sure. I've never made guacamole by hand before. I've bought those small plastic containers they sell at the store, but that's it."

Ally swallowed. "You're gonna make this again, right?"

"Is it really that good?"

Chase nodded fervently. "Sure is," he chimed in. "This is some good stuff. I taste extra garlic."

"Yes," Grace said. "There's a lot in there."

"I love garlic."

As her friends filled their mouths, complimenting Grace on her cooking, Grace found herself blushing. She looked down at the table, contentment coursing within. At that moment, she wanted to be nowhere else but right there in her home. And with nobody else but Ally and Chase.

They finished their meals, and Ally sat back in her chair, grabbed her stomach, and said, "I'm full. That was awesome."

"I hope you're not too full," Grace said.

"What?"

"I... made a cake."

"You what?" Ally laughed. "Are you becoming the next Betty Crocker, Gracey?"

Grace smiled. "I'm not sure if it came out well," she said, "but I really wanted to try. I think you'll like what I did."

"What you did?" Ally looked confused.

"Yes," Grace said. "You'll see."

"I want to know," Chase said.

"What I did?" Grace asked.

"Well, that too," Chase replied. "But I want to know about this kid of yours, Ally. Are we bringing a screaming boy or girl into our apartment?"

"Screaming, huh? That's what you think of first? Not cooing or smiling or babbling? Not even drooling? Just screaming?" Ally asked with a grin.

"Got that right. This kid will scream." Chase smiled. "But I love it already."

"I can get the envelope," Grace suggested.

"Yes!" Both Ally and Chase simultaneously exclaimed.

Grace laughed. "Goodness. All right." She stood from her chair and walked to the kitchen, where the envelope was still resting on the countertop. She brought it back to the dining area, held it to her chest, took a deep breath, and then handed it off to Ally.

"This is it," Ally said. "It's not a big deal. I don't care what the sex is. Seriously. But somehow… it actually is a big deal. I don't know why, it just is. Does that make sense?"

"Sure does," Chase said.

Grace nodded. "I have to admit that I would like to know, too."

Ally inhaled a deep breath then let it out. "Well, here goes, I guess." She slowly began to open the envelope then abandoned all restraint and tore it down the side. She removed the sheet within and immediately unfolded it.

Grace concentrated on Ally's face, attempting to decipher her emotions and glean a hint as to what the paper divulged.

Ally looked up, first at Chase and then to Grace. "It's. Holy shit! I'm having twins!"

"What?" Grace exclaimed, feeling flustered and utterly overwhelmed. "But… how? Wouldn't they have told you that well before now? I mean… Oh, my goodness, Ally!"

Chase sat at the table, his eyes wide and his jaw hanging slightly open. His face was devoid of color.

Ally began to laugh hysterically, clutching her belly. "You… you should see… your faces!" she managed to say. "So. Funny!"

"What?" Grace asked, clearly confused.

"I'm joking," Ally said, her laughter beginning to subside.

"What?" Grace repeated.

"You are both so gullible."

Chase narrowed his eyes at Ally. "Not funny," he said.

"I thought it was funny," Ally said.

"I… I was scared," Grace admitted. "Well, maybe not scared. I don't think that's the right word. I was just… overwhelmed. Two babies?"

"I wouldn't know what to do!" Ally admitted. "One's enough for me."

Chase lifted his chin, nodding toward the small sheet of paper in Ally's hand. "What does it really say?"

Ally smiled. "I'm having a girl."

Grace gasped with pleasure, and her hand flew to her mouth. "A girl?"

"Or a boy," Ally said.

"That's enough now," Chase chastised.

"Sorry," Ally said. "It's just too easy. No. Seriously though, I'm having a girl."

Grace's lips began to quiver, and a tear found its way down her cheek, the salty liquid leaving a streak in its wake. She wiped it away. "You're having a girl."

Ally nodded. "Yep. I guess it's official now. I'm pregnant. I'm going to be a mom. And I'm having a daughter. Holy shit. I'm having a daughter. I'm responsible for another human being."

"You're going to be a wonderful mother," Grace said wholeheartedly. "And if this baby girl is anything like her mom, then the world will inherit another wonderful person."

"Aw, all sentimental, now, are we?" Ally said.

"I am," Grace said. "I'm feeling very emotional."

"Chase?" Ally asked.

"A girl?"

"A girl," Ally confirmed.

Chase nodded. "I'm going to be surrounded by estrogen."

"You sure are," Ally said.

"And yet," Chase added, "I don't mind. Kind of cool, actually."

"Cool?" Ally teased.

"Yeah, cool."

"Would you like to see my cake now?" Grace asked.

"That was kind of random," Ally replied.

"Not really. Here… you'll see." Grace walked back to the kitchen, lifted a small cake into her hands, and brought it to the middle of the dining room table along with a large knife. "Here. You do the honors."

Ally accepted the knife then brought it toward the middle of Grace's creation, where she proceeded to push down through the frosting and moist cake. When she placed a small slice on a clean plate, she smirked. "No way! You told me you didn't peek!"

Grace looked down at the pink slice in front of her best friend. "I didn't peek," she said. "I just made two cakes. One pink and one blue. That way, I'd be ready for whatever was in that envelope."

Ally laughed. "You're too much."

"Mmm…" Grace turned as she heard Chase mumble.

"This is good stuff!" His mouth was full of pink cake and white frosting. He had surreptitiously pulled a chunk off the slice Ally had cut while Grace and Ally were busy talking.

"Hey!" Ally protested. "That's *my* cake!"

"You were too slow."

"Cut your own slice."

"Might just have to do that. Don't have much room after that dinner, but Grace is a good baker."

Although Grace, too, felt that she had gorged herself with dinner, she enjoyed a couple of bites of the cake she had made. The three friends sat and chatted for a while longer until Ally announced that she and Chase should probably head out. "Work tomorrow and all. Not all of us have the summers off."

Grace smiled. "Just the lucky ones."

"See you this weekend?"

"I'm looking forward to it," Grace replied.

CHAPTER 11

"Do you think you should tell your parents about your pregnancy?"

Grace and Ally were sitting outside their favorite cafe on a Saturday morning in mid-October, sipping cups of coffee—decaf for Ally—and enjoying two ginormous blueberry muffins. A gourd rested in the center of the table, and several large pumpkins lined the narrow walkway from the sidewalk to the main entrance. There was a chill in the air, and Grace hugged her thick sweater tighter to her chest as her blue boots tapped against her leg. Ally didn't seem the least bit chilled; in fact, she was only wearing a thick long-sleeved T-shirt with the depiction of a large jack-o'-lantern at its center, a baby jack-o'-lantern smiling at its base.

Ally's stomach had grown considerably since her ultrasound. She was now six and a half months along, and Chase's statement the night of the gender reveal had proven correct—the baby didn't have room to grow anywhere but out. From the back, Ally looked like her typical prepregnancy self, but viewed from the side, it was unmistakable that she was expecting. She had recently converted to walking with her hands propped on her lower back and grimacing at times when she stood from a low-lying couch or chair.

"I'll tell them," Ally insisted.

"But when? You're going to have this baby soon. If you don't tell them, then you'll show up on their doorstep with your daughter in your arms."

Ally grimaced. "I won't be showing up on their doorstep anytime soon."

"I know you're not close to them, and I know they don't live around here, but they should still know, don't you think?"

"Sometimes I wish you weren't so practical about everything," Ally replied. "I'd be just fine not telling them at all."

Grace paused for a moment and then said, "Do you think you'll see them again? Do you *want* to see them again?"

"I really don't have any desire," Ally said. "They weren't good to me, Grace. And I know we're related, I know we share the same blood, but I learned a long time ago that you make your own family. I can decide who my family is, and for me, blood doesn't have anything to do with it. Trust and love are deserved, not given. It's like you and your father. You haven't seen him for all the time I've known you, and if you have, then you haven't told me about it."

Grace shook her head and looked down at the table. "I haven't."

"And has he tried to contact you?"

"No."

"And when you see him, do all your memories come back to the surface? You once told me they did," Ally said.

"They do," Grace acknowledged.

"It's the same for me. I haven't seen my parents for a really long time, maybe a few years now. But the last time I saw them, it took me a couple of weeks to heal. I told you I don't people. I don't do jerks. And that includes my own family. Relationships go both ways. Trust and respect go both ways. I wouldn't exist without them, so I'm thankful for that, but that's where it ends. They are not good people, Grace. I've learned to break free. I don't want to regress. Seeing them would set me back."

"Purge that shit?" Grace smirked, thinking about the phrase Ally had once used with her.

Ally laughed. "You've got that right! And I'm proud of you, Gracey. I hardly ever hear you swear!"

"You're proud of me because I swore?"

"That's what I said," Ally replied with a wide smile.

"Since you won't show up on their doorstep, do you think you'll call?"

Ally pondered the thought. "Yeah. I'll call. I suppose they deserve to know. But I don't want them to have anything to do with this baby, and honestly, I don't think they'll want to."

"That just makes me… it makes me really sad."

"I get it," Ally said. "Seriously. But I've had years to come to terms with my childhood and everything I went through. I'm an adult now. And I'm happy. I'm good with my choices, and I'm good with the people I keep in my life. I've got some good friends, but you and Chase? I don't think a girl could ask for anything more than you and Chase. You're not just good, you're exceptional. You and Chase are my family."

Grace smiled wistfully. "Why does there have to be so much hurt in the world? I mean… I know things aren't all gumdrops and butterflies. I know that. But why is my mother an addict? Why did my father treat me the way he did? Why are your parents the way they are? And when you're a child, you see things so differently. Children ache for the love of a parent. Some people aren't as fortunate as we are. I feel like there are issues I struggle with on a daily basis with my anxiety and nervousness, but I also feel that I'm very lucky. I have a good job. I have you. I'm not on medication like my father, and I never resorted to drugs or alcohol. I think… I think I'm very blessed. And so are you."

"Yep," Ally agreed. "And I want to keep it that way. So… I'll call my folks, but it won't be a pretty conversation, I guarantee you."

"Well, I think maybe it's still good you're going to call."

Ally's brow furrowed. "I'm not so sure. But whatever. It is what it is."

Grace took a sip of her coffee, looked at Ally's belly, then said, "Have you thought about names?"

"Heck, yeah," Ally enthused.

"So have I. I know I don't have any say in the name department, but I still think of them all the same."

"I get it," Ally said. "It's hard not to think about it. Especially because this little girl's coming in just a couple of months."

"So?"

"So what?" Ally looked up through her lashes at Grace, a smirk on her face, her tongue slightly peeking out the side of her mouth to tap her upper lip.

"You're terrible."

"Don't I know it," Ally said. "I've got a few names I've been throwing around, but nothing that's stuck with me.

I've thought about Genevieve, and I've thought about Greta. Lately, the name Maggie has been on my mind, but I don't know. I'll figure it out."

"I know you will," Grace said. "But I think this is one of the exciting things, yes? A name can mean so much, and you have the power to give it to her. I know you'll choose well. You always do."

Grace and Ally finished at the coffee shop, deposited their dirty plates and mugs inside, then began walking back to Grace's house.

"No way! I totally forgot it was Breast Cancer Awareness Month," Ally said. She was looking intently at a decal stuck to a salon window. "Oh, you know what? I need a change. I've just decided. And what better way to change than to cut and dye my hair? And if I'm gonna dye my hair, then I might as well go pink. Bright pink. For Breast Cancer Awareness Month. Or maybe just the tips of my hair should be pink. I could go short again and make my hair look a mess, sticking up and all, and the tips will be pink. That would look great!"

Grace laughed. "Where did this come from?"

"From this window. And hey, we might as well, right? Spur-of-the-moment decisions can sometimes be the best decisions you make. And definitely the most fun too. What do you say?"

"You can do whatever you'd like," Grace replied. "I don't have anywhere to be."

"No," Ally said. "I mean, what do *you* think? Want to make a change?"

Grace's eyes widened. "You mean... me? Pink?" She shook her head. "No, I couldn't. That's really not like me at all."

"You don't have to go pink," Ally said. "You don't have

189

to dye your hair at all if you don't want to. But if you want to give it a try, just do the semipermanent stuff. That way, if you don't like it, it'll wash out in a month anyway, so no worries, right? And if you do like it, then awesome! Go red. Or blond. Or whatever. I'm definitely doing pink though. Or maybe bright orange for Halloween. No, no… pink. And you can cut your hair. Have you ever thought of that? It's pretty long, and it's nice and all, but a change is always good."

"I… hadn't really thought about it."

"That's because you're always wearing it under this hat of yours." Ally reached over and ran her finger along Grace's orange knitted hat. "Love the hat and all, and I know it's special to you because of your nana, but you've got nice hair. Show it off!"

"I don't know, Ally…"

"Okay. No pressure. Seriously. But you don't mind if I go in and see if they can take me?"

"I don't mind at all," Grace said.

Grace and Ally walked indoors, a bell chiming above to indicate their entrance.

A young woman with short jet-black hair was sweeping her station and looked over when she heard the ding. Three other women were currently working on other customers, smiling and chatting, looking through their large mirrors, brightened by the glow of several lights. "Can I help y'all?"

"Yep. I hope so," Ally said. "Do you take walk-ins?"

"We do."

"And do you have time right now?"

"For what, hon?"

"A cut and some pink. Bright pink."

"I can do that," the young woman said.

"Sweet," Ally replied as she moved farther into the room. "That's great news!"

The young woman looked over at Grace. "And what about you?"

"Me?"

"Yeah, you. You gettin' anything done?"

"Oh... I... I don't know," Grace replied.

"Don't know?"

Ally interjected. "She hasn't made up her mind just yet, but I'm working on her." She smirked at Grace.

"Barb's almost done, and I don't think she's got another appointment right away. She can take ya."

"Oh," Grace said. "Okay. I'll think about it."

"You can come with me," the young woman told Ally. "My name's Tory."

"Hi, Tory. I'm Ally."

While Ally followed Tory to her station, Grace sat down in a chair in the small waiting area and lifted a magazine. She opened to the first page and attempted to skim the contents but found she couldn't concentrate. She looked over at Ally, who already appeared to be in animated conversation with the stylist.

Leave it to Ally.

Twenty minutes passed.

Grace stood from her chair and slowly made her way to where Ally was comfortably situated in a different chair in the back corner of the room, her foiled head under some sort of semicircular contraption. When Grace stood in front of her, Ally looked up from the magazine she was reading.

"Hey," Ally said.

"Hi," Grace said softly. "I... okay."

Ally laughed. "Okay? Okay, what?"

"Okay, I think I'm ready for a change."

Ally's eyes shot up. "No way!" she exclaimed. "That's fantastic! You going pink too?"

Grace shook her head. "No. Absolutely not. I think that's way over my comfort level. But I'll get a haircut. And... maybe you can make a suggestion? I don't know what to do."

"Definitely," Ally replied. "A bob. Your hair is thin, so short is good. But not too short because I don't think that's you. Right under your chin, that's the way to go. But I'm sure Barb can help you out there. She'll know what to do."

"I sure do." Barb had apparently heard their conversation and had silently sidled up next to Grace.

"Oh," Grace said. "Okay."

"Don't you worry," Barb said. "You're in good hands."

"Barb is one of our best," Tory confirmed, her voice raised from her station. "You'll be walkin' out of here feelin' like a whole new you."

"I... don't think I want to feel like a whole new me." Grace was beginning to question her choice.

"Then you'll be walkin' out of here feelin' like everyday you, just lookin' great. Not that you don't already look great. But that's our job, you know. Makin' people feel like they can strut out that door and heads whip in their direction because we've done such a damn good job."

Now Grace was *really* reevaluating her decision.

Ally looked at Grace and laughed. "You look like you're gonna puke," she said. "Don't worry. It's just a haircut. Don't do a color. We can save that for another time. Baby steps, right?"

Grace swallowed. She couldn't remember the last time she had gotten more than just a trim, and even that had been over a year ago. "Okay."

"You ready?" Barb spoke beside her.

"I think so."

Barb chuckled. "Come with me."

"You've got this, Grace!" Ally shouted as Grace turned and began to follow Barb to her station.

Grace appreciated the encouragement, but she found her stomach was quaking. And then, as she took a deep breath in, she began to calm the slightest bit. It was just a haircut, after all. What was the big deal?

The attention. That was the big deal.

Grace hated attention. She loathed when people noticed something about her and mentioned it. It made her uncomfortable, nervous.

Barb extended her arm, and Grace sat in the indicated chair. "Let's see you without that hat," Barb said.

"Oh, yes. Of course." Grace scrambled to take her hat off and then rested it in her lap. She had no other place to put it—she had left her purse at home and just carried her credit card in the pocket of her jeans. She hadn't thought she and Ally were stopping anywhere other than the coffee shop that morning.

Barb placed a black apron over Grace's neck and then ran her fingers through her hair, flipping it to one side then the other. She tousled it then said, "Shampoo time. You can leave your hat on the counter." She motioned with her chin.

"Oh," Grace said. "Okay. Thank you."

After a shampoo—during which Barb massaged Grace's head, and Grace had to admit to herself that it felt rather good and even had the effect of calming her nerves a bit—Grace followed Barb back to the chair. Her long hair was combed out, and then Barb got to work. "Heard what your friend said. Just below the chin. That good with you?"

"Um... yes."

Barb laughed. "Don't sound convincing."

"This is just new for me," Grace explained.

"Your friend's got a good eye. You'll look good with chin-length hair."

"Okay."

Barb cut and cut, and just when Grace thought she was done, her hair was lifted and cut some more. "Layers," Barb explained when she saw the perplexed look on Grace's face.

"Oh, okay."

Barb eventually put her scissors down, tousled Grace's hair again, then reached for the dryer. The noise was loud in Grace's ears, and she closed her eyes because of the strong, hot air blowing into her face. When she opened them again, her hair was nearly dry.

"Finishing touches," Barb said. She put the blow-dryer back in its holder and filled her palm with product. She stood in front of Grace and ran her fingers through Grace's hair then stood back with a large grin. "Well?"

Grace's countenance was blank as she stared at her reflection in the mirror. She looked at the point at which her brunette hair met her forehead. She looked at the strands parted on the side. She watched as they gently flowed and wound into each other, and she stared at the tips as they touched her chin. Her eyes began to well.

"Ah, good," Barb said. "You weren't saying much. Thought you didn't like it."

"No," Grace said as she gently shook her head. "That's not it at all. It's… I've never looked like this before, but… I like it. Thank you very much." She stood from her chair and turned toward Ally, who was now at Tory's station. Ally had gotten her hair shampooed, and Tory was currently lifting wet strands, slicing through with her scissors. Clumps fell to the floor. When Grace approached,

Ally looked at her through the large mirror as she beamed and whistled.

"You look awesome!" she enthused. "Holy crap! Grace, you're hot!"

Grace felt herself flush.

"I'll go pay and then wait for you by the door."

"Deal. And seriously, Grace. You look fantastic."

As Grace made her way to Barb and the front counter, her eyes were trained on the floor, but her lips were lifted into a smile.

Grace paid and then sat down in the waiting area. She watched as Tory worked on Ally's hair. Even through the saturated strands, Grace could clearly see that the pink Ally had chosen was going to be bright indeed.

When Tory finished, Ally stood and made her way to the counter. Grace grinned when she saw her best friend, all smiles, with a hop to her gait. Her cut was reminiscent of when Grace had first met Ally on the park bench in the city just over a year ago, though it wasn't shorn on the sides. It was short, though. Very short, both at the sides and at the back. The top was longer and styled messily, and bright-pink strands shouted their appearance.

Grace couldn't help but think that Ally's hair now complemented her personality entirely.

Grace stood and met Ally at the counter. "I like it," she said.

"Me too," Ally said jubilantly. "Why didn't I do this sooner? And seriously, Grace. Your hair is gorgeous. I love it."

"Thank you," Grace said. "I have to admit that I really like it a lot."

"See?"

"See what?" Grace asked.

"It's all good." Ally smirked.

Ally finished paying, then Grace and Ally said goodbye to Tory and Barb. Ally flung her arm around Grace's shoulder, and the two women walked out the door and into the chilly autumn air.

~

The bell rang, indicating the start of lunch period for Grace's first-grade class. She walked them to the cafeteria, the handle of her lunch sack slung over her shoulder. She said her goodbyes with a smile and walked down the hallway to the staff room, where she expected to find her coworker and friend, Kathy. Kathy's class went to recess while Grace's students ate lunch, so the two women had been eating together, and Grace found she liked it very much.

Grace turned the knob on the door and walked through.

Kathy was reaching into a brown paper bag and looked up when Grace entered the room. Her eyes went wide. "Whoa," she said. "What did you do to your hair?"

"I… it's…"

"It looks so, so good!"

"Oh…" Grace looked down at the floor with a smile. "Thank you."

"What a big change, huh?"

"Yes. It really was." Grace walked toward Kathy and sat down in a chair beside her.

"Looks really good, Grace," a coworker named Brian said across the table.

"Thank you very much." Grace felt herself begin to blush, the slight warmth expanding to her ears.

"I should cut my hair," Kathy announced. "I need a change. It's always the same old thing. But I can never think of what to do."

"I really liked the woman I went to see," Grace said.

"Maybe next time you go, I could go with you," Kathy suggested.

Grace smiled. "I'd like that. I was... I was thinking of maybe getting some red highlights. Nothing bold; I don't think I'd like that. But just some subtle color, maybe?"

Kathy looked at Grace's hair and nodded. She brought her sandwich to her mouth and took a bite. "Yeah," she said. "You could pull off red. Go for it."

"You think so?"

"Totally."

"Yeah," Brian agreed. Grace hadn't expected him to have an opinion about something so purportedly mundane as her hair, so she felt flattered he'd joined the conversation.

Grace unzipped her lunch sack with a smile. She felt like she was about to soar.

CHAPTER 12

"*Happy* new year, Gracey!" Ally rushed at Grace over the threshold of her apartment door and crushed her in a hug, her distended stomach forcing her to lean far forward to complete the task.

"Thank you." Grace could hear music in the background and the chatter of gay voices.

"Hey, Grace." Chase sidled up next to Ally with a contented smile.

"You look happy," Grace observed.

"It's New Year's. Who's not happy on New Year's Eve?"

"I guess I don't know," Grace said.

"I didn't go crazy with the invites," Ally promised Grace. "Just a little over a handful of people are here, and they're all seriously nice. You'll love them, I promise. I'm so glad you could make it tonight."

"Of course," Grace replied. "I wouldn't want to be anywhere else."

"Aw," Ally crooned with a goofy smirk. "I love you too. Come in!"

Although Ally had promised that the additional friends in her apartment were friendly people, Grace still found herself rather uncomfortable upon initial intake. They all seemed to either know each other already or were at ease when meeting new people, unlike Grace herself. She was extremely relieved that both Ally and Chase were here tonight, and she vowed she would try her very best to be social.

"Want a drink?" Ally asked. "I put some out in the kitchen, so help yourself. And we've got tons of food. Chase cooked."

Grace turned to Chase. "You did?"

"Sure did," he confirmed. "I'm not the worst cook when I actually get around to doing it."

"Hmm… but should I trust it?" Grace teased.

Chase frowned. "Maybe not," he said then laughed heartily.

Grace smiled.

Yes, thank goodness both Ally and Chase were here, and even though she would have much preferred to spend New Year's Eve with just her two closest friends, she understood that they both had others that they enjoyed spending time with.

Grace inhaled a deep breath, slowly let it out, and then started for the kitchen. "Let me go see what you've made."

Yes, she'd try her very best.

A half an hour had passed, and Grace was in the living room, speaking with a girlfriend of Ally's, finding that she felt rather comfortable after all, thank goodness. It also helped tremendously that both Ally and Chase had broken into Grace's conversations several times to ensure all was well.

"Yeah, that's my husband over there," the woman said

as she pointed off in the distance. "We were so excited to find a sitter for tonight."

"How many children do you have?"

"Two boys."

Grace smiled. "I'm sure they have energy."

"They're just two and four, so yes! Do you have any children?"

Grace shook her head.

"Ally's due any day now, right?"

"Yes," Grace said. "Her due date is actually tomorrow."

"Oh, yes! Now I remember. How wonderful is that? Wouldn't it be great if her daughter was the first baby born in the new year?"

"It would not," Ally interrupted. "Too cliched." She brushed against Grace with her shoulder and leaned in to whisper conspiratorially in her ear. "My water just broke."

Grace gasped. "Are you… are you sure?"

"Positive."

"Oh my goodness! Oh, Ally… I… um…"

"I'm fine," Ally whispered. "I'm not feeling much of anything. I've been cramping all day, but I've been cramping for the past month, so I didn't think anything of it. But my water has definitely broken. It's trickling. I've got a damn hand towel in my underwear!"

Despite Grace's tension with the situation, she laughed out loud before lowering her voice again and whispering, "Do you want to head to the hospital now?"

Ally shook her head. "I just called the doctor. They said they don't need to see me until my contractions are more intense and closer together. And my water is just trickling, so it shouldn't be an issue. Let's just have fun."

"I see something is going on here," Ally's friend said

amicably as she pointed and moved her finger between Grace and Ally. "I'll leave you to it."

When she walked away, Grace discarded her whisper and spoke in a normal tone of voice. "Have fun? How can you think about having fun at a time like this?"

"The company is already over," Ally said with a smile. "And I'm feeling okay right now. My bag is already packed because I did that last week. There's nothing left to do. I just need to tell Chase."

"Is he coming to the hospital?"

"No, he'll stay here. I don't need Chase looking at my girl parts."

As Grace laughed, she felt the restraints against her heart begin to loosen. "You mean you wouldn't feel comfortable with him staring in between your legs?"

"Even my best friends don't need to be seeing me squeeze a baby out of my vagina! Well, except for you, obviously. I hear it can be gory, messy stuff. I hope you're ready." Ally smirked.

"I'm ready," Grace promised. She reached for Ally's hand. "I cannot believe you're going to have a baby."

"And on New Year's Eve or New Year's Day. How freaking annoying is that? Whenever I tell someone when this baby was born, that's all they'll gush about. Help me now…"

"I suppose your daughter will come when she wants to come."

"But she seriously had to begin her life now?"

"New year, new baby."

Ally smiled. "New year, new baby," she agreed. "My daughter."

"Your daughter!" Grace tightened her grasp on Ally's hand.

"Let me go tell Chase, then we can get back to the party. I promise I'll let you know when we need to leave."

"And you're sure you don't want to rest?"

"Even if I kicked all these people out of my apartment, do you seriously think I'd be able to rest right now?"

Grace laughed. "No. I suppose not."

"There's no damn way!"

Ally left to seek out Chase. Grace remained rooted to her spot in the living room, where smiling faces were abundant and good-spirited chatter reigned. But Grace could think of nothing but Ally and the impending birth of her daughter. She watched as Ally found Chase at the other end of the room, talking to a mutual friend. Ally leaned in, stood on her tiptoes, and whispered in Chase's ear. His brows lifted, his eyes widened, and the grasp he had on his plate became precarious. Chase fumbled as the plate slipped from his fingers, and although he managed to save it from crashing to the floor, the food that had been placed on top wasn't so lucky. Grace watched as Ally laughed and awkwardly bent down to pick the food up, depositing it back on Chase's plate. Chase brought the plate to an end table, and Grace could see even from her distance, that his hands were shaking. Chase grabbed Ally and crushed her in an embrace. Ally laughed and wrapped her arms around his waist before turning to speak with a friend who had just approached her.

How Ally had the ability to remain calm in such a situation eluded Grace.

Grace made her way to Chase who had abandoned his conversation with his and Ally's mutual friend and was walking toward the small kitchen. She caught up to him as he entered the space.

"Hi," she said.

Chase turned his head and glanced her way, though Grace could clearly see his mind was elsewhere.

"You've heard." It was a statement of fact, not a question, that came from Grace then.

Chase nodded, running his fingers through the hair at the front of his head. "Sure did. Ah, man…"

"I know," Grace agreed. "We both knew this could happen any moment, but now that it's actually here…"

"I know, right? I mean… shit!"

"And look at her," Grace said as she turned to find Ally through the open entryway. "She's acting like nothing's amiss."

"To her, nothing is amiss. That's Ally for you."

"Yes," Grace mused. "That's Ally. She really does live it up, doesn't she?"

"That she does," Chase said. "Always has."

"I wish I would have met her a long time ago. You too."

Chase cocked his head. "Nah," he dismissed. "She came into your life when she was supposed to."

Ally grinned. "That's something Ally would say."

"We do spend a lot of time together. She's rubbed off on me."

"Not a bad thing," Grace said.

"Nope. Not bad at all." He paused, his eyes transferring to Grace's hair. "I like the red."

Grace looked down at the floor and then slowly lifted her gaze. "Thank you. It's not permanent, but I… I like it, too."

Chase lifted his hand, his fingers slowly reaching toward a strand on Grace's cheek, then quickly retreated, placing both hands behind his back. "So… you're going to the hospital with her, yeah?"

"Yes," Grace confirmed. "I am."

"Lucky you were here tonight."

Grace looked back at Ally again. Her friend was smiling and joyful. She gesticulated wildly as she spoke to a group of friends. "Was it luck?" she whispered.

"What?"

Grace turned to Chase. "Never mind. It's nothing. I was just… thinking, that's all."

"Okay then," Chase said. "And hey, Grace?" He reached for Grace's hand, and her heart quickened when his skin touched hers.

"Yes?" She looked over at him, into his light brown eyes. A loose curl hung over his forehead.

"I'm glad you're going with Ally tonight. She talks about you all the time. I've known Ally for a while now, and she's got a lot of friends. Always has. But never like you."

Grace found herself blushing before she said, "And you."

"Yeah, we're great friends, but she's always telling me there's nothing like a friendship between two women."

"Does… does that hurt you?"

"Nope," he assured her. "Not at all. I get it. The way I am with my male friends is different than I am with Ally. She's my best friend, yeah, but it's still different. I'm not a woman. I don't know all of what you two talk about. But I respect it, your relationship. So no, it didn't hurt. *Doesn't* hurt. Our relationship hasn't changed." Chase's brow furrowed. "Actually, it has."

"What do you mean?"

"Now that I'm thinking out loud, I think it has changed. A bit. It's better."

"Better?" Grace was surprised.

"Yeah, better. Ally's always been a happy person, but since she's known you? She's even happier."

Grace chuckled. "I don't know how that's possible."

"I do," Chase said. He squeezed her hand.

Grace had to look away.

Chase released his hold and backed up a step. "Anyway, I'm glad you're going with her. She'll need you there. And as much as I love Ally, I don't want to be in that room."

Grace laughed. "I'm glad I'm going to be there as well. This is all so amazing to me, Chase. Just amazing. I… I love Ally."

Chase nodded slightly. "I know."

An hour and a half later, Grace watched as Ally stood on her sofa and clapped her hands. "Listen up, everyone!" she shouted.

The chatter in the room dissipated until the last sound floated into the air and all eyes were on Ally. "I just want to wish you all a happy new year!"

Cheers abounded from the partygoers, and clapping ensued.

"But," Ally added. "This is it for me. Chase will be here, so stay and have a great time. But I'm out. I'm in labor!"

Gasps sounded, and murmuring began. Guests looked to one another, expressions unmistakably surprised.

"I'm starting to really feel it now, so it's time," Ally explained. "Happy new year, everyone!"

Drinks were lifted into the air, and choruses of "Happy new year" were spoken. Ally hobbled down from the sofa, Chase offering his hand to help guide her way since she couldn't see her feet with her distended belly.

One last hug to Chase, a few goodbyes to friends, and

Ally made her way to her bedroom, where she grabbed her hospital overnight bag and purse, and she and Grace left the apartment, jackets and hats on to stave off the frigid late-night winter air.

"This is it," Grace said as she opened the front door to the building.

"That's right," Ally agreed. "This is freaking it!"

By the time they arrived outside the hospital, Ally was hunched over, hands on Grace's shoulders, so she could attempt to breathe through an intense contraction. They had been coming on stronger and stronger, with little time in between each one.

"I think we should have left sooner," Grace said.

"I'm…. ugh… I'm okay." Ally righted herself, and they walked through the front door and to the reception area, where Ally checked in. An orderly with a wheelchair arrived moments later and wheeled Ally to the elevator and to the maternity ward.

Minutes passed in which Ally was asked several questions about her progress, obliged to sign paperwork, and given a maternity gown to change into. Grace helped her into it since Ally had a contraction just as she was slipping her pants down her legs.

Once in bed, Ally was hooked up to a monitor and given an IV. Eventually, the OB-GYN on call strode into the room and introduced herself, asking Ally some of the same questions she had answered upon arrival and checking her dilation.

"Wow, Ally," the doctor said. "You weren't kidding. You're almost there."

"This hurts like a son of a…" Ally's face scrunched, and she clenched her teeth. Grace rushed to her side and offered her hand, which Ally willingly took and squeezed.

"Holy shit, Gracey. This is like nothing I've ever felt before."

The OB-GYN smiled. "It's not pleasant, but it is normal. It's not too late for some meds or an epidural. Let me know if you want either. If you want an epidural, you should think of saying so soon though. The anesthesiologist is swamped tonight."

"Okay, I..." Ally's head rolled back onto the pillow as another contraction coursed within.

Grace looked at the obstetrician. "They're really close together. She's having..." She turned to Ally, whose eyes were closed. "She's having trouble."

"From what I see, there are no complications. This is all just part of the birthing process," the OB-GYN said.

"Oh, goodness gracious," Grace replied.

The doctor smiled. "I have another patient to check up on, but it won't be long, Ally. You let the nurse know if you need any meds for the pain."

Ally merely nodded, pink strands of hair caked in sweat and plastered to her forehead. She looked at Grace. "Holy crap, Grace."

"I know," Grace swept a strand of Ally's hair to the side. "I've never watched a birth before. All I know is from TV, which sounds ridiculous out loud. I'm so sorry you're feeling this way."

"It's all good," Ally said. She lay back on the bed in its seated position, closed her eyes, and let her shoulders fall forward. She rested her palms on her swollen belly.

"Do you... do you think you need an epidural or something?"

Ally shook her head almost imperceptibly. "She said I'm almost there. I just... I just want this to be over with."

"Maybe—"

Ally shook her head again and then opened her eyes, looking directly at Grace, and although the smile she offered was strained, and her features denoted her exhaustion, Ally's eyes were clear and spoke volumes. She was good. She had this.

Her daughter was almost there.

The clock turned; the minutes passed. New Year's Eve melded into the first day of an entirely new year.

And then it was time for Ally to push.

With sweat dripping down her forehead, Ally lifted her legs to her chest and bore down with all her might. Grace stood at her side, there if Ally needed anything at all. Anything!

A half an hour passed them by, and Grace found her eyes begin to water with unshed tears. How much longer was her friend to endure this? How much longer would she have to push, have to feel the pain?

And just as Grace turned from Ally to the obstetrician between her bare legs, her mouth open and ready to utter her questions, the doctor called out, "I see a head!"

Ally appeared too exhausted to speak, but Grace saw the glimmer of a smile.

Grace walked forward. Slowly. One small step then two. She peeked over Ally's leg, and there, right beside her, was a mass of wet, dark hair.

The tears that had been threatening to let loose cascaded down Grace's cheeks. She didn't bother to wipe them away, for others would soon follow.

Grace looked from the baby's head to her best friend sitting in the maternity bed, her hands still wrapped intently over her knees, and they exchanged a look. A look that needed no words.

Awe. Adoration. Reverence.

Love.

"Now's the time," the obstetrician announced to Ally. "Give it all you've got."

Ally leaned forward, clutching her knees until her knuckles shone white.

And then Grace watched, tears streaming down her face, as Ally's daughter was brought into the world. She couldn't contain her emotions. Her shoulders were shaking, her tears so plentiful that she was continuously blinking heavily so that she could view the miracle before her.

Grace watched as the obstetrician cut the umbilical cord and placed the newborn in Ally's waiting arms. She saw the smile on Ally's face, the tears running down her cheeks. Tears from a woman that Grace had never before seen cry.

And then Ally looked at her, at Grace. "My daughter," she said, merely above a whisper.

Grace's nose scrunched and her lips quivered as a fresh set of tears formed in her red eyes. She nodded. "Your daughter."

The next half hour was a whirlwind to Grace. Ally had what felt like mere moments with her daughter before the baby was then whisked to the side of the room, where she was weighed and measured and cleaned up. She was wrapped in a blanket, and a security device was attached to her ankle. Then she was handed back to Ally, who eagerly scooped up her diminutive body and placed her daughter on her chest.

The staff eventually exited the room, and Grace and Ally were left alone with the baby.

"Congratulations doesn't seem like a strong enough word right now," Grace said with a smile.

"But I'll take it." Ally paused, looking down at her

daughter's small features. "Can you believe it, Gracey? I'm a mom."

"I can believe it."

"This changes everything."

Grace nodded. "We knew it would."

"Thank you for being here with me."

"Ally, I honestly wouldn't have wanted to be anywhere else. Anywhere! I can't believe... that was just amazing, Ally. Amazing. And you were like a superhero."

"I wouldn't go that far." Ally laughed.

"I would," Grace said with a smile. "So... we've talked about it a little bit, but I don't think you decided what you'd like to name her."

Ally looked from Grace to her sleeping daughter. "I know now. I knew the moment I saw her face."

Grace gave Ally a moment to impart the news, and when she didn't, she anxiously asked, "So? Are you going to tell me?"

Ally laughed. "Nope. I'm gonna make you stand there and guess."

"You're not being fair! Not okay, Ally."

Ally's laugh intensified. "I'm just kidding, of course." She looked back at her daughter and then said, "Her name is Evangeline."

"Oh, that's really pretty," Grace said. "And it's not one we had talked about."

"No, it's not. But... do you know what your name means? What Grace means?"

"No," Grace admitted. "I've never really thought about it."

"I looked it up. It means charm or goodness or generosity, and I know you don't have a good relationship with your parents, but they did something right when they named you

Grace, because that's exactly what you are. You are all good. So it got me thinking: what other name means good? And then I found Evangeline. It might be a bit biblical, I don't know, but whatever. What caught my attention was its meaning. Evangeline means good news or messenger of good news. So it's been in the back of my head since I heard it. Then, when I saw this little girl here, I just knew. Evangeline it was. She *is*. She's kind of named after you in a way. I want my daughter to be like you."

"I... I..." Grace choked. "But you're amazing, Ally. If your daughter turns out to be even a little bit like you, then we are all going to be very lucky."

"I know I'm a good person, but..." Ally looked directly at Grace. "I'm thinking about you right now, Gracey. If my daughter has you in her life, then she's guaranteed to have an awesome role model. And if she's anything like *you*, then, well... goodness knows we all need more Graces in the world. Jesus, Gracey, you're blubbering!"

Grace laughed through her tears. Eventually, she was able to calm down enough to look at Ally's beautiful new daughter and say, "Welcome to the world, Evangeline."

CHAPTER 13

$\mathcal{G}$race blew into her party blower, the length of it uncurling and emitting a sound reminiscent of an elephant's trumpet. "Happy birthday, Evangeline!" she cried.

Much to her delight, Ally had told Grace that she'd prefer her daughter's first birthday celebration be with just close friends. This included Grace and Chase, as well as two women that Ally had met through a mommy-and-me class she attended a couple of times a month on the weekends when she wasn't working. Henrietta and Chloe were these women's children, and they were both the same age as Evangeline, give or take a couple of months.

Grace had been quite surprised when Ally had told her she'd found this class online about six months ago and was interested in checking it out. Sure, Grace had an outgoing personality, and yes, she harmonized well with other people, but even when Evangeline was six months old, Grace was still awed by the notion of Ally as a mother. And yet, the mommy-and-me class had proven fruitful in Ally's further transition to motherhood, and it had extended her circle of friends, allowing Ally to bond with other mothers her age, which Grace was thankful for. However much she'd like to understand what Ally was going through with Evangeline, she knew she lacked the ability to fully comprehend everything.

After all, she wasn't a mother herself. She hadn't been the one to nurse Evangeline when she was a week old and crying hysterically at one o'clock in the morning. It wasn't Grace that had rushed to the hospital with Evangeline one night when the baby wouldn't stop crying, just to be told that she was colicky, and Ally would have to wait it out, that there was no underlying explanation for her daughter's excessive fussiness. And although Grace had been frequently present, it wasn't she that picked up her daughter from daycare every day after work, just to have the smiling child crawl over to her mother with her chubby, padded legs, sit back on her heels, and extend her arms, asking to be picked up.

Her mother.

For that was what Ally was.

She was Evangeline's mother.

And nobody could top that.

But other mothers could certainly understand more than Grace could what motherhood entailed and what Ally was experiencing. Grace was pleased they were here at Evangeline's birthday party right now, and Grace thought it was adorable the way Evangeline poked Henrietta and Chloe, the way she crawled toward them, threw her arms around their midsections, and mistakenly propelled them to the floor.

And their giggles. Oh, their giggles. The way Evangeline's chubby cheeks would lift beneath her blue eyes, her wet lips a wide O, her gummy smile one that shot explosions through Grace's heart. She had four teeth total: two on the top and two on the bottom—small, white, and square.

To Grace, Evangeline was perfect. The amount of love she bore for this miniature one-year-old girl was immense, but it felt different, too, which was unexpected for Grace. Her love for Evangeline was different from her love for herself, different from her love for Ally. This love was… no. No, she couldn't explain it even if she tried. This love made her feel protective. This love made her feel… fierce.

When Grace had thought about family prior to meeting the three most important people in her life, she never thought that her family would be this unconventional. But a family they were.

Grace, Ally, Chase, and Evangeline.

That was undisputed.

And Grace didn't believe she could be any happier than she was right now.

"Happy, happy birthday, Evangeline!" she shouted again, surprising even herself with her enthusiasm.

Ally turned to her and beamed. With her face lit up, she looked like—at any moment—she'd explode from love and appreciation.

"Can you believe it?" Ally asked.

"I most definitely cannot," Grace replied. "One year old today. Who would have thought?"

"Definitely not me. This last year has been a whirlwind. I didn't know what to expect being a mom and all, but I guess I didn't expect this. All of it. This year has seriously been crazy and has flipped my world upside down, but man —it's been awesome, hasn't it?"

Grace smiled brightly. "It sure has."

Grace looked at Ally's daughter sitting in her high chair, her gummy smile on display. A droplet of drool lined her lower lip as her tongue poked through the corner of her mouth to touch the lip above—a movement that Ally often made too. Evangeline's hair hadn't changed much in color since Grace had first seen her in the birthing room of the hospital, still a medium-hued brown, but it had grown. A lot. While Henrietta's head was nearly bald and Chloe's scalp was covered in a downy fuzz, Evangeline had a mass of thick tufts that covered her ears and tickled the back of her neck. Evangeline was a cuddler, and each time she placed her head on Grace's chest—thumb in mouth—Grace found herself brushing those luscious strands off Evangeline's forehead almost instinctively. And each time the tip of her finger grazed the girl's skin, Grace was reminded that her own mother had fled, that she hadn't seen her since she was a girl herself.

Grace knew that drug addiction was a disease, and she was convinced that without that addiction consuming her mother's life, she could have been loving, could have held the ability to calm, to soothe, to simply be there when Grace was growing up. Grace had had years to come to terms with her mother's absence, but even so, when she held Evangeline in her arms, she couldn't imagine leaving the precious, innocent little girl. She couldn't envision living her life without her, without Ally. Without Chase.

And not for the first time, Grace was full of gratitude that she had never picked up a needle, never inserted it into her vein.

Didn't follow in her mother's footsteps.

She'd look down at Evangeline as the beautiful girl nestled against her chest, and these thoughts, these memories, would flood her, overwhelming her with their insistence.

Ally walked to the kitchen counter, returning a moment later with a small cake, the pink frosting vibrant, the amount generous.

"Have some frosting with that cake," Henrietta's mother joked.

"The frosting's the best part," Ally said. "But her poops are going to be pink tomorrow." She laughed heartily.

"I bet they will," her friend said with a chuckle. "Those will make for some interesting diaper changes."

Ally shrugged her shoulders. "It's the weekend. I'll bug Chase to change Evangeline's diaper. Or maybe Grace will be over. She's a diaper-changing pro."

Grace laughed. "Is that what I am? I didn't realize you thought so highly of me, Ally."

"And if they're pink, I'm outta here," Chase chimed in. "A buddy of mine wanted to meet up for a beer, anyway."

"Oh, I see how it is," Ally said. "You're here for all the cuddles and smiles and when she tries to say your name— you know you love that, yeah? But right when I need you the most, you bail on me."

"I don't think a diaper change is when you need me the most," Chase said with a sly grin.

"Oh," Ally cocked her head and smiled up at Chase, batting her eyelashes playfully. "I always need you, Chasey."

"Ugh," Chase scoffed. "Do not call me 'Chasey.' You know how much I hate it."

"And that's why I do it."

"Incorrigible," Chase said.

"I know I am," Ally replied. "And you love me."

"You're lucky I do."

Ally lifted her chin and kissed Chase on the cheek before turning to a very eager Evangeline in her high chair. She placed the small cake on the tray. "Go at it, baby!" Ally said enthusiastically. "It's your first taste of cake. Oh! Where's my phone? I need to get pictures."

Grace held up her cell. "I'm on that."

"You're the best," Ally said. "Thanks a bunch." And then Ally began to sing. "Happy birthday to you…"

Grace joined in the chorus. "Happy birthday to you. Happy birthday, dear Evangeline, happy birthday to you!"

Evangeline clapped her chubby little hands together and then flung them out to the sides, looking at the cake on her tray, not knowing what it was she was supposed to do with it, which made the partygoers laugh and grin.

"You eat it, baby," Ally said. "Yum!"

"She's looking at it all funny," Grace said. "Hasn't she ever seen a cake before?"

"Nope."

"Maybe show her she can eat it?" Grace laughed. "Look at the expression on her face."

Ally dipped her finger in the pink frosting and brought it to her mouth. She licked it off. "See, E? You eat it. Seriously yums!"

"Yums." Grace laughed. "The words that you've been using this past year…"

"I know," Ally cringed. "I even annoy myself."

Evangeline looked up at her mother and then to the other adults surrounding her high chair. She glanced at both Henrietta and Chloe, who were propped on their mothers' hips. Then she looked back at the cake on the tray in front of her. She slowly brought her hand to the top of the cake, and then, with surprising speed, she smashed her hand into the cake, smearing pink frosting all along the tray.

Evangeline began to laugh hysterically, her baby enthusiasm proving infectious as the adults laughed in turn. Evangeline pressed her fingers into the cake—vanilla—and then brought her hand to her lips, where she proceeded to stuff a large portion of the contents into her mouth. Her eyes widened, and she bounced up and down in her high chair, the motion eliciting even more laughter from the adults in the room.

Before Evangeline had chewed and swallowed her first mouthful, she plonked both of her hands into the cake, large chunks crumbling to the tray, and stuffed more into her mouth.

"Slow down." Ally laughed. "You're gonna choke, E!"

"She knows a good thing when she tastes it," Grace said.

"Looks like she does. Her next cake will have to be baked by you, yeah? If you make a cake like the one you made me when we found out Evangeline was going to be a girl... yep, it'll ruin her appetite for all those veggies I've been trying to get her to eat."

Evangeline's first birthday progressed splendidly. She ate a good portion of her cake before she told her mother she was done, her adorable tiny voice echoing in Grace's ears. Ally unbuckled Evangeline from her high chair and brought her to the kitchen sink, where she stripped her daughter down to her diaper, turned the faucet on, and washed her off. When Ally set Evangeline onto the floor, Evangeline crawled off and into the living room, where she found a basket of her toys and began to play. Henrietta and Chloe were both brought to the floor beside Evangeline, and the three girls explored the basket's contents individually.

Ally brewed some peppermint coffee, festive for the new

year, and the adults soon found themselves on the sofa and chairs, enjoying the warm contents in mugs cradled within their hands, occasionally reaching over to pick at platters of snacks on the coffee table. The children played on the floor with Evangeline's toys. Smiles flourished, and the adults reveled in one another's company.

When Henrietta and Chloe were whisked away by their mothers to head home, Grace and Chase remained to help Ally clean up after the party. Ally put Evangeline down for an afternoon nap, and the friends got to work. Once done, Chase announced that he was leaving to meet up with a friend. Grace and Ally took advantage of their time alone together and sat on the living room couch.

"Oh, you know what we need?" Ally asked as soon as her bottom hit the cushion.

"What's that?"

"A glass of wine," Ally said. "Want one?"

"Actually, yes," Grace replied. "I think that would be nice."

"Red, white?" Ally smoothed down the material of her jeans.

"Either is fine with me."

"You've got it." Ally left the room, soon returning with two full glasses of wine, the burgundy liquid vibrant to Grace's eyes and aromatic when she accepted the glass with her fingers and brought the rim to her nose.

"I think this is going to hit a spot," Grace said.

"Yep," Ally agreed as she plopped back down on the couch, careful not to spill. She tucked her bare feet under her thighs. "Cheers." She held her glass out to Grace.

"Cheers," Grace said before bringing her glass to gently clink against her best friend's.

Grace took a sip of her wine, smacked her lips with

pleasure, then lowered it to her lap. "That was amazing, Ally."

"What was?" Ally brought the wine to her lips and took a large, satisfying gulp.

"The party."

"Oh, yeah. Wasn't it great? I know Evangeline won't remember anything about this day, but how could I not have a party for her?"

Grace nodded. "She might not remember the day, but she'll have the photos to look back on, and I think those are things that she'll really appreciate when she's older."

"When she's our age."

"And maybe has a family of her own," Grace added.

"A family like ours, I hope. One that's super awesome."

Grace laughed. "I think we are kind of awesome." She paused for a moment and then said, "Ally?"

"Yep?" Ally took another gulp of wine, her back resting against the high cushion, her body relaxed.

"I... I made something for Evangeline. And for you."

Ally lifted her eyes with anticipation. "You did, huh?"

"Yes. I... well, here." Grace stood from the couch, deposited her wine glass on the coffee table, and walked toward the door, where she had left her coat and a backpack. She lifted a scrapbook into her arms and cradled it against her chest before returning to Ally. When she sat, she relaxed her arms and transferred the book to Ally's lap.

Ally leaned forward and placed her glass on the coffee table next to Grace's then ran her palm along the front of the book. A photo was at its center, square, with serrated edges: a photo of a newborn Evangeline, a thin hat on her head that she had been given at the hospital, her body wrapped in the blanket Ally had brought with her to the maternity room. Evangeline's eyes were closed, her chin resting against the blanket on her chest. Her nose was small, her lips too. When Grace closed her eyes, she could remember the exact moment she had taken this photo, Evangeline in her mother's arms, and although the picture didn't show Ally, she had been looking adoringly at her newborn daughter.

Yes, Grace remembered it well.

Above the photo of the angelic newborn was one word: a name.

Evangeline.

"How… when did you do this?" Ally asked. She slowly lifted her head to look at Grace.

"I…" Grace found herself blushing slightly, though she didn't comprehend why. "I've been working on it since I came home from the hospital, since you left with Evangeline."

"You… no freaking way. You've been working on this for a full year now?"

Grace nodded, her movement nearly indiscernible, while Ally lifted the thick cover of the scrapbook to the first page, where Grace had written, *To Evangeline. You are loved.*

Ally's smile was awe-filled as she turned from page to page, exploring the contents of the book: Evangeline as an infant and one of Evangeline's first grins. There were photos of Evangeline reaching for her mobile and a picture of her sucking on a toe. A photo of Evangeline naked in the bathtub, the water bubbly, Evangeline's face set into a look of utter shock, made Ally laugh. "She's obviously splashing herself here. Her face is all wet."

"Yes," Grace said. "And look at her mouth. She doesn't have any idea how it happened to her, does she?"

"Nope." Ally chuckled as she turned to the next page.

221

"The only thing missing are pictures from today," Grace said. "I'd like to add those if that's okay."

"Of course it's okay," Ally said. She closed the book and reverently caressed the cover. "I can't believe you did this. It must have taken you so much time."

Grace shook her head. "Not really. Well, okay, yes. But it made me really happy doing it."

"See? That's why you're so awesome," Ally said.

Grace laughed. "Because I made a scrapbook?"

"Because you even *thought* about making a scrapbook in the first place," Ally clarified. She looked Grace directly in the eye. "I think you are an incredible person, Grace Clarke. And don't let anyone tell you otherwise."

"I..."

"Nope." Ally shook her head. "I know what you're going to say. You have a mom that bailed, a dad that's an ass. You had a husband that cheated on you. And none of that, none of it, is your fault. None of it. They didn't do that shit because of who you are, Grace. They did it because of who *they* are. And you've come out of it all an amazing person. Seriously. This right here," Ally pointed to the scrapbook resting in her lap. "This is who you are. A person that thinks of other people. A woman who is kind and considerate. You're pure and innocent, words I wouldn't use to describe myself—"

"I sometimes wish I could be more like you, though," Grace interjected, speaking words that had been spoken before. "I think I've gotten better. I'm not as anxious, but things still scare me. All the time. *Life* scares me."

"Life should be the last thing to scare you," Ally said. "Life is what brought us together. Life is something to hold on to, to embrace. Life is what gave us Evangeline. And I need you, Grace. More than you know. I might have a lot of friends, I might be an outgoing person, but I need you. Friendships come and go, but it's the extraordinary ones that last a lifetime. So no, don't be scared of life, because without it, I wouldn't have you. We wouldn't have each other."

Grace felt her chest begin to constrict, her shoulders start to quiver. A single tear found its way down her cheek and then another, until she was weeping freely, a smile on her face.

"Now, I'm not gonna cry," Ally said. "Because that's not me. But you do you, Grace. It's just one more thing I love about you."

"That I cry?" Grace chuckled through her tears. She attempted to wipe them away with the tips of her fingers, but they were so plentiful that she eventually gave up entirely and let them flow freely.

"Yep," Ally said with a smile.

Grace inhaled deeply several times, her tears eventually diminishing in volume. "Ally, I need to tell you something."

"What's up?"

"I need to thank you."

"Thank me for what?"

"For allowing me to be who I am. For not judging me. For not dismissing me when I'm nervous about something but encouraging me to come out of my shell all the same. But not... not in a pushy sort of way. I don't even know if I'm making sense. I think I'm just trying to say that I don't think I knew what I was missing until I met you."

"Missing?"

"Love," Grace said as she took Ally's hand. "I didn't truly know what love was until I met you. Friend love. Real love. Love for another person love." Grace paused and then continued, "I don't think I even knew what true love was with Gary. I know I loved him. I loved him very much, but I've come to question if he truly ever loved me or if he just went through the motions by rote. I don't know... I don't know about Gary.

"But I do know that since I've met you, I've been really happy. Because I know what love is now. And I know that real, pure love doesn't have to be romantic because that's not what we have. But love... love has to be caring and kind, and... it has to be free. Free to let one be who they are, no holding back. Free to speak, free to show affection, free to... just be. So yes. That is why I have to thank you. Because you have shown me this. You have filled this missing piece of my life that I didn't truly know I was lacking.

"I'm happy, Ally. I'm so very happy. I'm happy in my wonderful friendship with you. I'm happy with Chase in my life. And I'm so happy with Evangeline. She's brought us more love, more laughter. And I thank you so much for allowing me to be such a big part of her life this past year."

"Seriously, Grace, I wouldn't have it any other way. I should be thanking you for actually wanting to be such a big part of her life. My daughter is one lucky girl, there's truth to that for sure. And Grace?"

Grace looked over at Ally as Ally squeezed her hand. "I love you too. Very much. When you say what we have is real, well, yep. It is. You say you've never had a friend like me, but I'm here to tell you that these feelings are mutual. I think that's why we're so good together. I think that's why our friendship is so freaking amazing, yeah? It's not one-sided. We're both seriously lucky women."

"We really are," Grace said. She leaned over and embraced Ally with gratification.

And she smiled widely as Ally embraced her right back.

CHAPTER 14

$\mathcal{T}$he winter progressed. Snowstorms flourished in New England, and the white substance blanketed the ground in Grace's small front yard. She, Ally, and Chase took Evangeline for her first sledding experience, and the young girl enjoyed herself so much that the three friends set aside time to take her on several other occasions throughout those frigid months. Chase would watch Evangeline some Saturday mornings, brushing aside thanks from Ally, dismissing her demonstrations with the statement that he wasn't much of a morning person, so he'd already be home anyway. Grace and Ally took advantage of these opportunities to meet for coffee at their favorite coffee house down the street from Grace's townhouse, where conversation never lacked and smiles never ceased. Ally continued with her mommy-and-me classes, and Grace, Ally, and Chase found increased comfort spending time together in their own homes.

The snow began to melt, icicles dripped from tree

branches, and the drains along the sides of the roads swelled with running water.

Winter made way for spring, the icicles gone. Flower buds displayed their beauty, fresh renewal revealed.

Grace awoke on a chilly early April weekend morning, pushed the blankets from her body, and standing to stretch. She had made plans with her co-worker, Kathy, that would take place in just a couple of hours, so Ally had taken advantage of Chase's being home and his offer to watch Evangeline so she could take her bike out for a long-awaited ride. Last summer, Ally had purchased a trailer to attach to the back of her bike so she could take Evangeline along with her and adorned it with a pink unicorn flag, just as she had joked about when she had first found out she was pregnant.

Grace was pleased that Chase would be watching Evangeline that morning. Ally deserved some time alone, and this way, she could go unhindered, without the necessity of altering her speeds. When Evangeline was with her, Ally often took things slowly, stealing glances behind her to ensure all was well and that her daughter remained entertained. She didn't ride in the winter months, but although the sides of the road were still laden with dirtied snow, the streets themselves were bare now. Grace knew Ally was eager to head out once again.

Grace walked to the kitchen to prepare her morning coffee and thought about Ally, thought about her dear friend lifting her face to the sun in the sky, feeling the rays on her exposed skin, soaking in the crisp morning air. She thought about the thrill Ally would receive when she sped down hills—something she didn't do with Evangeline in tow—and it made Grace smile that Ally would feel such exhilaration.

This was going to be a wonderful morning for her friend.

Grace would spend time with Kathy, and then she, Ally, and Chase had dinner plans.

A half an hour before she was set to meet Kathy, Grace was sitting on her couch, her morning coffee long finished, reading her latest novel with Ennio Morricone's melodic classical compilations playing in the background, when she heard the unmistakable sound of a vehicle pull up in front of her house. Perhaps it was a delivery worker, though she wasn't expecting any packages to arrive today. She dismissed the thought and went back to her book. A minute later, a knock sounded on the door, slight and hesitant.

Grace furrowed her brow, closed her book, and rested it on the end table beside her empty mug. She stood and walked toward the door, turning the cold knob in her hand. Chase stood in front of her, Evangeline propped up on his hip, and the sight of him stalled Grace's breath.

Chase's hair was disheveled, his eyes red, watery, and unfocused. Grace stepped forward slowly and grasped the sleeve of his shirt. Chase's face contorted, and Evangeline began to slip from his grasp. Grace swept in and caught Evangeline, bringing the fifteen-month-old to the living room floor and handing her a chunky wooden puzzle from a small shelf that housed various toys for Evangeline's visits. Evangeline busied herself with the puzzle, and Grace guided Chase to the sofa. Eventually, she looked at his haggard appearance and whispered, "What is it?"

Chase didn't utter a word, merely turned to look at Grace with tormented eyes. When he spoke moments later, his voice was hoarse, drained. "She's gone."

Grace began to tremble, not allowing herself to believe

what her mind was screaming to be the truth. "What... what do you mean?"

"She's gone, Grace. She was..." His voice broke. "She was out on her bike... car... didn't stop... hit her, sped away..."

"What? Chase, you're not making any sense." Grace's entire body was shaking. She went to reach for Chase then brought her hand back. She clutched the material of her jeans, attempting to calm the trembling in her hands, but to no avail. The trembling remained, intensified. Her chin quivered, her lips parted.

"Ally was hit by a car when she was on her bike. She left early this morning. She was hit, and the car took off."

"What... I don't understand."

"People saw it. There were witnesses. I don't know if anyone got the license plate number, but someone went to help. It was... it was too late. The ambulance got there and..." Chase's voice cracked. "She was dead. I got a phone call... came right here. I need to... need to go to the hospital."

Chase sat on the couch in a daze, his eyes glazed over.

Grace's reaction was raw. She looked from Chase to Evangeline, and when she turned back to Chase, the look he gave her was unmistakable. His heart was breaking.

Grace began to sob. Louder and louder, more intensely as the seconds passed, until she and Chase were clutching each other furiously, grabbing onto shirts, arms, shoulders, backs. Grace's tears wet Chase's collar. His own tears emerged fully, streaking his skin. Saliva dripped from Grace's lips as she moaned, the pain she felt within coursing to the surface, unhindered, rampant.

Grace's face was buried in Chase's chest when she felt Evangeline's little hands on her thighs. She dared a look and turned her head ever so slightly. Evangeline was looking up at her, her tiny lips trembling, her eyes inquisitive, concerned. "You 'kay?" she asked.

Grace wiped tears from her cheeks, from her chin. She swept under her nose and rubbed her fingers on her jeans, then she lifted Evangeline into her arms and cradled her, gently stroking the girl's hair off her forehead and rocking her back and forth. Evangeline began to cry. Though Grace was sure Evangeline didn't understand what had occurred that very morning, though she couldn't comprehend that her mother was gone, Grace knew Ally's daughter possessed the ability of the young to intuit emotions, and her little mind was telling her that something was gravely amiss.

Chase leaned over and kissed Evangeline on the forehead. He wiped her tears away. He took a deep breath then wrapped his arms around Grace, cocooning Evangeline between them.

While Evangeline wept, Grace and Chase looked into each other's eyes. No words were spoken, for words were not needed. They understood. In their arms, they comforted a little girl who had just lost her mother, a woman who had been an integral part of all of their existences, a woman who was loved dearly. Neither of them knew how their lives would continue to evolve without her vibrant, vigorous presence.

Evangeline's mother was gone.

Grace and Chase had lost their best friend.

And now they were alone.

"How is that possible?" Grace asked the following weekend when Chase and she were in a lawyer's office, a lawyer who

Ally had evidently hired after she had given birth to Evangeline and who had helped her develop a living will.

"I knew Ally did this," Chase explained, "but I didn't say anything because she asked me not to. Plus, I never, not in a million years, ever thought we'd be here right now. I never thought Ally would die so young. Why would I? I didn't think we'd ever be sitting here talking about her will, talking about Evangeline. I thought we'd all be together for years. I thought Evangeline would graduate high school, go off to college, start a family of her own before Ally died."

Grace shook her head. "I just don't understand it. Why would she do this?"

"Because she trusted you," Chase said. "With her life."

"Evangeline."

Chase nodded. "Was her life."

"But how can I be her guardian? How can *we* be her guardians together?"

"I don't know," Chase replied. "All I know is that this is what Ally wanted, and she knew she had to get it down in writing. Her folks are shit; they haven't even met Evangeline. They won't ever fight for custody, I can assure you, but Ally knew she had to make it legal."

"I just… how are we going to do it? I don't even understand the logistics of it all."

"I don't know," Chase repeated. "But we'll figure it out. Ally trusted us. We need to trust ourselves. I guess it's kind of like how Ally used to say, 'Let it be. It's all good.'"

"Yes," Grace said. "But… I… I don't know if I can do this, Chase."

"Of course you can do this," Chase said. "Ally had faith in you, in us. And I think she knew that we'd be the best people to raise her daughter if she wasn't here to do it, and now look at us. Here we are. We've got this. Unless…"

"Unless?"

"Do you not want Evangeline?"

Grace's eyebrows shot up. "No!" she exclaimed. "That's not it at all. I can't imagine not being in Evangeline's life or her not being in mine. I just… I'm not Ally, Chase. She was such an excellent mother. She got out there, she connected. She would have been the one to fight for Evangeline if there was a bully in kindergarten. She'd be the type of person who would tell another kid that they were being a jerk if she saw them on the playground pushing another child around. I'm not like that. I don't know if I can do that. I don't know… I don't know if I'm the best person for Evangeline."

"You are," Chase said with conviction and finality. "Ally got this one right. We can do this together. I don't know how, what with two different places to live and all, but we'll figure it out. Evangeline is young. She'll take this better than we will, I bet. She'll help us figure this out."

Grace nodded. "Perhaps you're right."

"I know I'm right." Chase paused and then offered a self-deprecating smile. "Let's hope I'm right."

"So you're nervous too?"

"That's an understatement," Chase said. "I'm terrified."

Grace sighed. "That actually makes me feel better."

"Glad I could help," Chase said. "But really, Grace, would we want this to happen any other way?"

Grace shook her head vigorously. "Absolutely not. Evangeline needs to be with us. And honestly, I need *her*."

"So do I." Chase's voice was soft. He reached over and took Grace's hand. "We can do this."

Grace looked into his brown eyes, almost pleading yet hopeful.

"Yes," Grace agreed. "We can do this."

"And," the lawyer interrupted, "Ally gave you each one of these." He handed sealed white envelopes to both Grace and Chase.

Grace accepted hers hesitantly. "What is it?"

"Don't know," the lawyer said. "She didn't say. But they're for you."

Grace looked down at the envelope within her hands, clearly marked in Ally's curvy handwriting with Grace's name. Grace looked over at Chase. "Did you know about these?"

"Nope. Not at all."

Grace clutched her envelope possessively. Just inside were contents from her best friend meant just for Grace.

What were they?

Grace would have to wait. She wasn't about to tear into the envelope in the middle of the lawyer's office. Instead, she clutched it to her chest, breathed in, exhaled.

Reveled in the fact that she had a piece of Ally with her now.

Perhaps from Ally's pen. Ally's words.

For Grace.

They left the lawyer's office, already contemplating how they'd share guardianship of Evangeline. "So, how about this," Grace suggested after several scenarios failed to play out in their minds. "She attends the same daycare she's been going to all this time. That way, we won't be uprooting her life completely. You pick her up after work every day but Tuesdays and Thursdays. I'll come into the city then and pick her up. Even with the travel, I should get there before you would on a typical workday, since my day ends several hours before yours. It doesn't matter what days I have her with me because I'll have to go back to the city to drop her off at daycare before I head to work. She'll have to get there pretty early, but I don't know what else to do. You shouldn't have her every day of the week. That's a lot to take on alone. We can split weekends, but I'm sure we'll be together a lot anyway."

Chase looked beyond Grace, apparently pondering her words. Eventually, he nodded. "Gotcha. I think we can at least give it a try. It's a lot. I think Evangeline will be confused at first, but I think you're right. I think it's something she'll get used to, this new schedule of hers. As she gets a little older and is in school, we can reevaluate. Honestly, the school system in your town is superior to where she'd go down the street from me, so we should probably send her there. But yeah, we can talk about that when the day draws near. For now, let's try this."

Grace sighed. "It is a lot, isn't it? Not only for Evangeline but for us, too."

"Sure is."

"But we can do it," Grace said.

"Sure can." Chase smiled, though Grace could detect the sorrow masked behind his eyes.

Grace walked into an empty home later that afternoon. Chase had returned to his apartment to relieve the friend who had agreed to watch Evangeline so he could attend the appointment with the lawyer without worrying about having to entertain a one-year-old. It didn't matter in the least that Evangeline was adorable or that she often possessed the ability to occupy herself well; what mattered was that Grace and Chase felt the need to give their undivided attention to the lawyer at this important time, to learn what Ally's last wishes had been.

Grace closed the door behind her and leaned against it. She let her purse drop from her hand, and her keys followed, clinking to the floor. Grace hadn't relinquished her hold on Ally's envelope.

She walked to the sofa and sat. She brought the white envelope to rest on her lap and ran her fingers over its smooth surface, over the curving of her name. Ally had written that. Ally had placed pen to paper, thinking of Grace as she had done so.

Though Grace wanted desperately to open the envelope and discover its contents, she was also afraid. Afraid that this would be the last bit of Ally that she would possess, and once she had cracked the seal, there was no going back.

And yet...

Grace turned the envelope over and slowly brought her fingertip to the edge, where she slipped it into a small opening and gently tore the top free. Inside was clearly a sheet of paper. Grace lifted it, inhaling deeply before she unfolded the paper and gently deposited the envelope on the cushion beside her.

The writing she saw was unmistakably Ally's.

Gracey,

If you're reading this, then I'm gone. Sorry about that. But also not sorry, because I will have left the world knowing that I lived it up. I did good.

My lawyer would have told you by now that I want you and Chase to share guardianship of Evangeline. I bet that shocked the shit out of you, huh? Don't try to deny it—I know you all too well.

I choose you, Grace. I choose you because you're you, not me. Yep, I'm gone, and there's nothing that can be done about that now. I seriously never thought I'd be gone so soon, but it is what it is, I suppose. And E loves you. She loves Chase. We're a family. Now it's just missing a member.

But I know how you'll raise my daughter. You'll raise her with love and compassion. You'll raise her not to be one of the people that makes me not want to people, right? Remember that saying? "I don't people." Can you see me chuckling right now? You won't raise her to be a jerk. Because seriously, how can my daughter grow up to be a jerk with you and Chase as her parents? And that's what you are, Grace. You're her parent. You always have been.

I love you. And don't you ever forget that. I'm me, and you're you, and we're better together. Even though I'm gone now, even though I'm not right there with you in person, I'm still there. We're still together.

Because nothing can tear best friends apart.

And my daughter is one lucky girl to have you.

. . .

I promise. I promise it will be okay. I promise it'll be good. And I promise that everything will turn out the way it should be, because that's just what life does, right? It turns and it turns, and we live and we evolve. We love, and we love, and we love.

Don't forget that, you hear me?

We love.

And I love you.

I know it's a lot I'm asking of you and Chase. I know that. I didn't bring it up to you because I didn't think you'd ever have to read this thing you're holding in your hands right now, but I guess here we are. Sometimes life throws you the middle finger, but you still have to decide how to react to that.

It's a lot, raising my daughter in my absence. I know that. But I don't trust anyone else. I've got a nice amount of savings, and it all goes to you and Chase for Evangeline's care. Funeral arrangements have been made, but we seriously don't need to go into those details in this letter. This is my note to you, Grace. My note to tell you that you've been my guiding light. You've been a beacon. Sometimes I'm not the best with words, but I hope you never questioned my actions. I hope they spoke for me.

. . .

I hope asking you to raise my daughter is proof enough that you and Chase are the two most important adults in my life. You, Grace, are amazing.

Until we meet again, because I kinda know we will,

Ally

Grace folded the letter and brought it to her chest, careful not to crease the paper. The room was blurry through her tears, though she did nothing to remedy the situation. Let it blur. It unequivocally bespoke her feelings, her torment.

And yet—

Through her angst, through her heartache, Grace felt a sense of alleviation. Perhaps Ally had known Grace would need this letter. Perhaps Ally had known Grace more than Grace knew herself.

Perhaps.

And Ally trusted Grace. She trusted Grace with a piece of herself. The biggest, most important piece of herself.

She trusted Grace with her daughter.

And Grace was determined to live up to Ally's expectations.

CHAPTER 15

*T*wo weeks passed, and Grace found herself banging on Chase's apartment door, the apartment he had shared with Ally such a short time ago. Evangeline was propped up on a hip, and a bag filled with diapers, a sippy cup, snacks, wipes, and toys for entertainment hung from the opposite shoulder.

Please be home, please be home, Grace pleaded. She had taken Evangeline out for a walk around her neighborhood prior to arriving on Chase's doorstep and had a severe and sudden desire not to be out on that walk, in her neighborhood, surrounded by strangers. She wanted—needed—to be anywhere else, to run away.

She had jogged back home, grabbed her car keys and Evangeline's bag, loaded the toddler into her car seat—one of several new additions to Grace's severely altered life—and set off. At first, she didn't know where she was headed, but once she saw the city looming before her, she knew she had been pulled inevitably in Chase's direction. The thought hadn't even crossed her mind that she should text him to ensure he'd be home when she arrived, and even if it had, she lacked the ability, as she had left her cell phone on a small stand by her front door when she had buckled Evangeline into her stroller.

Please be home, please, please…

"Grace? What in the world is going on?" Chase stood just beyond the threshold, his hand clutching the side of the door.

"I… I…" Grace broke down then and sobbed. Chase leaped forward and took Evangeline into his arms. He pushed the door open more fully and gently led Grace inside and to the couch, the couch that held so many memories for them both, the majority of which Ally had been an integral part of.

Chase stooped over and brought Evangeline to the floor beside a basket of toys. He ensured Evangeline was happily playing before returning to Grace and taking the bag off her shoulder, a bag she had entirely forgotten she had brought with her. She had done things by habit. Even after just three weeks' time, her life had been set on a new trajectory. She had picked up the pieces. She was trying.

It's all good… Ally's voice in her head.

"It's not," Grace said, tears coursing down her cheeks. "It's not!"

"What's not what?" Chase sat next to her now, his hands in his lap. More gently, he said, "What's going on?"

Grace's shoulders rounded, her chest heaved. She released her emotions, let her agony free.

Chase sat at her side.

Eventually, Grace's body calmed. She shivered once, twice. She swiped at her tears and under her nose. She looked at Chase, into his brown eyes: gentle, kind. Waiting. Pleading.

"How do you do it?" Grace asked.

"Do what?"

"Everything. Every day. How are you taking things so well?"

Chase sighed and ran his fingers through his hair. When they dropped back to his lap, his curls were standing erect, maddening, electric.

Grace saw the dimple in his left cheek, slightly evident even when he wasn't smiling. She lifted her red-rimmed eyes to meet his gaze.

She looked at his clothes, a gray hooded sweatshirt with a circular stain on the collar, the sleeves fraying, old. Sweatpants with a small hole in the thigh.

Perhaps he wasn't doing so well after all.

Chase looked over Grace's shoulder then lifted his eyes to the ceiling. Finally, Grace followed his gaze out the window and to the busy street beyond, people going about their day, friends laughing, chatting, gay, delighted. Lovers holding hands, a stranger texting on his cell phone, bumping into a passerby. The accosted person flipping him off, expletives flying, muffled through the dirty windowpane.

Dirty.

Ally's windows were never dirty.

But Ally wasn't here.

"I'm not, Grace," Chase said. "I'm not taking things well. I'm just… not."

A fresh tear found its way down Grace's cheek, but her chin didn't quiver. Her lips didn't shake. Her energy was spent. In its place was a shell of who Grace had once been. Defeated. Deflated.

"I think of her every day," Grace whispered, the tear dripping from her chin to wet the top of her shirt.

"So do I."

"I wonder what would have happened if she had never gone on that bike ride that morning. I wonder why she did. I wonder why it happened. Why… how… why Ally? Why one of the best people in this world? Why someone so young? Why a new mom? Why… why our best friend?"

Chase made no reply. He merely looked into Grace's eyes, watery and red.

"I don't understand it, Chase. I don't understand any of this. Why was she hit? But it's not even… okay, she was hit. But why did the person leave? Why did they leave, Chase?" Grace's voice was beginning to rise. "I can't even imagine it, but no… that's not right, is it? Because I imagine it all the time. Every moment of every day, it seems. I see Ally in my head. I see her on her bike. I watch as she smiles and as she breathes in the fresh air. I can see her face so clearly, Chase. I see her happy.

"And then… and then I watch as she's hit from behind. I watch that smile transform. I watch as she's catapulted into the air…" Grace choked out a sob. "And I watch it when she falls to the ground, her body broken and shattered. And… when I see her… her eyes are open. Her beautiful blue eyes are still open. But they're lifeless. I know it.

"And this image haunts me. All the time, it haunts me. I can't let it go. I can't unsee it. I don't even know if that's how they found her, but this is how she looks in my head, and I can't stand it. Because that's not the Ally I know. Knew. See? Past tense. And that's not right, Chase. It's just not right!" Grace swiped fresh tears while Evangeline spoke to a doll on the floor as she fed her a mound of plastic peas.

Chase continued to stare at Grace, looking into her eyes, finding in their depths her anguish.

"Why didn't they stop, Chase? That's what I don't understand. Hitting someone from behind, I question that. I question it all the time, how that could even happen in the first place. But had they stopped… the fact that they sped away, that they left her there, dead or dying… that takes it to an entirely new level. And they haven't been able to find the person yet, and then I think… I wonder… will they ever find them? Will Ally ever get to rest? Will *we* ever get to rest?

"I wonder if maybe it was a teenager. Maybe it was someone who just got their license, and they were so freaked out that they just left, fled, maybe not even knowing what they were doing. For a moment, I think of Ally and what she would have said. I think of her letting things go… and for that moment, I find myself if not forgiving then at least maybe understanding a bit. And then my thoughts turn again. They turn to anger. Because there she is again, this image I have of our beautiful friend. Our friend who was so full of life. Dead. She's right there in my head, her eyes open but staring at nothing.

"It doesn't help that we just had her funeral. It doesn't help that she had hundreds of people there, people that she had touched in some way, whether they were good friends or just acquaintances. The word got out, and people showed up. Ally made a difference in all of their lives. I'm sure of it. I know this because of the difference Ally made in mine.

"But her parents weren't there. How can her parents not even come to her funeral? Chase, you did call them, didn't you?"

Chase nodded. "I did. Several times. They never answered. I had to leave a message. Sucks to get a message like that, and it's not the way I would have liked them to find out, but it's all I could do under the circumstances. Didn't know what else to do."

"That just makes no sense to me. I know Ally and her parents didn't get along. I know she didn't have a great childhood, and I know, too, that she and her parents didn't talk or keep in touch. But goodness, wouldn't you think they'd come to her funeral?"

"You'd think," Chase said. "But who knows, Grace? Ally and I didn't talk much about our pasts. Ally was a very in-the-moment type of girl."

"I know," Grace acknowledged. "I just don't understand."

"I get you. But maybe it's not up to us to understand. Ally didn't want to have a relationship with her folks, so maybe them not being at her funeral would have gone along with her wishes. Maybe they knew that. Or maybe they didn't even get the message. I'm pretty sure it was a landline. Maybe they're on vacation. Ally did say they traveled a lot."

Grace pondered the notion. "Maybe," she conceded. "But still… no phone call back? They have to know by now." She paused and then said, "Do you think they'll ever find the person that hit her?"

Chase shook his head. "Don't really know. But do you think it will really change anything?"

"What do you mean?" Grace asked, stupefied.

"I've been trying to think like Ally too, and here's what I've come up with: Say they catch the guy—or girl—say they catch them, right? Maybe that person fled because they were scared shitless, like you said. Maybe they were terrified. Maybe they've got a kid back at home the same age as Evangeline. Maybe they're a single parent of that kid and know that if they had stayed, they'd be jailed, and their kid would be sent off to foster care or to live with a relative. Maybe they made a split-second decision. A bad one, yeah, but maybe that's what they did, and when they sped off, they realized it was too late to turn back, that if they did turn back, their sentence would be even greater."

"Greater than it would be if they got caught now after running away?" Grace's eyes had gone wide, her voice shrill. Evangeline turned her head to look at Grace with curiosity.

"Don't know," Chase replied. "I'm just thinking out loud. These are things I think Ally would have asked me. I'm just playing devil's advocate."

"I have trouble thinking like that. Even when I try, it doesn't last long," Grace admitted. "Right now, I'm having trouble waking up in the morning, knowing that Ally isn't here anymore. I'm having trouble getting to sleep at night. And I can't stand the thought that the person that killed her —be it an accident or not—is still out there. They're living their life, while Ally is gone. And they did this to her. They're getting away with it."

"Don't be mad at me for saying this," Chase began, "but maybe they're not getting away with anything."

"How can you say that?"

"They have to know what they've done, yeah? Whoever did this to Ally is going to live with the decision they made for the rest of their lives, whether they get caught or not. I guess... I don't know if I could live with something as big as that looming around me every day."

Grace inhaled deeply. When she let it out, she said, "I see what you're trying to say. And I understand it. I really do. And I think you're right—those are words that Ally would probably use with us. But I just can't agree right now. I just can't, Chase. I can't think of that person out there living their life while Ally is gone. She's been taken away from us. She had so much more life to live. Evangeline is going to grow up never having the privilege of remembering her mother. This person has taken that away from her. Even if they're feeling guilty. Even if this is absolutely tearing them up inside, they are still out there and living. And Ally is not."

Chase nodded.

"I want this person to be caught. I want to see who they are. How old they are, what they look like. I want to look them in the eye."

Chase's gaze dropped to his lap, at the fingers he was lacing together, then back up at Grace. He paused for a moment and then ever so quietly said, "So do I."

"I'm having such a hard time with all this," Grace said. "I go home to an empty house when I don't have Evangeline, and I don't want to be there. The silence is deafening. It bothers me when it never bothered me before. Work is a respite. It keeps me busy, and it keeps my mind off of Ally even if just for the time that I'm with the children and don't have the ability to think of anything but them and what we're doing at any given moment. But then work is done. I come home. And I think.

"I like the days when I have Evangeline, but even after just two weeks of knowing I'm one of her guardians, I'm beginning to realize that this is really difficult for us both, me coming here, you heading to my place sometimes. I'm not sure how long we'll be able to do it before it just gets too hard. And not just on us either. I wonder if things are going to get hard on Evangeline sooner rather than later. I know we both thought things would be tough when she was school aged, but I think things are tough now, and it's been such a short amount of time."

"I'm not sure what else to do."

"And neither am I. You have to work, and so do I. If she stayed with you the entire week, I think it would be tough on you with your work hours and all. She could stay with me during the week, but... would I be taking her away from you then? Would you feel I was taking her away from you? And then... I also think about her daycare. We wanted her to stay there so she wasn't uprooted from everything in her life. I think she's doing very well considering the fact that her mother isn't here, but I'm also wondering if maybe she just doesn't know this yet... maybe soon she'll look at me or look at you, and she'll ask for Ally in a way that goes beyond how she's asked for her up until this moment. A way in which she'll just lose it. And Chase, when that happens... I think it's going to break my heart all over again, and I don't know how I'll keep things together for her. I don't know if I can stop myself from breaking down."

Chase lifted his eyes as if he was thinking things over. Eventually, he said softly, "I wouldn't think you were taking her away from me. It might be a more stable environment for Evangeline if you took her during the week. I could have her on the weekends, or we could keep it every other weekend. And we can spend time together on weekends, too. You and I. With Evangeline. We're still..." Chase paused, looked at Grace. "We're still friends."

"I know that," Grace said. She reached over and rested her palm on the back of his hand. "Very good friends. That's yet another thing I thank Ally for. The fact that she brought you into my life. I honestly don't know if I'd be able to make it through this if you weren't here, Chase. I really don't. You've helped me tremendously, even though your heart is breaking, too. Please know that I see that. I know you're hurting. I don't want to make this all about me. I just... I know I can come to you. I think... you're the only person who understands me right now." Grace paused. She pulled back her hand and looked down at her lap. In a whisper, she said, "I'm not sure I've ever told you this before, but I love you, Chase. You have been such an amazing friend. Not only to Ally but to me as well. Thank you."

Her eyes still trained on her lap, Grace could sense Chase's body relaxing beside her. He leaned back on the couch, reached his hand over, and rested his palm on her arm. "I feel the same way," he said, his voice soft and low. "I have from the beginning."

～

"How are you holding up?" Kathy asked in the staff room at the elementary school the following Monday morning, lunch sacks open in front of them. "I know things have been cuckoo lately."

"That's an understatement," Grace replied.

"Yeah, I bet. But for real, how are you?"

"Honestly, it depends on the day. No, actually," Grace said, "it depends on any given minute in the day. Things fluctuate. It's good to be here with the kids. I find it helps. The children have always been so dear to me. Their innocence is comforting in a way. They have no idea what has happened. They don't know me outside of school. To them, I'm just Ms. Clarke, their first-grade teacher. And I like it that way."

"How's Evangeline?"

"I'm not exactly sure how to answer that just yet. Evangeline seems to be taking things in stride, but she's just so small, so young. She doesn't understand any of this. She's asked for her mother several times, but when I tell her that her mom can't be with her, Evangeline dismisses it. Mostly, anyway. There have been a couple of times that she's protested. I think she's always been so used to being with both me and Chase that, for her at least, things aren't completely out of the ordinary. It hasn't been long enough for her to realize that her mother's never coming back."

"How are you holding up with the guardianship? I mean, gosh, one minute, you're living alone, and the next minute, you've got a little girl to take care of."

"I've been around Evangeline so much, and she around me, that being together more hasn't been an issue. It's the logistics of it all. I'm having a really hard time. But Chase and I have come to an agreement. I'll take Evangeline during the week and every other weekend, so I'll have her for the majority of the time. We thought this would be easier on her, and honestly, I know it will be much easier on him as well. I get out of school so much earlier than he gets out of work. I'm going to talk to that developmental center just down the street to see if they have room for Evangeline. She loves her current daycare in the city, but it's proven entirely too difficult for me to go there as often as I have been. She's a very resilient little girl, so I think she'll do all right with the change."

"I hope they have room," Kathy said. "And I hope you like it there when you go visit."

"Yes, thank you. I hope so too. But I think I will. I know that several of the teachers here send their younger children to the center."

Kathy nodded as she took a bite of yogurt. "True."

"And it would be really convenient to have Evangeline

right down the street. I've been worrying quite a bit with her being so far away from me during the day."

"Let me know how everything goes. When do you visit?"

"Tomorrow, actually," Grace said.

"Well then," Kathy held her spoon aloft. "Good luck!"

And luck there was. The developmental center—Susan's Saplings as it was appropriately titled—did have an opening for Evangeline, so Grace told Evangeline's current daycare center that Friday would be her last day there. She'd start at her new center on Monday. As much as the change frightened Grace, she couldn't help but admit that it would help ease this ever-changing transition to guardianship for her. Now she would have the convenience of dropping Evangeline off before heading to the elementary school just down the road and picking her up when the day was done to bring her home, where she and Evangeline could finish their day together. So much easier than heading into the city several times a week!

Monday arrived, and Grace dressed Evangeline in an adorable jumper adorned with ladybugs and butterflies, something Grace herself had purchased. She swept Evangeline's soft brown hair off her cheeks and positioned the strands under a large headband to get them off her face and out of her mouth. She had nearly purchased a set of barrettes at the department store the other day, but Ally's voice spoke in the back of her mind, reminding Grace that barrettes were choking hazards. She knew that even before she got to the center, Evangeline would probably rip the headband off. And Grace understood. Grace still found she wore her strands covering the skin of her cheeks instead of tucked behind her ears. And although Grace hid behind her hair and Evangeline just preferred hers messy, old habits certainly died hard.

A sneeze.

"Oh, bless you," Grace told Evangeline.

"'Kay," the little girl replied, which made Grace chuckle.

"Well, are you ready to go?"

"Uh-huh," Evangeline said.

"That's good. Let's head out then. Today's a big day." Grace scooped up Evangeline's bag from the sofa, stuffed to the brim with extra clothes and her favorite blanket, as well as a pink bunny that she had been sleeping with lately. Grace didn't know if she'd need the bunny, but she figured she'd pack it anyway. She was nervous. So very frightened that Evangeline wouldn't take well to her new environment. Perhaps the bunny would ease any of Evangeline's misgivings if they arose, a piece of home.

Her new home.

"Let's get your shoes on," Grace said. She walked Evangeline to the front door, the bag slung over her shoulder. She had to tip her opposite shoulder to the side in order to reach the little girl's raised hand, her fingers small and soft, delicate in Grace's palm.

When they reached the entryway, Evangeline let go of Grace's hand and plonked down on her bottom. She grabbed a closed-toed sandal and attempted to slip it on the opposite foot, jamming it on her toes in the process. She grunted, a look of frustration lining her face.

"Want some help?" Grace suggested. Evangeline lifted her gaze and let go of the sandal. It hung from the tip of her big toe, eliciting a smile from Grace.

"Here we go," Grace said as she brought the shoe to the correct foot. "See... that's right." She adhered the Velcro at the top of the sandal, grabbed Evangeline's other shoe, and secured it to her bare foot. "Oh, I hope it's not too chilly for sandals. I hadn't really thought about that until now. Oh, gosh. Your other daycare didn't say anything to me... are there rules? Oh, Evangeline, are there rules?" She looked down at the little girl as if she had the ability to answer her inquiry.

Grace shook her head. "Too late now. We've got to go. I think you'll be warm enough. But why did it take me until now to even think about your shoes?"

She scooped Evangeline up in her arms and stood. She exited her townhome, closing and locking the door behind her. As she turned toward her car, her stomach knotted. Ally had been the one to find Evangeline's daycare center in the city. It had been Ally who interviewed the teachers and the director. Ally was pleased with that center; it had been why she'd settled on sending Evangeline there. And now Grace had uprooted Ally's daughter. Grace was changing yet another thing in the young girl's life.

Was she doing the right thing?

Grace strapped Evangeline into her car seat the exact way in which Ally had shown her. She was about to shut the back door when she saw the pink bunny sticking out of the top of Evangeline's bag. She lifted it by its ear and handed it off. "Want your bunny?"

"Bunny," Evangeline said with a smile. "Yeah. Bunny."

Evangeline was stroking the bunny's fur when Grace closed the back door and climbed into her seat behind the steering wheel.

"Ice Bunny. Ood bunny." *Nice bunny. Good bunny.*

She'll be okay. She'll be okay, Grace thought to herself. She took a deep breath and started the car.

Grace was reminded anew just how convenient Susan's Saplings was to get to, since it only took her about eight minutes to arrive in the small parking lot. She turned the key in the ignition and allowed herself a moment to still her beating heart before exiting the car and unbuckling Evangeline from her seat.

"Here!" Evangeline declared with gusto. She held the bunny out to the side, its feet dangling.

At least one of us is excited, Grace thought. And then she smiled. If Evangeline was as happy and eager as she appeared to be, then perhaps Grace's fear of transitional difficulties wouldn't come to fruition. Perhaps—just perhaps—everything would be fine after all.

"Up we go." Grace lifted a willing Evangeline from her car seat and onto her hip. She stuffed the pink bunny back inside the bag and grabbed it by the handles. She closed the car door behind her and looked at the building that appeared to loom before her. "Here we are, I suppose." When Grace looked down at Evangeline, she saw the little girl was wearing a confused expression.

"Where we?"

"This is… this is your new daycare, Evangeline," Grace said, plastering a smile on her face. "Like I was telling you about. There are lots and lots of toys and kind people, and you'll make all sorts of new friends."

Evangeline's lower lip began to tremble. "Where we?" she repeated.

"Let's go inside. You'll be able to see all the wonderful things they have for you." Grace set off and headed for the front door. She punched the four-digit code she had been given by the director the previous week into the keypad, and the mechanism beeped as it unlocked. Grace pulled the door open and stepped inside. Evangeline clutched Grace's shirt, her nails digging into Grace's skin. Grace hadn't even realized how sharp Evangeline's nails were, and it wasn't until that moment that she realized that she hadn't cut Evangeline's nails at all since Ally had died. Had Chase? How did one even go about doing so? Regular clippers? Baby clippers? Would Evangeline squirm? Was Evangeline used to it? Would she put up a fuss?

Do not cry! Grace scolded herself as she shut the thick door behind her. *Don't you dare cry!*

Grace passed a couple of doors, peeking surreptitiously inside at the children and teachers, until she came upon a bend in the hallway. She turned the corner and slowly, hesitantly, entered Evangeline's new room. Several young children, all around Evangeline's age, were already present. Some were playing with toys on the floor, a couple were eating breakfast at one of the child-sized tables, and one little girl was sitting on a young female teacher's lap as she read from a picture book.

"Oh, hello. This must be Evangeline."

Grace turned to see a woman who appeared to be in her thirties with short strawberry-blond hair and thin-rimmed glasses.

"Ye..." Grace's voice croaked. "Yes. This is Evangeline."

"Hello, Evangeline," the woman said pleasantly as she tilted her head.

Evangeline immediately buried her face in Grace's shirt, flinging her arms around her neck and holding on tightly.

The woman didn't seem deterred, and her smile didn't falter. "I'm Morgan. We were told that Evangeline would be joining us today. You were so lucky! We had a child leave just a couple of weeks ago because his parents moved out of state. Otherwise, we wouldn't have had an opening. Your timing was perfect."

"I… that's nice." Grace winced. *Nice?* She couldn't have come up with anything better to say?

"You're… Grace, right?"

"Oh, yes. Yes. I'm Grace." Grace felt herself flush.

Evangeline's hands were splayed on her neck, and her face was still buried in Grace's chest.

"Here," Morgan said as she extended a hand. "Why don't you come and have a seat? Maybe if Evangeline sees the other children playing and all the toys we've got— maybe then she'll want to play, too."

"Okay." Grace slowly walked forward, and Evangeline began to kick her legs.

Please, no. Please, no.

Grace bent down, her movements awkward with Evangeline protesting in her arms and the bag slung over her shoulder. Just as she neared the floor, she lost her balance and landed hard on her bottom. The heat spread even farther throughout her face, and she pretended that nothing had gone awry, that everything was just as it should be. That she had most definitely not just fallen clumsily to the floor in front of two adult strangers.

"Evangeline, do you like puzzles?" Morgan asked. She placed a chunky wooden puzzle beside Grace on the floor, directly below Evangeline's hidden face. "I love puzzles." Morgan continued to speak as if Evangeline and she had begun playing together moments before and were having a marvelous time. "This one is my favorite. It's got a puppy on it, and it's even got a bunny just like the bunny I see in your bag there. Do you like bunnies as much as I do, Evangeline?" Morgan's voice was soft and soothing, and Grace appreciated her efforts very much, even if they didn't seem to be working as Evangeline buried her nose even deeper into the folds of Grace's shirt.

"Oh my goodness, do you know what I have?" Morgan asked, her cadence raised with excitement. "I bet you'll just love this toy."

Grace watched as the woman reached behind her to a small wooden shelf and brought a brightly colored plastic toy to rest between her and Evangeline. She pushed a large knob at the top of the toy, and several small balls began spinning feverishly in a clear plastic cylinder at the toy's base.

"Oh," Morgan clasped her hands together. "Here they come. Watch this, Evangeline!"

Evangeline did no such thing. Her head remained buried in Grace's chest, but then the balls shot out of the toy and up into the air, piquing Evangeline's attention. The little girl poked her head out from under her arm and stole a glance as the balls plummeted back to the ground.

A little girl with pigtails on either side of her head toddled over to Morgan, bent her knees, and bounced up and down over and over again, her smile wide. She squealed with glee and then exclaimed a very fervent, "More!"

"You would like me to do it again, Lily?" Morgan asked.

"Yes!" Lily clapped her hands and beamed.

"Okay... here we go. Ready, Lily? Ready, Evangeline?" Evangeline's entire head was now turned toward the toy on the floor, though her hands still rested on Grace's neck. "One, two... three!" Morgan pushed the knob at the top of the toy again, and the balls started spinning, round and round, then so fast it was hard to follow them visually, bright colors streaking the clear, thick plastic like a camera capturing movement at night.

Evangeline's hands fell from Grace's neck, and her body relaxed. Lily squealed again, clapping as she bounced. Evangeline looked from Lily to the toy then back at Lily again. When the balls spurted out of the toy and flew into the air, Evangeline slowly climbed off of Grace's lap and stood. A small smile began to form on her lips.

"More, more!" Lily demanded enthusiastically.

"You'd like more, Lily?" Morgan crawled on hands and knees to retrieve the balls then placed them back in the cylindrical part of the toy.

"Yes!"

"And how about you, Evangeline? Would you like more, too?"

Evangeline nodded, the movement slight but noticeable.

"Here we go…" Morgan's voice lingered in the air as her palm hovered over the top of the toy. "Actually, Evangeline, would you like to help me?"

Evangeline's smile faltered momentarily. She looked at Grace—who immediately plastered a smile of encouragement on her face—then back to Morgan. Her lips lifted minutely, and then she said, "'Kay."

"Come on over," Morgan said gently but with enthusiasm. "All you have to do is push this down. That's right." A slight chuckle. "It's tough, isn't it? Want me to help you?"

Evangeline nodded. Morgan covered Evangeline's hand with her own and then said, "Ready?" When Evangeline nodded again, Morgan counted down. "One, two… what comes next, Lily?"

"Twee!"

"Three!" Morgan said. She pushed down gently on Evangeline's hand, and the balls went spinning furiously. As

Evangeline and Lily both exclaimed their appreciation for the toy's antics, Morgan leaned over toward Grace and whispered. "It might be okay for you to go now. I'll have her say goodbye, but we should be sure to let her know that everything is good here. If we look worried, she'll think there's something to be worried about."

"Okay."

"I promise I'll tell you all about her day when you come to pick her up this afternoon."

"Okay," Grace repeated. There was nothing left to do but stand. "Oh. Where do I put this?" She indicated the bag still on her shoulder.

"We've given Evangeline her own cubby. Tomorrow when you come in, we'll take her right over to it so she knows her morning routine, but for now, she's having fun, and we want to be sure she feels comfortable here. You can just leave her bag in her cubby."

"Okay." *Okay?* Was that all Grace was capable of replying? Didn't she have a more extensive vocabulary than that?

Grace moved forward, and just as she began to step away, Evangeline caught sight of the movement and grabbed onto her pants. "No. No go," she protested.

"Mommy has to go to work," Morgan said. "She'll be back really soon, I promise. Evangeline, do you want to help me with the toy again? We can try to catch the balls! Come on over. Ready, set..."

Mommy.

Grace knew she had to leave, knew it was best for her to make her exit now that Evangeline was occupied and happy, but she felt rooted to the spot.

Mommy.

It was such an innocent word, truly, but for Grace, it held an abundance of meaning and elicited several emotions, all of which spiraled within her now. When she felt her bottom lip quiver and her eyes grow damp, her feet found their purpose, moving hastily toward Evangeline's new cubby. She plonked the bag down and headed for the door.

"Bye, Mommy!" Morgan called over. She was looking at Evangeline and waving her hand animatedly. Evangeline looked rather hesitant, but she wasn't crying, and neither was she making any protest, so Grace feigned a smile of indifference at the endearment, waved back, and walked out the door.

Morgan might not have been told about Evangeline's circumstances. Perhaps she didn't know that Ally was dead, that Evangeline's mother was gone. Maybe she didn't realize that Grace was her legal guardian. Even if Morgan had just forgotten, Grace was sure that she would be privy to the logistics of their situation shortly, and Grace was not looking forward to that conversation whatsoever. She didn't want the look of pity, didn't want to hear that Morgan was sorry. It would have all been so much easier had Morgan known—or remembered—their situation prior to Evangeline's arrival this morning, but there was nothing to be done about it now. Grace was so shaken that she was left stupefied.

She hadn't been expecting this, not one bit. And she didn't like it. Evangeline's mom was gone. Gone. Ally was dead. She wasn't coming back. Grace's best friend was not coming back. If Ally was still alive, then Grace would have left her house that morning and headed directly for the school. She would not have detoured to take Evangeline to a new daycare center that she had never been to before. Where Grace had been mistaken for the girl's mother.

Grace loved Evangeline. She loved the little girl with

her entire being—fully, wholeheartedly, she loved her. But she wasn't the one that was supposed to be caring for Evangeline now. She wasn't the one that was supposed to drop her off at daycare, to pick her up, to take her home. Ally was supposed to be the one to have those pleasures. With her daughter. *Her* daughter.

Grace swiped at the tears flowing down her cheeks as she hastened to her car. Her vehicle beeped as she pressed the unlock button on her key. She climbed inside and shut the door. She rested her head on the steering wheel and let the tears flow freely.

Chase. She needed to talk to Chase. Maybe he hadn't yet arrived at work.

She inhaled a gulp of air, held it in her lungs. Her shoulders shook, but she forced them back. She lifted her chin and wiped the fresh tears from her cheeks and from under her eyes. Not for the first time these past weeks was Grace thankful that she didn't wear makeup. She'd look a wreck right now, she was sure of it. More of a wreck than she inevitably already did.

"Grace?" Chase's voice sounded panicked. "Grace, is everything okay?"

"Ye... yes," Grace choked.

"What's going on? You're crying."

"Yes," Grace said. She pursed her lips and let out a breath, attempting to calm her emotions. "I'm okay. I just... I needed to hear your voice. You're the only one... you're the only one that will understand."

"Understand what?"

"They called me her mommy."

"What?"

"They called me her mommy," Grace repeated. "Here at the daycare. They think I'm her mom."

"Oh," Chase said. "Shit."

"Yes. It is. And I… I've lost it. I was good in front of Evangeline. She had a bit of trouble at first. I think because it's a new place and all, but I think she's okay now. The lady seems really nice. But she called me Evangeline's mom. And I just… Chase, is this how it's going to be? Are we going to have to continuously correct people? Will I have to explain all the time that I'm not Evangeline's mom, that Evangeline 's mom died when someone hit her bike with their car and then took off? Because I can't do that. I can't tell this story over and over again. I know that I don't have to give people details, but shouldn't they at least know that we're not her parents? Ally deserves that. She can't be forgotten, Chase. We can't let that happen. Evangeline calls me Grace. I want it to stay that way. I need it to stay that way. Because Ally… I can't… we can't…" Grace choked on a sob. "Ally."

"I know," Chase said calmly, smoothly. "We won't let that happen. Evangeline will always know who her mom is. Always."

Grace said nothing for a while. Eventually, she found her voice again. "Thanks, Chase. I… I need you."

"And I'm here. Promise. Hey! Want to hear a funny story?"

Grace smiled slightly. She knew that Chase was trying his best to cheer her up. "Sure," Grace said. "Go ahead."

"You know I take the T into work because traffic's a shit show, yeah?"

"Yes, I know."

"So I'm there this morning, got my nice pants on, shirt, tie, suit jacket… I'm lookin' snazzy."

"Snazzy?" Despite Grace's emotional state, she nearly snorted.

"That's right. Snazzy. I'm lookin' good. Always have to look my best when I head in to work. So there's this young girl standing next to me, maybe seventeen, eighteen. Maybe going to school? Who knows. This guy hobbles over, all wobbly because hey, it's the T, right? And he looks right at her, lifts up his hand, and shows her…"

"What?" Chase had kindled Grace's curiosity now.

"An egg."

"Um… an egg?"

"Kid you not," Chase said, and in Grace's mind, she could even see him lifting his hand, palm outward, eyes wide. "The man had a freaking egg with him. And it had eyes and a nose and a mouth and was even wearing some sort of cloth like a diaper."

"Really?"

"Really! The girl looked at him like he was nuts, and he probably was, because the look on his face as he held up this egg of his… oh, boy. She walked away and left me there with Egg Man. He looked at me, and then you know what he did?"

"What?" Grace found herself smiling.

"He stroked the top of the egg like he was brushing hair or something."

"No way!" Grace chuckled.

"Kid you not. I can't make this stuff up."

"It's stories like these that make me happy to live where I live. And this one isn't even all that bad. Strange, but not bad."

"You've got a nice place and a nice neighborhood, I'll give you that. But I'm the one with the stories. Gotta love the city for that, right?"

"I suppose."

"And hey, my story made you smile. I can hear it in your voice."

"Yes. It made me smile." After a pause, Grace said. "Chase?"

"Mmm?"

"Thank you."

"My pleasure, Gracey. Now, you go have yourself a great day at work. Those kids need you. You are, after all, the best teacher ever."

Grace laughed. "And how would you know that? You've never seen me in my classroom."

"Oh, I just know," Chase said.

And Chase had been right. She could hear it when someone smiled.

Grace was in her classroom during the last period of the day. Her first graders were sitting at their desks, working as teams at their circular tables to play a math game of Grace's own devising. A beep sounded in the room, and then a voice came over the intercom.

"Grace?" It was the main office.

"Yes, I'm here."

"Call for you. Line two."

"Oh," Grace said, her voice filled with confusion. Who would be calling her at school? She never received phone calls at work. Never. "Thank you."

Grace walked to her desk, picked up her phone, and clicked on the red flashing button. "Hello?" She said hesitantly. "This is Grace Clarke."

"Grace, hi," a chipper voice sounded at the other end of the line. "This is Morgan from Susan's Saplings."

"Oh. Hi?"

"I'm so sorry to call you at work. I know it's almost time for you to come and pick up Evangeline, but she seems to be sick. I'm so sorry. She was fine this morning. She really had a good day until just about an hour ago. At first, I thought it was because she was missing you, but she just got fussier and fussier, and when I felt her forehead, she was really hot. She's got a temperature now, and her nose is running. I think she might have caught a virus."

"Oh, my goodness," Grace replied. "I didn't know."

"Not a problem. It probably came on quick. But because of our sick policy, I'll need you to come and pick her up early."

"Oh," Grace said. "Yes. Of course. I... um... okay. I'm coming."

"See you soon."

"Okay. Bye."

Grace hung up the phone then looked at the children in her classroom. She had to leave.

But how?

Grace had never been in this position before. She had to get Evangeline. There was nobody else that could help her out. Chase was also at work and was much farther away from Evangeline than Grace was at the moment. And yet she had a classroom full of first graders that couldn't be left alone. What was she to do? In the past, when Grace hadn't felt well, she had toughed it out until the end of the day. She wasn't used to leaving work on the spur of the moment.

Grace walked to the door of her classroom and hit a black button on the side of the wall, paging the front office.

"How can I help?"

"I, um... that was Evangeline's daycare. She's sick."

"Alrighty then. That stinks."

"Yes. Well… I need to go pick her up, but I've got my students here…"

"I'll send someone down to fill in for you until the end of the day."

"Oh, wonderful," Grace said. "Thank you so much."

Grace turned back to the class, feeling a bit flustered.

"Someone is sick?" It was a young girl named Elizabeth who spoke from her chair.

"Yes," Grace answered. "It's… well… I'm taking care of someone's daughter. Well… indefinitely."

"What does that mean?"

"It means… forever. It means I'll be caring for her forever."

"Like a mom."

Grace's stomach flipped. "Well, kind of. But I'm not her mom."

"That doesn't make sense."

"Course it does, dummy," the boy at Elizabeth's side pronounced. "Like when my mom got sent away and my dad got married to my stepmom. And when my friend got adopted. He's got a new family. My dad tells me that families don't mean a mom and dad. Families are all different."

"Well, aren't you just a smarty pants," Elizabeth retorted.

"I am when you're being dumb."

Elizabeth opened her mouth to reply, but Grace intervened. "That's enough, now. Yes, it's correct that there are all sorts of families in this world, and they are all different. Families are special. They can have one parent or two. They can be adopted families. They can be foster families. They can be with no children or with ten."

"Ten kids?" Elizabeth exclaimed. "That's a lot."

"Yes," Grace agreed. "It is. But it's also a choice, and

just because someone does not have a family like yours doesn't mean they are not a family, and a special one at that."

"Like you and the girl?" Elizabeth asked.

"Yes," Grace replied, attempting desperately not to cry. "Like me and Evangeline."

"And she's sick."

"She is, yes. I will need to leave to go get her."

"Who's gonna be with us?"

"I don't know just yet," Grace said. "But whoever it is will be here very soon, and I'm sure you'll have a wonderful end to your day today."

"Will you be here tomorrow?"

"I'm not exactly sure," Grace said.

"I hope you're here tomorrow," Elizabeth pouted.

"I'll try my best."

A slight woman entered the room. The vice principal. "Sorry about Evangeline, Grace," she said. "I've got it from here."

"Thank you so much. I really appreciate it." Grace grabbed her bag and lunch sack from under her desk, said goodbye to the children, and swiftly walked out of her classroom.

Evangeline was waiting.

When Grace arrived at the developmental center and walked into Evangeline's room, she saw the little girl sitting on Morgan's lap, her head tilted to the side and resting on Morgan's chest, and her thumb in her mouth. When Evangeline looked up to find Grace standing in front of her, she broke out in tears.

"Oh, oh, goodness," Grace said. Evangeline lifted her arms, and Grace snatched her up and onto her chest. Evangeline wrapped her legs around Grace's hips and sobbed into her shirt. The secretions from her nose and the tears she shed wet the material.

"Probably not the first day you had hoped for," Morgan said gently. She stroked the hair off the back of Evangeline's neck. "Give us a call and let us know how she's doing. I hope she's feeling better really soon."

"Thank you," Grace said.

She made for the door, but Morgan called out to her. "Don't forget Evangeline's bag."

"Oh," Grace said. "Oh, yes. Of course." She felt entirely too flustered with Evangeline sobbing into her chest, feeling at a loss about what to do to calm the little girl's tears.

"I bet she'll be back to herself once she's got some Tylenol in her," Morgan said. "She probably caught a little virus. Poor girl. It doesn't feel good to be sick."

"Yes," Grace said. "I'm sure she will." Tylenol. Medicine. Of course! But Grace didn't have any baby Tylenol at home. In fact, she didn't have much at all in the way of first aid for a one-year-old girl. She'd have to stop at the pharmacy on the way home. With a sobbing child. A sobbing child that she couldn't leave in the car.

God, help me, Grace pleaded to herself. *I have no idea what I'm doing.*

Grace placed a tearful Evangeline in her car seat. She attempted to hand her the pink bunny, but Evangeline immediately discarded it to the seat. Grace slid behind the wheel and pulled out of the parking lot and into the road. Luckily, there was a pharmacy a few minutes down the street that she could stop at. Once she arrived, she parked the car, took a protesting Evangeline out of her seat, and headed inside. The customers within turned their heads when they heard Evangeline's sobs. A man at the cash register glared daggers at Grace as he grimaced. One woman looked at Grace with kind, empathetic eyes and a slight encouraging smile. Evangeline wailed, spittle dripping onto her lips and down her chin. Grace wiped it with the corner of her sleeve.

Please stop, Evangeline. Please, please, please stop.

Grace walked into an aisle and realized she was nowhere near the medicine. She feverishly looked at the signs hanging from the ceiling and hovering over the various aisles until her sight rested on the one she thought she'd need. She hastened its way, hoisting Evangeline higher onto her hip. Grace skimmed over the contents of the shelves until she found what she was looking for. Medicine to reduce a toddler's fever. But there were so many kinds! Which one did she need?

Grace settled on the Tylenol—desperately hoping she had made the right decision—and brought it to the front counter to pay. The cashier rang up her transaction and announced the price. Grace reached for her purse, and—

It wasn't there.

No, no, no! This is not happening right now.

"I… I…" Evangeline was flailing, and Grace thought she was about to lose the last modicum of composure she possessed. "I left my purse in the car. I… I'll go get it." Her eyes glassed over.

"Never you mind." The voice was beside her, and when Grace turned her gaze, she noticed it was the woman she had seen upon entrance into the pharmacy. "I have three kids myself. I know how it is. And it looks like you could use a little help right about now."

"I… I…" Grace was so overcome with emotion that she didn't quite know how to answer.

The woman smiled. "You just go right ahead. I'll pay for this with my other stuff."

"I... how do I thank you?" Grace asked.

"You just did. Go on now. Get that little girl of yours home."

Grace snatched up the Tylenol, looked over at the woman, and said, "Thank you," the words sounding fruitless on her tongue. She wanted to express so much more.

Grace arrived home soon thereafter, took Evangeline into the house, and set her down on the living room floor, where Evangeline protested even louder. Surely this wasn't normal, was it? Surely this couldn't just be a fever? Was there something else going on? What had Grace missed?

She was so utterly confused and flummoxed!

Grace tore open the little box and grabbed the medicine bottle. Under duress, with a screaming Evangeline in the background, she read the directions. With shaking hands, she filled the syringe as instructed, brought it over to Evangeline, and placed it in her mouth.

Evangeline swatted it away.

"Oh, please don't," Grace pleaded. "I don't know how else to help you." She tried once again, and Evangeline turned her head, her chest heaving.

Grace began to cry. She felt her efforts were futile. She had no idea what she was supposed to do. She hadn't grown up babysitting, and when a child in her class said they weren't feeling well, she sent them to the nurse's office. She had never been in this predicament before now.

With a deep breath, Grace plunged the dropper deep into Evangeline's mouth and pressed down. Evangeline choked, but much to Grace's relief, it appeared that most of the medication had been swallowed, since she saw only a small amount of purple liquid seep out with Evangeline's saliva as she cried. Grace swiped at her own tears, and her knees gave out, sending her to fall hard onto her bottom on the floor. Together, their sobs commingled in the air, louder and louder, until Evangeline's came to a crescendo and her body, exhausted, began to calm. Evangeline's tears slowed until she spent them all. Her little chest heaved. Once, twice, and then she reached for Grace.

Grace eagerly lifted Evangeline into her embrace and made her way to the couch. She brushed the wet hair off the little girl's cheeks and wiped under her nose and on her chin with the sleeve of her shirt. Evangeline rested her cheek on Grace's chest, her ear at the very spot at which Grace's heart beat. Grace began to rock from side to side. Evangeline's eyes drooped, opened, drooped again, until her mouth hung slightly open and her breathing slowed. Her lashes fluttered as she slept.

Grace sat on the couch, holding tightly onto Evangeline. She looked down at the sleeping child, at the movement of her eyes, at her chest as it took in air and expelled what she didn't need. She watched Evangeline sleep, peaceful, uninterrupted. And all the heartache, all the uncertainty of the last hour melted away until there was only one emotion left. One emotion that overtook Grace's entire being.

Love.

Love for this little girl that she held in her arms.

Love for the little girl who had uprooted her life so completely.

Grace held Evangeline until she awakened an hour and a half later. Her limbs were stiff, but she paid no mind. She had wanted to be nowhere else but on her couch, cradling the little girl.

She attempted to feed Evangeline dinner and was

pleased when Evangeline ate a few bites. She clearly did not have the appetite she typically did, but Grace was happy that she had gotten something down. It was better than not eating anything at all.

Evangeline played for a small amount of time after she ate, but as soon as Grace saw her rub her eyes, she whisked Evangeline away to give her a bedtime bath. Perhaps a bath would help her to feel better. Or perhaps not. Who knew? But it was what Grace's intuition was telling her to do, so she listened.

When Evangeline began to fall asleep in the tub, Grace toweled her dry, put on a fresh diaper, and walked her to the kitchen, where she administered another dose of Tylenol before putting her to bed early. Evangeline obviously needed her sleep.

"Goodnight, little one," Grace said as she brushed the brown hair off Evangeline's forehead. Evangeline's eyes closed, her eyelashes fluttered, and she was asleep.

Grace walked to the living room, where she plopped down on the couch, feeling utterly exhausted. She turned the television on and was in the middle of a show when a knock sounded on the door.

What?

Grace stood from the couch and turned the knob, tilting her head to see who stood on her threshold. "Chase!" she exclaimed with surprise. "What are you doing here?"

"Got off work just a bit early. Thought you might need this." He held up a bottle of merlot. "Let me in and lay it on me. I bet you need to talk." Chase winked at the same time he added, "Mommy," with an incorrigible grin.

And although Grace had had an incredibly trying day, Chase's words did nothing but make her smile.

She opened the door fully and let him in.

CHAPTER 16

race had never been so pleased to have summers off of work than she was now that she cared for Evangeline. In order to keep her placement at the daycare center, Grace still needed to pay for Evangeline's slot, so she sent Evangeline to Susan's Saplings twice a week. She thought it might help Evangeline to have this consistency in her life instead of taking her out of daycare entirely and then placing her right back in when school started up at the end of August. Plus Evangeline appeared to love daycare. Morgan said that she and Lily—the little girl who had been there on Evangeline's first day at the center—had taken a liking to each other, and the notion filled Grace with pleasure and, admittedly, relief.

It was now a hot and humid Friday afternoon in the middle of July. It was Chase's weekend with Evangeline, and Grace thought it might be nice to head into the city a bit early so she could take Evangeline to the park where she had first met Ally before dropping her off at Chase's. Evangeline could play on the equipment or in the sandbox. And although Grace didn't much like the city, she figured a change of venue would do her some good.

"Whee!" Evangeline lifted her arms as she zoomed down a small metal slide.

Grace couldn't help but smile as she watched her play. "Very good, Evangeline," she said.

She looked at Evangeline's thighs as the little girl lifted herself from the bottom of the slide, turned, and clumsily ran back to the stairs. She was eighteen and a half months old now, and the chubby fat of her baby years had melted away. Though still clearly a toddler, she was changing, her cheeks not as round, the elastic of her wrists long gone.

"How about the swing?" Grace suggested. "You do like to swing."

"'Kay. Let's go!" Evangeline set off for the swings.

Grace hoisted her into the air and placed her in the bucket. She faced Evangeline, grasped the chains, pulled toward her, and let go. Evangeline grinned widely and began to giggle.

After another half an hour of playtime, Grace told Evangeline it was time to go see Chase. Evangeline typically protested when it was time to leave a fun activity, but she adored Chase even more than she did the playground, so she made no protestation and, instead, led the way toward Grace's car.

Grace hated driving in the city. Hated it. It gave her a constant fright and only heightened her anxiety. But she had learned fairly early on that she hated taking Evangeline on the T even more than she loathed the city traffic.

Grace quickly caught up to Evangeline and grasped her hand. She was looking down, so she didn't see him at first. It was because she almost bumped into him that she lifted her chin and her eyes darted his way.

Her steps halted so suddenly that her pull on Evangeline's hand caused the little girl to falter backward. "What you doin'?" Evangeline asked.

"I... I..." Grace's eyes didn't leave him. *Couldn't* leave him. "Nothing, sweetie. I just..."

"Hi, Grace," Gary said. His voice was low, almost uncertain.

Grace made no reply. She lacked the ability. Her stomach roiled, and goosebumps formed on the skin of her bare arms despite the humidity. And then she glanced beside him.

Stephanie. This had to be Stephanie. Long dark-blond hair, graceful build.

And beside Stephanie, a young boy.

Gary's son.

"How've you been, Grace?" Gary's eyes slowly made their way to Evangeline and lingered.

"I'll take George to play," Stephanie announced. She avoided eye contact with Grace, tugged on her child's hand, and quickly walked away.

Gary nodded, still looking at Evangeline. Then slowly—ever so slowly—he turned his gaze back to Grace. "I thought you didn't want kids."

"And I could say the same for you." Grace didn't know where it came from, this sudden urge, the sudden stance. One moment, she thought she was going to be sick right there at the playground, and in a fraction of a second, her entire perspective changed. Her nerves wouldn't win. She was determined that her anxiety would not, could not peek through.

Grace wouldn't let it.

"Who's this?" Gary asked.

"I Evangeline," Evangeline declared. "Who you?"

"I'm—"

"Never mind, Evangeline," Grace interrupted. "Go on and play in that sandbox over there, okay? We'll leave in just a minute."

"You could have let me introduce myself," Gary said once Evangeline toddled away.

"And I don't see why I should." Grace crossed her arms over her chest. "You don't have that right."

"You caught me off guard."

"And you did the same to me."

"Didn't think I'd see you again," Gary explained.

"I would have been okay with that."

"Geez," Gary said. "Hold up. I'm trying to be nice here."

Grace took a deep breath in and closed her eyes. When she reopened them, she looked up at Gary, into the dark-brown eyes in which she had once lost herself so fully. "Okay," Grace said. "Thank you, I suppose. But see, Gary, here's the thing: I've learned a lot about myself these past few years. A lot. And I guess... someone once told me that we should just let things go. I suppose I thought I had until I saw you just now and a whole slew of emotions came bubbling to the surface. But... no." Grace shook her head, and then, much to her surprise, she laughed. "Oh my goodness, I think I *have* let things go! Seeing you right now... I realize that I really have. I was never right for you, Gary, and you most definitely weren't right for me, and I think... I think that you broke my heart, but maybe that had to happen for me to finally open my eyes. That had to happen in order for me to be... I guess for me to be who I am today."

"With a daughter." Gary motioned toward Evangeline.

Grace said nothing, merely stood her ground, looking

up at him. A slight smile broke out over her lips, and she uncrossed her arms. "Good luck, Gary. With everything. And I actually mean that. You have no hold over me anymore, and I guess… yes. Things do fall into place, don't they? Life somehow works itself out." Grace laughed then, hearty and light. She was thinking about Ally.

Gary merely looked down at her inquisitively.

"I hope you treat them well." Grace glanced over at Stephanie, who was attempting to stealthily look over at her husband and Grace from near the monkey bars. Somehow, this tickled Grace anew, and she chuckled.

"What's so funny?"

"I…" Grace started laughing again. "I don't even know. But what I do know is that I feel good right now. Mighty good. Now, if you'll excuse me, Gary, Evangeline and I have somewhere to be." Grace turned on a heel and walked toward Evangeline. She held out her hand, Evangeline took it with her own, and the pair walked to Grace's car, leaving Gary open-mouthed in their wake.

"I'm feeling so good right now," Grace cried as she stormed into Chase's apartment.

Chase grinned. "I can see that. What's gotten into you?"

"Oh, nothing." Grace knew she was being cryptic, but she wanted to keep that afternoon's miraculous progression to herself. "But I don't want to stay in. Let's take Evangeline to that tiny hole in the wall that you and Ally took me to that one time. Remember? That little Mexican place."

"Of course I remember. I still go there sometimes."

"Let's go tonight."

"Really?" Chase smiled and cocked his head.

"Yes, really. I'm in the mood."

"You don't usually like going out in the city with Evangeline."

"Tonight, I've changed my mind."

"All right then," Chase agreed. "Let's go. I just need to change. Your timing was perfect. I just barely got home."

When they arrived at the restaurant, Grace wasn't surprised in the least to spot an open table even though the venue was tiny and tables were limited. This afternoon had just been too fantastic. Her mood had lifted exponentially since leaving Gary at the park, and she felt as if nothing could go wrong. She felt exhilarated.

They ordered their meals and sat down. When their food arrived at their table, Grace cut Evangeline's quesadilla into tiny bite-sized pieces, and Evangeline ate with relish.

"She's goin' to town," Chase remarked.

Grace laughed. "Yes. She is. Just like her mom."

They were finishing up when Grace turned to Chase.

"What is it?" Chase asked. "You're looking at me all funny."

"I just... Chase, I know that we had planned on my heading back to your apartment with you and Evangeline. I need to get my car anyway. But..."

"But what?" Chase lifted his brows and smirked.

"There's somewhere I need to be."

"Somewhere you need to be? What does that mean?" Chase asked.

"I just... yes. There's somewhere I need to be. Something I need to do. For me. Do you mind? Can you take Evangeline back to your apartment on your own, and I'll meet you there later tonight?"

"Okaaay," Chase said. "You've got me curious, but okay."

"Thanks so much, Chase. I appreciate it."

Grace finished her dinner, said goodbye to Chase, kissed Evangeline on the forehead, and walked out the door, purse in hand. She wore a smile the entire way to the T station.

"Grace Clarke," Derrick said by way of greeting once Grace had seated herself at the counter in Ally's favorite bar. "Haven't seen you in a dog's age. Where you been?"

Clarke.

Grace hadn't bothered to change back to her maiden name. She was still carrying around Gary's. Identifying with Gary's.

She'd have to remedy that.

"I'm sorry, Derrick," Grace replied. "I know I haven't been back at all since Ally died a few months ago."

"We missed you." Derrick offered Grace a wistful smile. "Can't go losing two of my favorite girls now, can I?"

Grace looked down at the counter. "I'm sorry," she whispered. Then she lifted her chin, looked Derrick fully in the eye, and said, "But I'm here now. And I promise I'll come back every so often. It won't be as easy as it was before, since I have Evangeline to care for and don't live nearby, but Chase is wonderful and very supportive. I can come on by when I drop Evangeline off at his house sometimes on a Friday evening. I'd like to see you."

"And we'd like to see you, both Mark and me. Hey, you know what?"

"What's that?"

"Why don't you and Chase come to our place sometime, yeah? Bring the little one."

Grace's eyes widened. "Oh," she said. "Yes... yes, that would be nice."

Ally had been coming to this bar for years, more frequently prior to Evangeline's birth, yes, but even after Evangeline was born, Ally still came, Grace knew. She still ordered her signature drink, and she still enjoyed her conversations with Derrick, and on the nights that Derrick's boyfriend, Mark, was able to join them, she enjoyed his company as well. Grace had had nothing but a wonderful time when she accompanied Ally to the bar, but never, never had she been to Derrick's house. She knew that Ally had entertained Derrick and Mark on a few occasions in her apartment, but Grace never had. Their relationship hadn't progressed to that level, or so Grace had thought. Grace was shocked at the invitation. Shocked but also very touched.

"Thank you, Derrick," she said, finding her voice again. "I'd love that."

"Now, what can I get you? 'Cause I'm guessing you didn't come here just to see me, although I am pretty fantastic."

Grace laughed. "You are fantastic, Derrick. But you're also right. I'll get a sidecar, please."

Derrick tilted his head and looked at her with a sideways glance. "Ally's drink."

"Yes," Grace said.

"Thought you didn't like it."

"I'm willing to give it another try," Grace replied with a grin.

"Ally might have liked that drink, and I make it well, but it tastes like balls, you know."

Grace laughed. "You would know," she quipped.

"Ah… I see you," Derrick replied. "Our innocent Grace… Ally really corrupted you, didn't she?"

"Maybe she did," Grace said with a smile.

Derrick pushed off the counter. "Be right back." He turned and began preparing the drink.

Grace pivoted in the stool and looked out the front window of the bar. The sun had made its descent in the sky, the buildings surrounding the venue barring her view. An ethereal glow illuminated the street outside as Grace watched people go about their evening, walking toward one destination or away from another.

"There you go," Derrick said as he ceremoniously slipped the drink in front of Grace. "Enjoy."

"Thanks, Derrick."

"My pleasure."

Grace looked at the drink for a moment, at the thick orange liquid. She ran her finger slowly around the base of the glass. She pulled it closer to her chest, the glass sliding smoothly over the surface of the bar. She fingered the rim.

"This one's for you, Ally," she whispered. "I miss you so much. So much that I can't even put it into words. I know it hasn't been long and it's to be expected, but I still have really tough days without you here. It's like I miss you so much that I can feel the ache inside of me. But tonight? Tonight I think was the first time that I laughed and I truly felt happy since you were taken away from us, and... Ally, I felt you with me. But in a different way. I didn't miss you at that moment because I somehow knew you were there with me.

"I'll probably wake up tomorrow and cry while I make my morning coffee. Evangeline won't be with me, she'll be with Chase, so I'll be alone, and the house will be silent. Entirely too silent. And I'll think of you. I know I will. Because I always do. So yes... I miss you terribly. But right now, Ally? Right now at this very moment, I feel content.

"Something happened in that park this afternoon with

Gary, something that I can't even explain because I don't fully know what it is, but something happened. Something big. And it feels so darn good." Grace lifted her glass into the air. "And somehow, Ally, I know it's because of you. So cheers." Grace took a sip of the sidecar, the strong liquid trickling down her tongue and the back of her throat.

And then she laughed. "No," she said out loud. "I still don't love it. But you did, Ally. Cheers to you."

Grace took another sip and smiled.

CHAPTER 17

"Can you believe it's been a year already?" Grace asked Chase as they were sitting on his living room couch and Evangeline was at the table with crayons and paper.

"Nope," Chase replied. "Been thinking about that all week."

"Yes," Grace said. "So have I. Thanks for having me over today. I know it's your weekend with Evangeline, and you were probably wanting to do something special with her, but instead, you spent it with the both of us."

"Nope," Chase said. "It's good to have you here. Almost appropriate, if that makes sense?"

Grace smiled. "Yes. It makes sense. But thanks all the same."

"You're welcome."

"I've been reflecting a lot these past couple of weeks as today loomed closer and closer."

"Yeah?"

"Yes. I just thought about the past year. I've thought

about how much our lives have changed not having Ally around. Not just the fact that I miss her so much it hurts sometimes, but that we have Evangeline. I went from not being fully responsible for anybody but myself to being responsible for another human being. A wonderful, innocent, amazing human being who seems to remind me more and more of her mom every day."

"She does, doesn't she? Except for the hair."

Grace smiled as she looked at Evangeline, and her heart swelled over the twenty-seven-month-old girl coloring at the table, at her messy brown hair that she still refused to pull back into a ponytail or into a headband to get the strands off of her face. Then Grace watched as Evangeline leaned over the table, kneeling on the chair as she scribbled her picture. Her little tongue peeked out of the corner of her mouth to touch her upper lip.

Just like her mom.

"No," Grace said. "Her hair is different. But she has so many of Ally's mannerisms. Even now. Even at just two years old."

"Yep," Chase said. "She does. She's her mom through and through."

Grace smiled wistfully. "I miss Ally so much," she said. "But she gifted the best part of her when she trusted us with Evangeline."

Grace felt her eyes begin to water, and when a single tear dribbled down her cheek, Chase lifted his finger, slowly brought it toward Grace, and wiped the tear away. His finger lingered. Grace wasn't aware that she was holding her breath, but she was cognizant of the sensation inside, at the flip of her stomach, at the stiffening of her shoulders. She looked into Chase's light-brown eyes, eyes that bored into hers now. Eyes that bespoke words that had never been uttered. She looked at a curl that covered his brow, and she suddenly felt an intense desire to touch it, to feel its softness between her fingers.

But she held back.

And Chase's finger retreated to his lap.

A knock sounded at the door.

Chase rocketed off of the couch and answered the knock. "Hi, Kristen."

He pulled the door back to reveal a young woman, perhaps in her mid-twenties, with shoulder-length honey-blond hair, high cheekbones, and a rounded chin.

Grace found her stomach plummet but this time, for an entirely different reason. Chase hadn't dated anyone since Ally's death. Perhaps it was time. He certainly deserved to date, deserved to have a companion, deserved happiness for himself.

Grace was just surprised at her sudden reaction to the young woman's presence in his home.

Chase closed the door and turned to Grace. "Grace, this is Kristen," he said. "We work together."

Kristen walked toward Grace with an outstretched hand. Grace stood, slipped her palm into Kristen's, and shook. "Hello."

"Hi, there," Kristen said with a smile. My, but she was attractive.

"Kristen is a lifesaver and has agreed to watch Evangeline tonight."

Grace whipped her head in Chase's direction and looked at him with a quizzical expression. "I don't understand."

Chase smirked. "I'm taking you out."

"I... I mean... what?"

"I have a surprise."

"A surprise?" Grace asked.

Chase laughed with amusement.

"I don't understand. It's Sunday night. We both have to work tomorrow."

"I know," Chase replied. "But trust me. You'll understand when you see where I'm taking you."

"I... okay." Grace didn't know what else to say. "But... what about Evangeline? I was going to take her home with me... she has daycare tomorrow."

"I've already called the center," Chase explained. "They know she'll be in late tomorrow. I'll take her in once she wakes up. I'm going in to work a bit late myself."

"What?"

Chase laughed again, clearly pleased that he had baffled Grace.

"Where are we——"

"Doesn't matter where we're going right now," Chase interrupted. "And no, you don't need to bring anything. Leave your purse here. Just grab your jacket because it's chilly." Chase turned to Kristen. "Thanks a bunch for watching Evangeline."

"It's my pleasure," the young woman replied. "I'm sure we'll get along well. I love kids."

Chase spent the next few minutes introducing Evangeline to Kristen, and Grace watched as the new woman, this stranger, bent down and began talking to the little girl. Grace saw a smile form on Evangeline's lips and listened as she spoke excitedly.

"Ready to go?" Chase sidled up next to Grace, and she looked over at him. Still confused, still surprised.

"Yes," she said, her voice sounding hoarse to her ears. Grace walked over and gave Evangeline a kiss goodbye before returning to Chase.

Chase brought his palm to rest on her lower back as they walked toward the door. "Bye, Evangeline. Bye, Kristen," Chase called.

"Bye!" Evangeline said enthusiastically as she leaned on the table with one elbow and waved with her opposite hand.

Grace and Chase stepped out into the cool air of the April evening. "Are you going to tell me where we're going now?" Grace asked.

"Nope," Chase replied with a mischievous grin. "Just follow me."

They walked down the street and boarded the T. When they arrived at their stop, Grace followed Chase as he stepped onto the platform and headed down the sidewalk, obviously aware of his destination's location. Grace saw the red door and the sign even before they arrived at the entrance, bright, bold colors announcing the name of the venue.

"Oh, no, Chase. I don't think so."

"Aw, come on, Grace. You'll be great. You didn't want to go when we went with Ally, and look how much fun you had."

"Yes, I suppose so," Grace admitted. "But that was a long time ago, and Ally was with us, and... I don't know. It might have been a one-time thing. I'm not going to know anybody inside. Maybe there will be lots of people. Maybe it will be crowded. And it'll definitely be noisy."

"And you'll love it," Chase said as he took her hand. He squeezed. "I didn't want to tell you where we were going because I knew you'd be nervous, but it's the perfect place to be, yeah? We'll definitely think of Ally here."

"I was thinking of Ally back at your place," Grace protested. "I think I'd prefer to remember her by ending our day the way we were: just being at your apartment together. We don't need to go in there"—Grace pointed— "to remember Ally."

"Gotcha," Chase said as he ran his fingers through his hair. "But I wanna go in. I know you only came here once with Ally, but she and I came here a lot, especially before Evangeline was born. I didn't always love it, but she had a way of convincing me. She always had a way of convincing me to do things. When I thought about today, when I thought about Ally, this was the first thing that popped into my head. I was hoping you'd be game. Maybe give it a try? If you don't want to be here, we can leave."

Grace looked at Chase, at his hopeful expression. She slowly nodded. "All right. I'll give it a try."

"Great!" Chase exclaimed. "After you."

Chase opened the door, and Grace walked over the threshold. Voices chattering and the sound of glassware clinking accosted her ears. Music began to play, loud and clear. Then the singing.

Grace was back at the karaoke bar.

"Let's have a seat," Chase suggested, and Grace followed him to an empty booth. They ordered appetizers to share. Chase enjoyed a beer, while Grace took large gulps from a tall glass of water. Before too long, the food had been eaten and the glasses were empty.

"I'm going up," Chase said. "You don't have to come with me, but I'd love it if you did."

"I... I don't know, Chase."

"I get it. This place is out of your comfort zone. Just thought maybe it would do you some good. But honestly, Grace, if it's too much, I understand. I can get a song in, then we can head back to my place. You're welcome to spend the night if you don't want to drive home too late.

Or you can head home and enjoy a quiet morning without Evangeline before you have to go to work. Bet that would be nice for you. I know it's been a while since you've had some alone time during the week, and I know how much you like your alone time with a book. That would be a nice way to start off your day if you go home tonight. But thanks. Thanks for being such a trooper. I know this isn't your thing, and I dragged you into it."

"It's okay," Grace said. "It's definitely not my thing, and yes, it is out of my comfort zone, but I can see why you thought to bring me here. I think I'm going to sit while you sing, though."

Chase nodded, stood from the table, and walked toward the stage. The person currently singing was finishing with their song, and Chase spoke to the man in charge, purportedly announcing his desire to perform next.

The music died, and the person bowed dramatically then stepped off the stage.

Chase climbed the stairs, took the microphone into his hand, and looked directly at Grace with a grin. "This one's for Ally," he said. "Not a song I'd typically sing, and though most of you don't know me, you'll probably wonder what the hell I'm doing up here, singing a song from *The Golden Girls*, but hey, just trust me. It needs to be sung."

The music rang out, and Grace immediately found her eyes begin to well with tears as he prepared to sing "Thank You for Being a Friend" by Andrew Gold. As Chase sang the beginning lyrics, Grace was reminded once again that he was not a natural-born singer, but his voice, terrible as it was, made the moment all the more special, more meaningful. Grace looked at Chase up on the stage. Their eyes met, speaking volumes.

Chase continued to sing, uninhibited and passionate.

Grace closed her eyes and listened to the words. Tears fell from beneath her lids, wetting her cheeks and falling to her chest. Her mind conjured an image of Ally, her smile, her small lips parted to show her white teeth. Her blue eyes twinkling with mischief and pleasure. And then Grace heard it: Ally's laugh. Melodious and beautiful.

Hey, Gracey.

Grace opened her eyes, but Ally wasn't there. Of course Ally wasn't there. Not physically. And yet… she *was* there. Grace was convinced that she was. Ally was beside her right now. Ally was in front of her as Chase sang his song.

And then Grace gasped, for there she truly was.

Ally.

On stage.

Looking directly at Grace with a smirk on her face.

Ally, spinning in slow circles to the tune of Chase's song.

Ally with her eyes closed and her face uplifted, higher, higher, toward the ceiling, toward the sky.

Ally with her arms outstretched. Reaching out. Up.

Ally as Chase's song came to an end. Ally staring directly at Chase then turning her eyes to Grace.

Ally with her hand over her heart.

Ally as she mouthed *I love you.*

Her image began to fade more and more until she was gone, leaving Chase alone on the stage, gazing intently at Grace.

Grace's tears were plentiful as she held Chase's stare.

Chase climbed down the stairs and walked to Grace. He held out his hand, and she took it in her own. "Let's go home."

~

Ally spent the night at Chase's apartment. Evangeline had long been asleep by the time the pair arrived home. Kristen left, and Grace and Chase sat on the sofa, Grace's head resting on Chase's chest. No words were uttered. There was no need.

Grace called into work the following morning, something she hadn't done but for the few exceptions when Evangeline was sick and back when Gary had first left her. She needed this day for herself. She knew what she had to do, what she *wanted* to do.

Chase had left earlier that morning to take Evangeline to daycare and then to backtrack into the city for work. Grace picked up her purse and headed to her car. When she arrived at her townhouse, she entered. The silence wasn't so depressing to her right then; rather, it was a welcome respite. Although she had taken the day off, she didn't bother making herself a cup of coffee. She ate a breakfast bar instead then dressed in bright-colored exercise clothes and stepped into a small adjoining room that she used for storage.

It was there that Grace kept her bike. The bike she had bought with Ally.

The bike she hadn't ridden since Ally was hit.

Grace inhaled deeply as she looked down at her bicycle, the helmet hanging off a handlebar. She clenched her jaw with determination, grabbed her bike, and led it outdoors to her driveway. She swung one leg over the bar, snapped her helmet into place, and put her foot into the stirrup. She put her sunglasses on.

Then she set off.

She began slowly, hypervigilant. She was aware of every car, every pothole, every pebble on the road. After a couple of miles, she found her nerves if not satiated then at least diminished. Her shoulders relaxed, she pedaled a bit faster.

Grace approached a large hill, the hill Ally had taken her on that very first day Grace had ridden with her. She had every intention of coursing down when she suddenly stopped at the top of it, unsure of herself, unsure of the situation.

She turned to look in back of her.

No cars.

She looked from side to side. Water, trees.

She glanced in front of her, the hill so large, so long that it seemingly went on forever, indefinite.

Grace was about to turn back when an image of Ally entered her mind. Ally with her helmet on, a large smile on her face.

You're gonna love it, Grace!

And Grace whispered back. "I promise I'll try, Ally. I can always try."

She pushed off the road with her foot and found the free stirrup. Her bike began its descent, slowly at first and then faster and faster until Grace was coursing down the hill, the wind whipping her chin-length hair back, the crisp spring air filling her nostrils, entering her soul. She closed her eyes and lifted her head to the sky. The morning sun seeped through her glasses and warmed her cheeks.

When Grace opened her eyes, she was smiling. Wider and wider until she was giggling then laughing out loud. Her eyes watered from the wind, dripped from the corners. Grace screamed with joy, with glee, with remembrance.

The bottom of the hill eventually neared, the water of the lake off in the distance, the sun's rays glistening off the top. Grace's bike slowed until it came to a full stop. She hopped off, held the handlebars in her palms, and walked her bike to the edge of the lake. She gently laid it on the hard earth, took off her helmet and glasses, and sat, staring at the water, at how it glistened in the gentle morning breeze.

She thought of Chase, a man she had grown to love dearly. She didn't know what would become of them, but right now, she was content with the way things were. She had an amazing man, an amazing friend in her life.

For now, that was enough.

She thought of Evangeline, the daughter of her best friend, a little girl she loved dearly, with her entire being. She knew she was blessed to have Evangeline in her life and vowed she'd do all she could to ensure Evangeline grew up to know Ally, to know that she was loved and would always be loved.

And Grace thought about Ally. Her best friend. A friend who had shown her what true love really meant. How it felt to be loved and to love another.

Unconditionally.

And with her entire being.

Thank you, Ally, Grace thought. She plucked a yellow dandelion out of the earth and brought it to her nose, drinking in its gentle scent.

Thank you.

Grace's story continues…

Grace and Ally Book 2 is coming soon. Sign up here to be notified of its release: http://eepurl.com/gPCU1X

THANK YOU

It is with heartfelt thanks that I write this. With so many novels to choose from, I am always humbled when a reader chooses one of mine. Thank you for doing so.

I truly hope you enjoyed *Grace and Ally* as much as I enjoyed writing it. If so, would you please consider reviewing this book on the social media platform of your choice? Each and every review made is greatly appreciated and helps get *Grace and Ally* into the hands of new readers.

Thank you!

ABOUT THE AUTHOR

An author of both adult and children's fiction, Amy Fillion graduated from the University of New Hampshire with a degree in psychology. She worked in the field of early intervention before making the decision to leave and stay home with her growing children. Amy has an insatiable appetite for reading, and you can easily find her juggling between three books at any given time (paperback, ebook, audiobook.) When she's not reading or writing, she loves to walk and cycle outdoors. She lives in New Hampshire with her husband, three boys, one rescue dog (best office companion ever!), and three crazy rescue cats.

Never miss a book release or important news! Sign up here to stay informed and get a free copy of Amy's short story *Hold On* : http://eepurl.com/gPCU1X

Visit Amy at https://www.amyfillion.com.

ALSO BY AMY FILLION

Adult Novels

Secrets of Spaulding Lane: Nancy

Secrets of Spaulding Lane: Marni

Secrets of Spaulding Lane: Rose

Little Things

Broken and Breaking Free

Children's Books

Fairville: Room of Reveries Book 1

FenneGig: Room of Reveries Book 2

Esmerelda and the Courageous Knight: Room of Reveries
Book 3

Wonderwell: Room of Reveries Book 4

SkyTopia: Room of Reveries Book 5

The Ancient Curse: Room of Reveries Book 6

A Magical Farewell: Room of Reveries Book 7

Made in United States
Orlando, FL
08 February 2022

14606694R00182